A Quiet Wife

A Quiet Wife

LG Dickson

Copyright © 2020 LG Dickson

The moral right of the author has been asserted.

Apart from any fair dealing for the purposes of research or private study, or criticism or review, as permitted under the Copyright, Designs and Patents Act 1988, this publication may only be reproduced, stored or transmitted, in any form or by any means, with the prior permission in writing of the publishers, or in the case of reprographic reproduction in accordance with the terms of licences issued by the Copyright Licensing Agency. Enquiries concerning reproduction outside those terms should be sent to the publishers.

This is a work of fiction. Names, characters, businesses, places, events and incidents are either the products of the author's imagination or used in a fictitious manner. Any resemblance to actual persons, living or dead, or actual events is purely coincidental.

Matador
9 Priory Business Park,
Wistow Road, Kibworth Beauchamp,
Leicestershire. LE8 0RX
Tel: 0116 279 2299
Email: books@troubador.co.uk
Web: www.troubador.co.uk/matador
Twitter: @matadorbooks

ISBN 978 1838593 414

British Library Cataloguing in Publication Data.
A catalogue record for this book is available from the British Library.

Printed and bound in Great Britain by 4edge Limited
Typeset in 11pt Minion Pro by Troubador Publishing Ltd, Leicester, UK

Matador is an imprint of Troubador Publishing Ltd

For the Nanas – all the Nanas. The quiet ones and the not so quiet ones.

ACKNOWLEDGEMENTS

Thanks to the Marie Stuart Society for their sheer enthusiasm and commitment to the study of Mary Queen of Scots and in particular Society President Liz Manson, my dear friend, who took me round Linlithgow Palace and helped me to really see and feel the place.

To the uplifting 'Women of the West End' written by Sandra Marwick - thank you for telling Elsie Inglis' story.

Grateful thanks to my writing community- tutors Claire Askew and Sophie Cooke, the Golden Hare writers and their offshoot - the Leverets! Particular shout out to Julie, Sarah, Lucy, Antonia and Neil for being Sheila's greatest champions.

And finally, once again, thank you to those closest to me for your continued love and support.

PROLOGUE

She looked in the mirror but there was nothing there to tell her story. She knew she looked different but there were no bruises, no scratches – nothing. Her eyes stopped darting around and fixed their stare. Now she knew what it was. She looked beaten. Not in the physical sense, of course, it was more the notion of who she thought she was. Her character, her integrity – all of it crushed, beaten. But what had actually happened? Could she even put a name to it? It had felt brutal at the time but now she wasn't sure if anyone would think it was all that bad. Not when you consider what some women endure. Why then did she feel so degraded? In reality she'd just been taken down a peg or two. That's all it was. That's all he'd meant it to be.

CHAPTER 1

Sheila enjoyed her reputation as a ruthlessly efficient PA. Organised and industrious, she took pride in her ability to ensure that the Chief Executive's office ran like clockwork. An unobtrusive presence, she was always there, ready to support and on hand to silently intervene.

She had once overheard the Leader of the Council describe her as poised and elegant. She never forgot that. It stayed with her, joining the other little affirmations that all helped to formulate her personal mantra.

Smart look, smart mind.

Every morning, she dressed and applied make-up that was subtle and tasteful. When she got to the office, she would run a comb lightly through her still-auburn hair before striding along the richly carpeted corridors of the City Chamber's inner sanctum. Until suddenly the cackling sound of support assistants standing in the tiny kitchen, making teas and coffees, broke through her aura. They would abruptly stop their chatter and smile at her. Pained, disdainful smiles, and she would return the compliment.

Onwards and upwards. It was not for her to pass comment on their colourful language or inappropriate dress. She had far more important responsibilities to attend to.

And so how had this moment come to pass? How was it that she was now standing in the magnificent Dunedin Room surrounded by people pretending that they were sorry to see her go? They had, for the most part, put up with her demands and calls to action but she knew they resented her position. Many of them were professionals – highly paid professionals. They possessed qualifications and skills that she had never aspired to and she knew they despised her for it. She could be charming as and when required, feign interest in their little gripes and grievances, but she wielded a degree of power that was well beyond her pay grade. She knew it and she enjoyed it – a position of trust, authority and influence. And now, with every word uttered by Colin Meikle, CBE, she could feel that power, that influence slowly ebbing away.

'And so, ladies and gentlemen, if you could all just stop your chattering for a few minutes I would like to pay tribute to our wonderful Sheila who retires from the Council today after thirty years of invaluable service.'

He looked at her and smiled. Colin Meikle was tall, white-haired and softly spoken. She had loved working for him. He had been a godsend after the ineffectual John Grant, followed by the tyrant that was Keith Jamieson and then finally the turbulent reign of Clive Johnston. A man who threw himself into the world of civic hospitality with such energy it left him with little strength to attend to the trivial matter of running the Council.

Colin had emerged from the relative anonymity of corporate affairs. Promoted in order to steady the ship, it had often felt as though the Council was in danger of becoming permanently becalmed – but he'd surprised Sheila. His pleasant demeanour belied a steely resolve and he managed to get things done quietly and efficiently. It was an approach that was right up her street and they very quickly became a formidable team.

But now here he was standing with a sheet of paper in his hand, hesitantly reading his own near-illegible scrawls.

She should have typed that for him. Large bold caps and double-spaced. That's how he liked his speeches to be typed.

She suddenly stopped listening to his words and scanned the faces scattered around the room. The young office girls, chewing gum and knocking back tumblers of warm white wine, using the occasion as a precursor to hitting the pubs on the High Street. The jaded middle-aged men, all life drained from them, wishing they too could make their escape.

And then suddenly, he stopped talking and picked up a large square object that had been wedged in between the heavy mahogany chairs standing fiercely to attention around the highly polished boardroom table. She couldn't help but notice that the wrapping paper was cheap, not something she would have chosen. If only someone had asked her. She had plenty of supplies, someone should have just asked. He smiled warmly at her as he handed her the prize.

The prize for being a faithful public servant; the prize that told her it was time to go.

*

She sat on the edge of the king-size bed staring at the original oil painting propped against the wall. Her back was to her husband of thirty-five years and although she couldn't see his face, she knew it wore an expression of bitterness. She couldn't see it, but she could hear it in every word.

'Think they might have exercised a bit of imagination. Do we really need to look at the back of the City Chambers every day? Not much for all these years spent running after a succession of bloody fools.'

She turned to look at him standing in front of their gilt-edged full-length mirror tying his bow tie and turning his head from side to side. She had often wondered if other men took such care over their appearance. After the bow tie had been perfectly tied, he ran his hands through his hair. She watched as he savoured the image reflected back to him. The lines at the side of his eyes slowly creased and his mouth broke into an approving smile.

'Well, I think it's wonderful. Not sure where we'll hang it, but it's very imposing and I like that. Oh, and I got perfume too. Chanel. The one I like.'

'Well, that was big of them. And no, I don't know where we're going to hang it either. Maybe I could take it into the office. It's not going to work in any of the rooms here, is it?'

She looked down at the montage of images. Scotland's capital city from a variety of viewpoints. The monuments to intellectual and scientific achievements, the castle fortress, the City Chambers, all looking down at the untidy hordes that dodged and weaved along its once-proud central thoroughfares. She felt the impact of these dark depictions of the city's character. They spoke of strength and moral purpose. She let out a despondent sigh, knowing such sentiments were entirely lost on her husband.

He turned to look at her. 'You never really see paintings of the real Edinburgh, do you? The gritty reality behind the Festival façade. No one wants that do they? No one wants the real Edinburgh.'

She didn't say anything. It was a ridiculous point to make. Why was he making it? None of the other paintings adorning the walls of their Georgian terraced house were 'gritty'.

'I'll take it back downstairs. We can think about it later.' She got up and smoothed down the sides of her Jean Muir skirt that tightly covered the contour of her thighs allowing just enough room for the smart, sharp paces required to travel the corridors of municipal power.

'How does this look?'

She wasn't sure if the question was directed at her or to his reflection in the mirror. In either case, she wasn't given the space to answer.

'Well, it will have to do. Executive Committee at the Malt Whisky Society. Like to be on top of my game for that lot.' He turned round and picked up his jacket without even glancing at her.

'Executive Committee?'

'Chamber of Commerce. Come on darling, keep up.' His words were shouted back at her as he ran down the stairs.

John was the Chief Executive of Edinburgh Travel. Bus Operator of the Year three years running. They had recently taken over the running of the troubled tram project. Financial issues, operational problems, bad PR. Not much going for them until John McDonald and his team pulled them up by the scruff of the neck, brought them back from the brink, got them all shipshape again. Just a few of the metaphors that had flown across the breakfast table every morning for the best part of a year.

He'd always been an ambitious man. He liked to succeed, to be the best, all of which was undoubtedly a big part of why she had found him so attractive. But something had changed in the last few years. Winning and beating the competition didn't bring the same rush. He resented his competitors, grew bitter at anyone else's success and bemoaned anyone who gained recognition for their efforts. And all of that manifested itself in the honours system. Birthday Honours, New Year Honours. *How the hell did that idiot manage to swing a CBE? Must have paid someone. Only bloody plausible explanation.* A string of invectives shot out from behind the newspaper twice a year.

She looked down again at the dark painting. It wasn't just his comments that she minded. It was the fact that the gift had been dismissed as readily as the life-changing event itself. They'd talked about retirement over a year ago and, at the time, it had all sounded quite firm and fixed – for both of them.

It was something to look forward to. Time would essentially be divided between their homes in Edinburgh and Provence and she had started to feel genuine excitement at the prospect. A new phase was about to begin and because they so rarely spent time focussing on their lives together, she had relished the clarity of his thinking and the tenderness of his tone. Increasingly divergent lives were ready to reconnect. She was ready for it and it had seemed as though John was too.

Her own departure had certainly happened pretty quickly. Budget savings were the order of the day and the financial offer placed in front of her by her employer was too good to pass up. John had said so and of course she'd agreed. But maybe she'd taken his words back then and fitted them into *her* vision of the future. She always clung on to words more than he did. And now because he'd said nothing more and the interminable tram project dominated his every waking moment, she'd let it all drift. Concrete planning had turned to wishful thinking.

She brushed her hand along the top of the dark wood frame. There was so much to think about, to talk about, and she really didn't know how to begin.

After he left, she walked down the stairs and into the drawing room. The only sound was the solid ticking of the marble clock on the mantelpiece. She chose not to sit on the large three-seater sofa but perched on the edge of the French-style Napoleon chair that filled an awkward little space in the corner of the room. She was still in work dress and a soft seat just wouldn't do. As she looked round the room, she thought of all the redesigning projects she'd spoken to John about. Not just here. There was the house in France too. New colours, patterns, fabrics and then just as she was trying to bring a new colour palette to mind, a terrible sense of panic overwhelmed her.

She was lucky. Of course she was lucky but was this it? Redecorating until he decided on the right time to stop work? She thought of all the kind invitations from neighbours, most of whom had stopped working and devoted themselves to a myriad of charitable causes. Her old friends Agnes and Sandra whom she often met for coffee in town on a Saturday morning gushed about museum outings and talks at the National Library of Scotland. Of course she'd agreed. How wonderful it would be to have the time to just be indulgent – for a short time at least. No diaries to manage, no meetings to plan.

But that wasn't the issue. When she'd spoken to them in the run-up to retirement she'd focussed on the humdrum, the ordinary, but all the time what she had loved, really loved about her job, was being at the heart of things. And that was something they just would never understand. She was the gatekeeper to the Chief Executive. She knew how to oil the wheels, get him what he needed when he needed it. Without her, without Sheila McDonald at the centre, at the core of the machine that kept local services delivering for the people of the city, then what? What might happen?

Janet. Janet was going to happen. Not the sharpest but as Colin had said, she was 'efficient enough'. Sheila bristled at the thought. 'Efficient enough' in no way hit the mark for the Executive PA to the Chief Executive of Scotland's capital city. Well, it wasn't her problem, not any more. She stood up, once again smoothing down the sides of her skirt. *I'd better get something prepared for John's supper*, she thought.

*

She was trying to empty her mind and drift off. Stop thinking about tomorrow, stop thinking about the future. She hadn't heard him come in, but she had heard the dodgy latch on the drinks cabinet being slammed shut and then the clattering about in the kitchen. He'd be wolfing down the cold meats and potato salad she'd left him and knocking back a large malt. Satisfied that all was well downstairs, Sheila started to enter that blissful state where sleep begins to sweep over both mind and body. She slowly drifted off.

Suddenly she was jolted from her slumber.

'You've never heard such utter rubbish, Sheila.'

Turning, dutifully, to hear his complaint of the day, she saw he was sitting up, glasses on his head with a pile of papers in front of him.

'What rubbish?'

'A presentation on emerging markets. Utter bullshit. Just a bunch of investment managers spouting financial crap. Must have a word with Claire. That's not the sort of thing we need to be hearing about.'

'Okay dear. Put the light out soon.'

'Yes, yes. Now that you've got all this time on your hands maybe we could start hosting some drinks things, the odd dinner. I think I need a better "in" with this crowd. I'm just not making the right connections.'

Her heart sank. 'Oh right, sorry, darling. A lot to think about. Have you thought? You know, about filling your time. I know it happened a lot quicker than you expected but you know, this could be really good for you, for us.'

'Well, I've not really had much time to get used to the idea.'

'No, no, of course not. No rush. It's just I think we could maybe make a bit of a concerted effort now.'

'Concerted effort for what?'

'Just to get my name circulating. That's all.' He put the papers down at the side of the bed, placed his glasses on the bedside table and, as he did every night, patted the clean hanky tucked into the pocket of his pyjama jacket. 'Tell you what. Let's go out to dinner to celebrate your escape. Saturday maybe? Get Caitlin and Simon along?'

'Oh, I don't know, John.' Sheila turned to resume her normal sleeping position. Everything about their planned future had faded from his mind. 'Let me think about it.'

*

Later in the week, Sheila was in the kitchen with her daughter Caitlin, discussing if new kitchen units were required or whether sprucing up, even changing, the doors might be all that that was needed to give the place a lift. It was riveting stuff.

'Really looking forward to Saturday by the way. Dad rang me and I've arranged with Flora to look after Milo. Simon has a hockey game in the afternoon, but he'll be finished by five.'

'Dad rang you?' She went to make a pot of coffee while her daughter sat back on the two-seater, bouncing chubby little Milo on her knee. He was an adorable little boy, but she couldn't get over the fact that her daughter allowed some form of viscous substance to flow constantly from his facial cavities. This morning there was a line of yellow snot firmly stuck between left nostril and lip followed by a bubbly dribble from mouth to chin.

'Yes. Wasn't he meant to?' Her daughter looked quizzical for a moment but only a moment. 'Anyway I think it's a great idea to celebrate. Wonderful thing, Mum. The world's your oyster now.'

She didn't know how to respond but offered up a half-hearted smile and then turned back to push hard at the plunger on the cafetière.

'For God's sake, Mum. He's only trying to do a nice thing. The right thing.' Caitlin whipped out a wad of hankies and rubbed the mucus away from Milo's face, ready for the next discharge. 'That's all he ever tries to do.'

She couldn't look round. John could do no wrong in Caitlin's eyes. It was always them against her and it always would be. But maybe her daughter was right. Maybe she was just being ungrateful. He worked hard and after all it was his money that had bought them their Georgian terraced house in the New Town and his money that bought their place in Provence. Yes, she'd earned her own money but that was for the inconsequentials of life, nothing of substance. And that was at the heart of it. Her life, her work, her contribution to the McDonald family always felt like nothing of any great substance. And just at that moment the only place she wanted to be was sitting in the oak-panelled office of Colin Meikle CBE. Planning the week ahead. Making the calls that would have people at the other end of the line take note and take action. Organising papers and managing the diary. Getting him to the right place to meet the right people at the right time.

Now *there* was a position of substance. *There* was a meaningful contribution.

CHAPTER 2

Cafe Jardin, the little French Bistro that had been such a favourite haunt over the years, was once again buzzing. How many times had Sheila and John turned up here, on their own or with friends, and thrown themselves into an exchange of friendly banter with Jean? He liked to welcome his patrons with a glass of burgundy that looked like liquid chocolate in one hand and, up until the smoking ban, a large cigar in the other. There were always continental kisses and slaps on the back before they sat among their fellow diners.

Saturday night was her favourite night to dine out. Any lingering thoughts from Friday's missed deadlines or clashing diaries had completely dissipated and the spectre of Monday morning schedules wouldn't appear until sometime late Sunday. Saturday night was a free night. The only one of the week and they were all in it together. Relishing the simple hearty food and savouring the vintage wines was a restaurant group activity, not just for her and not just for her husband.

'Well, in the end it was just Bill and me. Two of us in a room together. No interfering Board members. Just two men who knew how to get a job done.' John emptied the breadbasket and waved it in the air somewhere in the general direction of the waiting staff. 'But to be honest he was a beaten man, Simon. Felt bloody sorry for him by that point.' John was recounting his one-man rescue mission of the tram project. It had been told before, but each new telling brought a different emphasis to his own time-critical role – repackaged by way of a new, sparky anecdote.

'Christ, John, sounds like you got in there in the nick of time.' She wasn't sure if Simon was feigning genuine interest or not.

She was used to these stories and they were just as much a Saturday night tradition as the *escargots a la bourguignonne*. But tonight they grated. Along with the incessant scraping of chairs on the wooden floor, the sudden bellowing laughter from the table in the corner, the witty exchanges with Jean. She didn't feel part of it anymore. She had always loved this little corner of France tucked away down a quiet cobbled street in Edinburgh but she loved *their* little corner of France even more. If only they were there now, sitting on the terrace, a salmon-pink rosé in hand, looking out to the Aleppo pines. Wonderful trees, bent almost double under the strain of early season winds that had swept across the fields of Provence since time immemorial.

Her mind suddenly switched back when she noticed an elderly couple sitting at a small table that was wedged up against the wall behind Simon and Caitlin. They jumped every time someone shouted or laughed. They peered over each spoon of French onion soup raised to their mouths, surveying the scene, watching it all from the outside looking in. They didn't quite belong either.

'What's wrong, Mum? You look a million miles away.'

Sheila was looking round trying to work out why her chair was so close to the one behind her. She turned back to see that same quizzical look on her daughter's face.

'Sorry dear. Just having a look round.'

The short exchange caught John's attention. She wished it hadn't.

'Well, Caits, she's not been herself since walking away from that place. Thought she'd be happy to leave it all behind.' He tucked his red napkin into the collar of his shirt waiting for the snails to arrive dripping in garlic butter. 'But apparently not.'

'Just takes a bit of adjustment, that's all.' Simon smiled at her. It was sweet of him, trying to be on her side. He often did that when she was up against the two of them.

'No, it's not that,' she lied. 'It's just I've got a bit of a head tonight. Don't know what's wrong with me.' She turned and put her hand on top of John's. She meant it to reassure, to let him know that nothing was amiss. It worked. He smiled and raised his glass. 'Okay then. Here's to your retirement from the Council and to whatever the next chapter brings – for both of us. To Sheila.'

'To Sheila,' Simon and Caitlin cried in unison and the boisterous table next to them joined in the toast. The old couple opposite wedged themselves further against the wall.

*

The night was finally over and she started to take the cushions off the bed.

'What the hell's wrong, Sheila?'

'Nothing, nothing. Please, I've just got a sore head, that's all.' But it wasn't sore; it was just full. Full of thoughts, confusing possibilities and fear. How could she be scared of the future? What on earth was there to be scared of?

'It *is* what you wanted isn't it? You know, when we talked about it? I thought it was what you wanted.' He was looking at her as she undressed and suddenly his expression softened. It had transformed into a confused look, a look that said he couldn't quite fathom what was going on and because she hardly ever saw him at a loss and because she wasn't terribly sure what was going on either, Sheila started to cry.

'Yes, yes of course it is.' She grabbed a tissue from the box on her nightstand. 'It's just you've stopped talking about the future, about your own retirement.'

He moved across to her side of the bed where she stood in her bra and pants, crying and shivering. His arms enveloped her and she buried her face in the crook of his neck. He held the back of her head with one hand and dropped the other down to the small of her back. 'Only because everything's so busy. Don't worry, we'll get there.'

The tension began to ebb away and she relaxed into his embrace. Then he began to move his hips. Short, sharp thrusts into her stomach. She didn't move, she didn't want him to see the pain etched on her face. The price for his comfort, for his affection, was going to be a simple act of sexual gratification. Simple, no frills, straight in and out –

sex. It was a familiar scenario – she recognised it as such and acted out her part. It wasn't a chore, it was never a chore, but how could she tell him what she really needed? How could she tell him something she didn't know herself. And so she focussed on the pleasure of holding him close to her until it was over.

'Just a bit of perspective. That's all you need.'

They were lying on top of the bed and John was holding her right hand and rubbing her thumbnail. It was annoying her, sending little shocks through her body. She wanted him to stop but didn't want anything else she did to create a scene.

'We've got each other, we've got our family. We don't want for anything.' The words were meant to comfort but it sounded like he was merely making up little affirmations for himself. She pulled her hand away and turned over, nestling into his neck. This is where she wanted to be, this was the space where she loved and felt loved in return.

'Well, time for sleep I think. It'll all be better in the morning. We'll talk it through properly. Start to set out a plan.' He manoeuvred himself away, letting her head slowly sink down into the cavernous space between them.

*

'Didn't know you were playing golf today.'

'No, sorry. Completely forgot about it. Roger and Martin.' He stuffed a piece of toast into his mouth and began filling the side pocket of his oversized golf bag with golf tees, gloves, energy bars and other assorted items.

She remembered her own father setting off for a few holes round the local municipal course with a bag half the size that held a few battered old clubs. This, however, was state of the art and looked as though it could double up as luggage for a two-week holiday in the sun. *That would be nice*, she thought. Maybe they could talk about holidays.

'No, it's fine. It's just I thought we were going to talk.'

He pulled the soggy half-eaten bread from his mouth. 'Talk about what?'

'Oh nothing. I just meant it would be nice to have a leisurely breakfast.'

'Well, you'll be having all the leisurely breakfasts you like from now on.' He stood up, pulling the mighty load of golfing equipment up and over his shoulder, then strode across the kitchen, clubs clanking at his back, and kissed her on the cheek. 'You lucky thing.' He smiled at her. One of his devilishly attractive, smart smiles. The kind that seduced people he was trying to impress.

She had thought about cooking up a full breakfast. Start the day with bacon smells, aromas of warm toast and freshly ground coffee wafting through the house. Good homely cooking smells would provide the right atmosphere for discussions about the future. Had he just forgotten about the promise to sit down and talk or could he just not stomach the thought of having to sit down and listen to her? Maybe it was more than he could give; or worse, more than he was prepared to give. But now that he was gone and her plans had been cast aside she started to think about cupboards, emptying cupboards. That would be a good place to start. Get rid of everything that was out of date, never used and never likely to be. That would make her feel better, like she'd accomplished something. Then just as she was about to start, the doorbell rang. Feeling mildly annoyed that she'd been interrupted before she'd really got going, Sheila whipped off her Marigolds and marched towards the front door.

'Oh good, you're in. Thought Milo might settle with a visit to his grandma. He's just been a nightmare all night and this morning for that matter.'

'Well, he's probably just teething. Just needs a bit of comfort.' She watched in exasperation as her daughter struggled to unstrap the red-faced toddler from the confines of his stroller. He kicked and wriggled until finally he was out and was thrust toward his unimpressed grandmother. Why did this feel like an unwanted intrusion? It was her daughter, her grandson. Sheila checked herself. What kind of grandmother thought like that?

Caitlin stood, hands firmly stuck to her ample hips, looking glad to be briefly free of all child-rearing responsibilities. The self-satisfied smile soon began to give way. 'Sorry, Mum. I should have rung but I was just taking him for a walk and he wouldn't stop crying and I just thought... well, I'm sorry. Shouldn't just barge in. Look, here's a rusk for him to chew on.'

'No, it's fine. It's lovely. Just best to ring ahead, that's all. In case we're going out or something.'

'Well, you've got the Marigolds at the ready so don't think you're going anywhere soon.'

'Actually, once I've finished cleaning out these cupboards I was thinking of going to see your granddad.'

Milo was now resting comfortably in her arms, sucking on the once-hard, dry biscuit and rapidly turning it into a pile of mush. Caitlin proceeded to make a pot of tea. 'Oh right. Well, that's a shame. Just seem to have got him settled here. Where's Dad? Maybe we could just hang out with him.'

'Sorry, he's off golfing. Why don't you come along? I'm sure he'd love to see Milo.'

Her daughter let out a short, sharp snort of derision. 'Really, Mum? He doesn't know what time of day it is. He barely remembers *you*. I haven't seen a flicker of recognition for years now so he's hardly going to recall the fact he's a great-grandfather.'

She turned away quickly towards her grandson. 'Okay, well – I'll go a bit later.' Sheila plonked Milo down into the high chair in the corner of the kitchen and pulled him in towards the table. Milo squealed in delight. 'Let's sit down and have some tea first.'

'Cool. I've already made a pot. What's there to eat?'

*

Alexander Shaw had been the Deputy Bank Manager at the old Trustee Savings Bank, not a million miles away from where Sheila and John now lived. He had left home at precisely the same time every morning with his fedora perched at a slight angle, plain navy raincoat buttoned up to the neck and a thin wallet briefcase, which never seemed to contain very much more than firmly pressed white bread Spam sandwiches wrapped in greaseproof paper, an apple and a chocolate biscuit.

He arrived home at five thirty on the dot every evening, opened up his case to hand Sheila's mother the carefully folded used sandwich wrapping and disappeared off into the kitchen with his wife to eat his evening meal. Only after eating did he turn into the father Sheila adored. Shoes came off, tie was loosened although never removed and he would sit in his chair in the lounge and ask his only child to tell him everything about school, friends, piano lessons – everything.

It was the highlight of her day and one that she never consciously placed in jeopardy. Not after the time she refused to eat her mother's grey tasteless stew and was sent to bed just minutes before her father was due home. She had sat up in her bed, arms tightly folded round the top of her legs straining to listen to her parents' conversation. Waiting for them to stop talking, waiting for the moment when he would defy his wife and race to see his daughter.

Sheila sat with her head on her knees, feeling sick and not letting herself cry in case she missed hearing the moment. The moment that would bring excitement to replace the misery as he strode across the lounge, threw open the door and ran up the stairs to ask her about her day and, if she was very lucky, to tell her one of his magical stories. But it hadn't happened and that night, that very night, she realised that this wasn't a love that came without rules. It would always depend on her being a good girl and, as a consequence, she really did try her best not to let anyone down. That night, she strained to listen as her parents tidied up, locked doors, went to the bathroom until finally their bedroom door was closed and that was that. She'd never let that happen again, that was for sure.

*

Sheila stood at the entrance to her father's care home – an impressive Victorian house located in one of Edinburgh's leafy suburbs. From the outside it looked no different to the other mansion houses in the area, originally built as second homes for rich families in the New Town or to house the shipping merchants of Leith. The outer reaches of Edinburgh were a strange mixture of areas considered to be country retreats when they were built in the early nineteenth century banging up against sprawling concrete labyrinths designed to house the poorest and dispossessed. No beautifully cultivated gardens and parks in those forgotten parts. She knew those places existed; she drove past them but never into them, not even through them. She didn't know anybody who lived in them. Her father had, growing up. Friends from his childhood. Good people, he used to say.

'These people are torn from their communities, Sheila. Their homes have been falling down about their ears. Is it their fault? No, of course not. They've had to live without indoor toilets, baths, barely anything to cook on for years. But did they complain? No, they bloody didn't. Because they were living in it together. They shared and looked out for each other. And now what? They get shoved out, away from the heart of their existence into these anonymous ghettos.'

He would rail at the system that sentenced people to this hapless existence. Yet there he had been, at the centre of a financial institution that offered little support other than to entice these same people out of their drudgery on the basis of false hope and an unaffordable existence. Not her words. It was John who had categorised her father's views as faux socialism and utterly hypocritical for a bank manager offering unaffordable loans and mortgages.

And now she stood carrying a dog-eared old photo album and a packet of sweets, pressing the doorbell and waiting to enter into her father's very own fantasy existence. Sometimes light, but more often than not, dark and confusing. She used to give her father money; cash to buy various sundry items at the home's little shop but they'd asked her not to bother anymore. It wasn't just that he'd lost any sense of monetary value. At first he'd struggled with counting and working out what coins to hand over. Now he had no idea what money was and Sheila reluctantly had to admit defeat. The day when he just stared at the five-pound note in front of him and then picked it up and started licking it was really the last straw. The man who had had money at the centre of his very existence just wanted to know what it tasted like.

'Ah, Sheila, lovely to see you. I'm sure he'll brighten up now you're here.' Carole was the home manager. She wore a look of understandably permanent weariness but always seemed to speak words that suggested happier days were just round the corner.

'Well, I don't know about that. Thought I'd just tell him my news and have a look through the photos again.'

'Well, it's always worth a try. Sometimes you get a glimmer.' Carole offered up a forced smile, turned and sashayed along the light airy hallway towards the communal lounge.

Sheila followed closely behind, the familiar feeling of dread enveloping her as she approached the room and its crazy maelstrom of wild, cackling happiness and cries of utter despair. No matter how much she prepared herself, there it was. A mixture of anger and sadness, feeling torn between wanting to scoop his hunched, frail body up into her arms or to make a bolt for the door and pretend that the glazed and lost-looking man sitting in the corner of that room was not her father. Not Dad.

She walked slowly towards him, all the while hoping that he might just turn and smile. She didn't look for much more than that now – just some fleeting glimpse of her father – but he didn't move and kept staring straight ahead. She quickly looked round for a spare chair and spied a small plastic bucket seat propped up against the wall opposite. She made a beeline for it and then turned to walk back, dragging the chair behind her. As she grew closer to him, she could feel herself entering the periphery of his closed and confused little world. He looked up with a jolt, the expression on his face turning to one of fear and panic. She quickly set the chair down alongside him and gently covered his hand with her own.

'It's okay, Dad. It's only me. Sheila.' And then for a brief moment she saw the muscles in his face relax, his eyes brighten and the almost imperceptible shape of a smile begin to form. His body seemed to strengthen, arching upwards and she felt him suddenly grow back into the mind and body of the father she knew – just as he had done a hundred times before. She didn't take her eyes off him, clinging on to the image in front of her until just as quickly, his shoulders fell, chin dropped to his chest and he closed his eyes. She'd lost him again. She sat back and began flicking through the photos. Holidays in Pittenweem. Mum, dad, daughter all wearing identical Aran cardigans with identical leather buttons. Happy faces full of anticipation. Happy to be at the mercy of the salty sea air and anticipating nothing more exciting than the fish and chip shop opening up at five o'clock on the dot.

CHAPTER 3

'You should come with me next time.'

'I'm going to need to get a new driver. The guys are just smashing it off the tee. Feel like a complete dick always being the first to hit my second shot. Complete wuss.'

'John.'

'Yes – what?'

'You should come with me sometime – to see Dad.'

'If you need me to.' He turned back to cleaning his golf clubs. 'Just not sure what purpose it would serve.'

She didn't say anything.

Her father hadn't much liked John in the early days – 'altogether too full of himself' he'd told her just a few dates in. But that was all he'd said. When it became clear that Sheila had fallen in love, he wasn't going to get in the way. She often wondered if it was because he too had fallen head over heels at a young age and nothing would have stopped him marrying the love of his life. Of course it was difficult to really know but it had seemed like a happy marriage right up until her mother's death more than forty years ago.

The protracted battle with cancer and painful death were seared into Sheila's memory, all happening just as her own unruly hormones were beginning to rage around her teenage body. Sometimes they just sat, father and daughter, saying nothing but feeling content and secure in each other's company. It was how she'd felt when she was little. He would kneel by the side of her bed, thinking she was fast asleep, and mumble his nightly prayer. She never knew the words, but the simple act had made her feel safe and protected as she drifted off into a worry-free sleep.

She had struggled to connect with her father in the immediate aftermath of it all but then as she got older they had moved on together. When he began his long journey into dementia she became as protective of him as he had been of her. She liked to think that in this final stage – the distressed state – the faulty wiring that so often misfired or disconnected completely would, from time to time, smoothly recreate images of his beautiful young wife and adoring little daughter. It wasn't a completely forlorn hope. She had seen signs when he was sufficiently 'present', glancing at the old black and white photographs she carried with her into the care home; a warmth in his eyes, a softness to his smile.

'Thinking about a springtime drinks party – once the garden's in a fit state.'

'Really?' She was abruptly torn away from her reminiscences but then checked herself. She really must try to get behind John's ideas – his ambition. 'Well, I suppose so. Who for? I mean who would you want to invite?'

'Oh, don't worry about that. I'll draw up a guest list.' He walked across the kitchen and put his arms tightly around her waist. 'Of course I'll go and see the old boy with you.

Don't look so dejected. Whole new chapter I keep telling you, Sheila, whole new chapter.'

*

Over the next couple of months, she busied herself with fabric samples and colour charts. She began to look into classes at the local library and the possibility of volunteering. None of it was really firing her imagination and, of course, the spectre of the drinks party hung over everything.

'What sort of people are coming to Dad's party?' Once again, Caitlin and Milo had just dropped in.

'What do you mean, what sort of people?' She was sick of the thing already and they were still four weeks away from 'Springtime Drinks at the McDonalds'. Her resolve to be more supportive was weakening. Although come to think of it, Caitlin had really just confirmed what she already knew. This was John's event. She was expected to organise the canapés and garden seating but really this was all about him.

'Well, is it golf club types, business types? You know what I mean.' Caitlin was absent-mindedly wiping peanut butter from Milo's mouth, but she'd merely succeeded in spreading it further round his chubby little face. The little boy was, once again, squealing in delight.

'They're all the same, aren't they?' She stopped writing her shopping list and looked up across the table to see Milo grinning from ear to ear and holding his hands out towards his grandma to show off his peanut butter fingers. His mother didn't look quite so happy with her lot.

'Good grief, Mum. Can't you summon up a bit of enthusiasm? This is important to Daddy. Anyway, I just wondered if it was something Simon might find useful.'

She knew it was the last thing in the world that Simon would find useful. He was a gentle soul and she always wondered how he'd managed to get on in the cut-throat world of fund management. She was sure it wasn't a career of choice – more likely one that her status-driven daughter had pushed for.

'Well, you'll need to talk to your dad about that. I'm sure I won't know half the folk who're coming.'

The day of the drinks party finally dawned and Sheila determined to dispense with any outward signs of negativity. As she laid out the pretty floral dress that John had bought for her birthday, it occurred to her that at no point since the retiral drama had John actually made good on his promise to sit down and discuss their future. But then why wait for him to suggest what the future might hold? This drinks party was probably just a taste of things to come.

Suddenly things started clicking into place. She needed to steal a march on her husband before any more plans to enhance their social status started to form. She needed to start making her own choices and they needed to be good choices. She would start thinking about new interests – she could just dip her toe in to start with and take it from there. She felt lighter and brighter, like the pink and yellow floral print covering her new dress, as she skipped down the stairs to check on the prawn tartlets.

'We've been bloody lucky with the weather, darling. I know there's a bit of a nip in the air, but I don't think we'll need to wheel them all inside. As long as everyone's got a decent jacket with them. That's Edinburgh for you – always a bloody nip in the air.' John was wandering round the garden checking his hellebores and primroses. She watched him from the kitchen doorway and just as she was deciding whether or not to join him on his tour of inspection, the doorbell suddenly gave out three shrill bursts. She wiped her hands on the front of her apron, marched through the hall and opened the door.

'Caitlin. Simon. You're two hours early.' She felt her shrillness had matched the abrupt tone of the doorbell.

Caitlin's face fell. 'Thought you might need a bit of help. We can always go away and come back later.'

She noticed her daughter had slapped on the make-up, was wearing a sharp, short black dress and stood teetering uncomfortably atop high-heeled black stilettos. 'Don't be silly, I was just surprised. You look lovely.' She stood back to allow Caitlin to make her entrance and to welcome Simon, looking slightly uncomfortable in what Sheila assumed to be his best formal occasion suit.

'Everything okay, Simon?' She took her son-in-law's arm as her daughter rushed out to her father in the garden.

'Yes, yes. Just not entirely sure what I'm doing here.'

Sheila squeezed his arm as they walked through to the dining room. 'Me neither.'

Assorted bottles of spirits, decanted bottles of red wine and port were lined up on top of the shining walnut sideboard. The matching dining table had been extended to its full length and was covered in dainty canapés and finger food. John had quietly nodded his approval as he'd walked round earlier making his inspections. The cheese wasn't out yet; John had decreed it was far too early and cited the Brie as the prime candidate to run away before anyone was near ready for a cheeseboard. He would give her a clear signal when the time was right. She wanted to laugh but he'd been deadly serious, so she merely nodded.

'Wow, looks amazing.' Simon eyed up the tasty morsels on offer. 'I'm guessing he'll notice if I snaffle one of those salmon things.'

'Blinis, Simon. And no, he won't. We'll just rearrange the rest.'

They gave each other a conspiratorial smile.

People were going to start arriving soon and she prepared to step effortlessly up to the role of hostess. As she removed all signs of Simon's food grab, it struck her that none of this entertaining at home came particularly naturally to her. Needless to say, she acted out the role to perfection and never let her husband see what an effort it was. She checked again the lactose-intolerant and gluten-free guests on the list her husband had given her.

After the 'intolerant' guests' food had been correctly labelled, she started to lay out napkins and her mind wandered back to the vast, echoing rooms of the City Chambers.

She loved all the organising that went into civic dinners and receptions but then maybe that was because she was never expected to be up front and centre. There was always the Lady Provost or some other dignitary to take on that role, until that was Colin became Chief Executive. He had been widowed some years earlier and Sheila had found herself increasingly stepping into the role of… no, she could never quite find the right word for it. Obviously she wasn't his wife but whatever it was seemed to be above and beyond the PA's job description and it wasn't something she was always entirely comfortable with.

Was that enough napkins? She'd just put the rest in the sideboard. She could get them out later, if needs be.

Best to get ready to meet and greet, make small talk, all the things she found so excruciatingly difficult when she had to entertain with her husband. Maybe she just enjoyed the 'purpose' behind her works events. Could be something to do with the civic good – attracting business, enhancing the city's profile. But why on earth did that matter more than her husband's ambitions? Did that make her an awful wife?

'All right, darling? You look miles away.'

Her moment of introspection was brought to an abrupt halt as she turned to see her husband standing with one hand in his trouser pocket and the other holding up a bottle of champagne. He was wearing a pale pink shirt, cream flannel trousers and a navy sports jacket. His blue eyes twinkled against his tanned skin.

'Yes, fine, sorry. Just wondering about the napkins.' She walked towards him and planted a kiss on his cheek. He was going all out to impress today, she thought, as she swept the greying hair back from his temple and then moved her hand down to the slightly crinkled skin around his neck. She always thought he seemed to wear all signs of aging as a badge of honour – show the young guys that he still had it. She was just starting to think about saying something supportive and complimentary when he moved away from her. It quite often happened like that. Small gestures, movements – anything that suggested intimacy and he would gently step away.

'Thought we'd crack this open – get a head start. Where are the kids?'

'Oh, I think they went out into the garden.' Her voice trailed off. John had already made for the kitchen doorway and was shouting to Caitlin and Simon to come in and get the party started.

*

'Yes, of course I remember you. Yes, the Andersons at Christmas. Of course.'

'Sorry, did you say Tony? Yes, that's right, John speaks very highly of you. How long have you been with him now?'

'Ah yes. Chamber of Commerce – and what's your business? Ah, yes of course. I've heard John speak about it.'

'Oh, just now and again. It's not a regular thing. John likes to get people together from time to time. And of course, so do I.'

'Yes, we do. We enjoy entertaining a lot. Don't we dear?'

What were these words tumbling out of her mouth? God, she almost sounded convincing. Oh well, she guessed it didn't really matter, as long as they all looked happy enough.

And then suddenly, and quite unexpectedly, a familiar face dropped into her view. 'Colin? Is that really you? Good God, what are you doing here?' She had turned to walk back into the house only to see her former boss filling the doorway. No sports jacket and casual trousers for him. Blue pinstripe suit and the Council's official tie. He stepped down onto the patio quickly followed by her husband.

'Surprise, surprise, darling. Invited Colin and didn't tell you.' John marched over, put his arm round his wife and now they both stood facing the slightly awkward-looking Colin Meikle. 'Thought it might perk you up. Getting the two of you together again.' Sheila was slightly bemused at this unexpected turn of events but at the same time felt relieved that she could finally strike up a meaningful conversation with someone she really quite liked.

Her husband stood there beaming, like he'd just turned up a prize catch. 'Leave you to it then. Some people you might want to meet later, Colin. Good contacts for the Council. Just let me know and we'll do intros. After you've caught up with my lady of leisure, of course.' He planted a painfully hard kiss somewhere between her left eyelid and eyebrow and marched back into the kitchen.

'Well, look at him all pleased with himself.'

It was only a passing reference to the demeanour of the host but it caught her off guard. She wasn't sure she liked it, the tone attached to the remark, more than anything. They were completely different men, of course. Outlook, character, sense of humour – everything. And yes, John could be unbearably full of himself sometimes but that had felt just a bit rude and also quite unexpected from a man who wouldn't normally say boo to a goose.

Suddenly Colin seemed to switch gear, leaving all thoughts of John McDonald trailing behind him as he moved in closer towards her, arms outstretched, face beaming. 'How are you? Lord, I've missed you.' And with that she was swept into a giant bear hug. Colin Meikle wasn't a man known for extravagant gestures.

She started to feel just a little bit uncomfortable. The hug was going on for too long and the little dig at her husband was playing on her mind. One arm had escaped and she held it away from her body, away from his body. She looked down and could see her wine glass. She was holding the stem tight, but it seemed awfully far away. Suddenly, he stepped back.

'All good, Colin, really, all good.'

'So what are you doing with yourself? What about John? I thought he had plans too.'

'Well, we've not really had the chance to sit down and talk it all through. I mean, to be honest I'm just enjoying the freedom.' She blurted out a little laugh, but she knew she sounded ridiculous, like a snorting pig.

'But I thought he was retiring soon. Thought that was why you wanted to jump ship early.'

'Well, we did talk about it. He was getting a bit frustrated with things last year, but you know John, something else spikes his interest and he's back on track again. It was the whole tram thing really and of course he got a lot of plaudits for that. But some time down the track – oh, some time down the track. Isn't that funny? You know the trams—'

'Yes, the trams.'

She was nervously twirling the stem of her wine glass now. She didn't want to talk about this and she really didn't want to see the expression of pity on Colin Meikle's face. If she thought about it too deeply she might come to doubt that her husband was absolutely right in persuading her that the financial package on offer was one that she would be mad to pass up on; that he would of course be stepping down just as soon as the time was right; and that very soon they would be spending so much more quality time together. Here, France, everywhere.

The world was her oyster. She must remember that. But that was the point – it was her oyster and it would be her plans for the future. She really needed to focus and that was exactly what she would be doing as soon as this God-awful party was over.

Colin's warm expression suddenly turned to something altogether more mocking. 'Well, don't be surprised if you find yourself doing a lot more of this type of thing. Seems a shame really. You were bloody good at your job, Sheila. I'm afraid Janet just is nowhere near as clued up as you – you're sorely missed, you know.'

She'd known from the start that Janet wasn't the right fit. 'Well, I'm sure she'll—'

'Mr Meikle, how are you?' Caitlin, for once, had appeared just at the right moment waving a champagne glass around and looking increasingly unsteady on her feet.

His expression softened again as he began to enquire after Milo. He'd barely finished talking when Caitlin grabbed his arm and started blinking wildly. Sheila, straight away, recognised the early stages of her daughter's descent into inebriation.

'You don't have a drink. Goodness' sake, Mum. How long has Mr Meikle been standing here without a drink? Come on, Colin, come with me. I'll show you where the good malt's stashed away.'

'Well, if you're sure your dad won't mind.' Colin turned and winked at Sheila. She wasn't sure what was going on. It wasn't a familiar, friendly gesture that she'd been used to in the office. It was something else, but she wasn't quite sure what. And then as the three of them made to walk back into the house, she suddenly felt Colin Meikle press his hand, fingers spreading, all too firmly into the small of her back.

CHAPTER 4

'Think we should go for a walk.' Sheila was busying herself hanging up shirts, putting away ironing and all the while ignoring her husband lying prone on top of the bed with a cold, wet flannel covering his eyes.

'Really? If my head would stop thumping then I might consider it.'

'Well, it might help. Couple of ibuprofen and then some fresh air. Come on, John, you can't lie there all day.'

She didn't want him to suffer but reckoned she had more of a chance to speak to him when he was at less than his active best. No racing about and no running rings round her with his reasoned arguments.

'Give me the painkillers now and I'll see you in half an hour.'

That would do nicely. Give her time to think about what she wanted to say and how she wanted to say it.

An hour and a half later they were walking in single file down the narrow cracked pathway to the world outside. She could hear him muttering under his breath. She lifted the latch on the black wrought-iron gate and turned to see John's contorted face and screwed-up eyes remonstrating against the bright spring sunshine.

'I'll need my sunglasses. I'll need to go back for my sunglasses.'

'Wait there. I'll get them.'

'Oh and a hat. Get the panama out of the hall cupboard.'

Eventually they were out, past the black cast-iron streetlamp that stood guard on top of their garden wall. Crossing the cobbles on the prestigious street that had been their home for the last fifteen years, they made their way towards St Bernard's Crescent. The dramatic sweep of porticos and pillars seemed to set this grand little street quite apart from its less ostentatious neighbours. She liked this place. She liked where they lived.

Sheila was keen to stride out, but John was taking his time, walking sedately by her side and so she took the time to peer through the large drawing room windows and admire the quality fabrics, paintings and assorted *objets d'art*. It wasn't nosiness, she told herself – she might just get some ideas for their own redesign project. Suddenly she spotted, through one window, an elderly couple engaging in what she imagined to be a quiet and unfussy conversation. Nothing like the conversations she and John had.

The wife was perched on the edge of one gold damask sofa and the husband was relaxed back into the other. A petite, elegant lady with grey hair tied up into a tight bun, she didn't look at him at all, but sat determinedly turning the pages of a magazine. As she talked, she smiled. It looked a gentle, contented smile. He wore the same expression while sucking on a pipe that didn't appear to be lit. They looked content in their surroundings. Content with all of life, Sheila imagined.

'Where are we going?' They'd come to the end of the crescent and John was not looking or sounding remotely content with anything. He pulled his shades off but tilted his hat down towards his eyes. He wore the hunched-shoulder look of a menacing mobster.

'Just thought we'd have a spin round the Botanics.'

'Oh God no, it'll be full of screaming children all running round after long-tailed rats. And we'll never get a seat anywhere – and the café will be full – again of screaming children.'

The rats were of course grey squirrels, but she sensed that the normally calming beauty of the Botanics was never going to wash away the pain of her husband's hangover. Where to go? She needed the right environment for a deep and meaningful chat about the future.

They walked on in silence for a little while.

'Water of Leith? St Bernard's Well?' She reckoned the quiet walkway was less likely to be overrun with energetic children. Nature's more subtle offerings were there – aromas of wild garlic, puffed-up crimson bullfinches and the odd flash of shining blue to signal a kingfisher speeding over the flowing water. They could sit by the well and start to make plans, finally.

'Fine, come on then.'

She slipped her arm into his and for a brief moment touched her head to his shoulder. She had always enjoyed the feeling of walking as one – together, a couple for all the world to see – but turning to look at him, all she saw was a furrowed brow and increasingly pained expression.

She supposed it was the effects of the hangover, but then maybe not.

They walked through the stone archway heading towards the well and took the lower path, away from the walkers to sit close to the stone base of the temple that housed the statute of Hygeia, the Greek goddess of health. The natural mineral spring here had been discovered in 1760 and, at the time, many locals had claimed the waters could cure everything. She never had that much faith, but she did enjoy the beauty of the place. The water here turned and twisted, channelling around and in between great hunks of stone. The course was set until finally the gushing, tumbling water could choose a more sedate pace further down its route towards the open sea. They sat on one of the few benches along this short stretch, away from the purposeful ramblers striding along the more elevated path.

Before she could say anything, a Japanese couple rushed down the steps, dressed in heavy-duty wet-weather gear, and began snapping away with oversized cameras, taking shots of the domed structure from every conceivable angle.

'Christ, they must be expecting some sort of deluge. Look at the state of them,' muttered John. She followed her husband's gaze but didn't appreciate his tone and so chose to say nothing in response.

The busy little twosome departed quickly enough and soon the only noise she could hear was the sound of rushing water and the chirping sound of chaffinches as they flitted from one side of the water across to the other, hoovering up the small insects that darted about the surface.

She turned to her husband who was sitting with his legs outstretched, crossed at the ankles, arms firmly folded across his chest. The hat seemed further down over his face, the sunglasses were back on and the collar of his checked sports jacket was turned up. She wondered if she'd ever seen a less welcoming sight.

It was time to move things along. 'I just wanted to talk about what we're going to do now.'

He said nothing.

'Look, I know now is not a good time for you to retire but we must have some kind of plan. It was the whole reason I left work. We talked about retiring early, the both of us. Not just me. And now I feel I've given up doing something I really enjoyed and now there's nothing – just nothing. You won't talk to me about anything.' It was all a bit more rushed than she'd intended.

He took his glasses off and turned to look at her.

'Nothing? You say there's nothing. Just think about that, Sheila. Think about what you're saying. We have a lovely home. Well, two homes, actually. You have a daughter, who by the way I know would appreciate a bit more help from her mother, and an adorable grandson. You don't need to work. We don't need the money and you could actually relax and enjoy life for a change. How many people are lucky enough to say that?'

He put his glasses back on, stood up and walked over to the iron railings, gripped them tightly and looked across to the tree-covered bank opposite.

'Look at where we live, Sheila. Over there, behind these trees. Our house is over there. You say there's nothing? I lived in a bloody room and kitchen growing up. Five of us did. That's *nothing*, Sheila. Now we have more rooms than we know what to do with. And by the way you *know* none of this fell into my lap, none of it. I've worked bloody hard. Christ, just when I really need your support you want me to rush into retirement.'

He turned now, leaning back against the railings.

'John, look all I'm trying to say is—'

'Trouble is you haven't had to scramble up the greasy pole. Your dad was a bank manager. Mine didn't know what a bank *was*. You've never had to do without, always had someone looking out for you.' Suddenly his voice dropped. 'Well *lucky* you, Sheila, *lucky* you.'

She'd heard it all before, of course. Every time he felt that his choices, perhaps even his character, were coming under attack, he lashed out like a cornered animal. She stopped listening and started to think about how to frame the next segment of her argument.

'This is nothing to do with how hard you've worked, John. How hard you still work. I appreciate everything your hard work has given us, you know I do.' She stood up and walked over to the railing placing her hands on top of his, covering the white knuckles that looked like they might try to rip the barrier away from its foundations at any minute. She was right in front of his face looking into his pale blue eyes.

'This is about us. Our future. What we're going to do with the rest of our lives. I can make decisions for myself, of course I can, but we're a partnership. We *are*.' She tried to smile but the muscles in her face seemed to have seized up, and so she pressed her face into the crook of his neck. This could go one of two ways. She might seem challenging and cajoling but she hoped he would interpret her words as loving and caring. These, however, were much subtler emotions and she was never really sure if her husband recognised subtlety in anything.

'Look, I just can't retire right now. I know what I said and it will happen, of course it'll happen. Maybe next year, maybe the next again. I need to make sure I'm leaving everything in really good nick and then maybe, you know, maybe it'll be my turn.' He was stroking the back of her head. She loved when he did that. Stroking her hair, gentle kisses.

'Turn for what?' She had lost herself in the warmth of his neck, the tenderness of his touch and ultimately had lost track of his argument.

His hands moved to her shoulders and she felt him tense up as he pushed her away from him.

'Just some kind of recognition. Whether it's some kind of gong or not I don't really care. Just something that says the establishment in this stuck-up city has finally taken notice. I want to show them, show them all that a boy from Leith, from a run down tenement and a bloody awful excuse for a school can do just as well as these idiots with their money, private education and stupid little uniforms.'

She listened. Of course, she listened. It was all he'd banged on about these last few years and to top it all off he'd had his application for membership of one of Edinburgh's most exclusive golf clubs turned down. It was over a year ago now, but he'd been furious. No reason had been given – they didn't need to give a reason. Up until then she'd always thought it was about accolades and affirmations. Recognition of a good job well done. But of course it was more than that and as he spoke to her now, she could see the sheer frustration of it all building and tears began to fill his eyes.

She remembered back to when they had first met – the handsome, ambitious young man desperate to escape the drunken beatings of an abusive father and make good. He'd told her of the crushing disappointment when he knew that, despite getting the grades that would have got him into university, his parents couldn't possibly have afforded to let him go. And then finally, the overwhelming grief of watching his gentle mother, who smothered him with love, die before she could see his success. Over the years these things would haunt him, never leave him. And now this desperate need for recognition was tarnishing his zeal for life. The glowing optimism that she'd found so attractive when they were young just grew dimmer as time went by.

'I just wish it didn't mean so much to you. You work so hard and well, it would be nice if you could start to enjoy it a bit, that's all.'

He looked down at the ground, unable to hold her gaze. 'I will, Sheila. Just not yet, not yet.'

She sighed a heavy sigh and stroked the side of his cheek.

He grabbed her hand tightly. 'You are with me on this, aren't you?' His heart, all too briefly opened, had once more slammed shut and she knew there was nowhere else to go with this conversation.

'Yes, of course. Of course I am.'

*

Sheila had arranged to meet her friends Agnes and Sandra at one of Edinburgh's oldest hotels on Princes Street. The three women had met at college decades earlier and had been firm friends ever since. The place she'd always known as the Mount Royal commanded wonderful views of Edinburgh's more dramatic sights, including the Castle and the Scott Monument. Unfortunately the hotel had been taken over by a succession of bland corporate chains over the years and now the decor was a depressing shade of mauve; a colour which seemed destined to offset the lift that your spirits encountered on walking into the lounge and seeing the sights from one of the large picture windows.

She was a tad early and walked in to find the hotel staff still clearing away after breakfast. The smell of disinfectant, the noise of the vacuum cleaner and the sight of tables still covered with toast crumbs really was doing everything to dial down the experience. A small group of elderly pensioners had bagged seats near the window and were now marching slowly and relentlessly like a band of hungry zombies to the counter, sniffing out the coffee as they went. Just as she took possession of one of the few remaining window tables, the doors suddenly swung open and in walked her friends.

Sandra was a vision in purple. A long sweeping mulberry raincoat, the hem of which grazed the top of a pair of swanky ankle boots with sharp shining stiletto heels. She wasn't sure she'd ever seen a purple raincoat before.

'Oh darling, how are you?' Arms were outstretched ready to sweep Sheila up. She readied herself for the tight embrace.

'Yes, great Sandra, just…' She knew it was coming but still wasn't quite prepared for the wind to be knocked out of her. '…great.' Sheila peered over Sandra's shoulder to see the older of the two friends, Agnes, quietly bringing up the rear, walking in Sandra's wake as she always did. Short grey hair cut in a no-frills style, and plain beige raincoat with simple brown shoes. Agnes was unmarried, a devout Catholic, and Sheila often wondered if she'd ever felt the calling to become a nun and devote her life to the Lord, following in *his* wake rather than Sandra's.

The three of them sat down and waited for the 'codgers' as they liked to call them to return to their seats for mid-morning feeding.

'Are we all lattes?' Sandra barked, whipping off the raincoat and then rearranging her pale lilac scarf so it sat loosely around her neck with the ends trailing over her ample bosom.

Sheila and Agnes nodded in agreement and off she marched.

'How are you?' Agnes tilted her head slightly and smiled. She could have started with the confessional there and then.

'Oh, I'm fine. Just getting used to the whole "lady of leisure" idea.'

'You'll get used to it, of course you will. The three of us are going to have such fun now too. There's so much to get your teeth into – if you're open to new things of course. I really have loved my needlework class and the local walking group for that matter.' A frown began to distort Agnes's saintly features. 'But I'm not sure that's you. You're not much of a walker, are you?'

Her heart was slowly sinking and she knew her face was going to be quick to follow.

'Never mind, you'll find your "thing" soon enough. Don't worry.'

'It's not that. It's that I always saw my retirement happening with John. Didn't really think about having to find "things" to do.'

Agnes shuffled forward in her seat. 'I hope you don't mind me saying this, Sheila, but it always struck me that John sort of ploughed his own furrow. Always very driven and I think after Caitlin was up and off doing her own thing you pretty much did the same. Understandably so. Now that it's just the two of you and you're both heading to retirement – okay, you've got there a bit quicker than anticipated – you probably should talk about what it means for both of you.' She sat back again. 'He's not the easiest, I can see that, but I've always found John to be quite engaging. Not like Sandra's Brian at all. And look my dear – you don't have to be living in each other's pockets. I think you both value doing your own thing, but you *do* need to talk about it at some point. What the future might look like, I mean.'

Sheila leant across and briefly squeezed her friend's hand. Whatever the future held, she knew she would need to be doing something of substance. Something that mattered to her. And that something probably wasn't going to be needlework.

Suddenly Sandra was back. 'She's going to bring them over. Probably didn't trust me in these.' She lifted her leg up so Sheila could properly inspect one of the lethal heels. 'So what am I missing? Are we starting to make plans?'

Agnes smiled. 'She's still getting her head round the idea.'

The young waitress appeared with a tray of steaming coffee and carefully laid down the cups. Sheila welcomed the brief break in questioning.

'Yes, John and I have some things to sort out too.'

Sandra picked up her coffee, sipped at it, all the while staring straight at her. 'Well, you can't wait for John to decide what he's going to do. I mean the man's a bloody workaholic.'

Sheila smiled across at Agnes.

'Seriously Sheila – don't wait for him to retire. That's not going to happen any time soon. I mean he's nothing like my Brian. *He* got out as soon as he could and look at him now. Pottering in the garden – "*Thirsty work Sandra, got a beer there?*" Then it's, "*I'm off to read for a bit,*" and that's him locked away in that miserable room with his endless volumes of Roman military history. I mean you'd think one invasion pretty much looked like any other. "*Think I'll just take a G&T in there.*" Honestly, Sheila, it soon all racks up and then you wonder what the hell am I living with? Not the man I married that's for sure.' She once more smoothed down the ends of her silk scarf. 'Keep him working as long as you can. Gets him out your hair and you can just relax and do your own thing. Also keeps them interesting – I mean Brian just sucks the life out of me, he really does.' She looked momentarily downcast but then suddenly cracked a wide beaming smile and toasted Sheila with her coffee cup. 'Anyway, enough of all that. Here's to lots of fun times ahead.'

CHAPTER 5

Sheila was in the kitchen preparing dinner. When she'd been working, weekday meals, by necessity, had been hurriedly thrown together. But today, she'd enjoyed thinking about what to cook – taking time to look through neglected recipe books, planning a menu and shopping for the ingredients. Shopping, as she'd just rediscovered that afternoon, could be pleasurable when you weren't running round a supermarket throwing items into your trolley at breakneck speed. Normally she was rushing past the folk in Waitrose who had all the time in the world to stroll up and down aisles and consider the merits of Colombian versus Guatemalan coffee and now here she was joining the chilled-out shopping brigade. In her working days, she'd often thought it would be a good idea for the supermarket bosses to create fast lanes after five o'clock dedicated to the sole use of harassed workers. And now here she was meandering behind an elderly gentleman and his chauffeur. Yes, a chauffeur. The white-haired, moustachioed old man weaved from side to side pointing to things and his driver, still with cap on, merely did his master's bidding. She briefly wondered if the young man felt at all demeaned by the experience. But then was it that much different to the young men and women working in the supermarket filling up trollies to order for home deliveries? They too were doing their masters' bidding; they just wore a less glamorous uniform and drove a delivery van rather than a gleaming Bentley.

Back at home, she propped the recipe book up on its stand and prepared to marinade skinless chicken thighs in chilli, garlic, lemon and mint ready for throwing on the griddle later to have with a green salad and fresh crusty bread. She glanced at the clock. John should be home in the next hour or so and it would be time for her to freshen up and get ready to pour gin and tonics as he came in the door.

Creating a domestic idyll wasn't something she'd really bothered about when she was working. Often, they'd been like the proverbial ships that passed in the night, or at least the early evening, and it was a rare occurrence for them to sit down at the same time and eat their evening meal together. But this felt important to her. They had drifted over the years; lost sight of what was important; lost sight of each other. Get this right and maybe other moments could be created. Moments he would come to cherish, moments he would want to recreate.

There would be no talk about retirals tonight – hers or his. There was no rush, really. She was just going to enjoy having a bit of time. It was all sorted in her head now, almost as if the chat with her friends had just given her the little jolt that she needed. *Thank God John was nothing like Brian*, she thought as she hammered at the clingfilm-clad thighs, flattening them so they were ready to take on the marinade. And as for Agnes's talk about needlework and other mind-numbing hobbies. Well, she didn't need hobbies. Needlework – good grief. She brought down the mallet one last time and with a little bit more force than was strictly required.

She skipped upstairs just before seven and changed. Nothing too fancy – crisp pink blouse and cream trousers. Two quick bursts of her lighter Guerlain perfume – not her "going out for dinner" three – she didn't want him to think tonight was about extra effort – and then finally, a hint of lipstick, just to give her some colour.

Seven o'clock came and went. He'd said he would definitely be home by then. She'd made a point of asking just as he was going out the door that morning. He'd looked a bit taken aback to be fair, unsure what lay behind the question, and so she explained she would be cooking – from scratch and with nothing microwavable. As she spoke she'd felt quite proud of herself, taking the initiative and taking steps to move them closer together. It might not last, it might only happen occasionally, but she wanted to show him that this was something they could create together, whenever they wanted to. He'd merely lifted his eyebrows, smiled and said, 'Well, that sounds nice.'

It was only twenty past seven, just twenty minutes late. The gin was in the glass and the lemon cut. Tonic and ice cubes were in the freezer ready to make their grand entrance. Bottle of Sancerre chilling. She glanced at the clock on the mantelpiece – seven thirty. That was fine, that was acceptable. Well, it was acceptable until five endless minutes later the clock hands moved closer to eight and further away from seven. She decided to call his mobile but it went straight to voicemail, so she headed back into the kitchen to check that the salad wasn't starting to wilt. Her senses, tingling in anticipation just moments earlier, quickly settled back into nothingness. He could have phoned, particularly given that he'd been quite clear about when he'd be home. Surely that wasn't too much to ask?

The phone rang but she didn't rush to answer – he could wait now. Slowly she picked it up and spoke. She was aware that her voice was sounding faint, monotone, disinterested even.

'Mum, is that you? Can you speak up? Are you okay?'

'Yes, sorry dear. Just caught me having a wee nap. Don't know where that came from. Not like me. Sorry, fine, wide awake now.'

'No, it's not like you. Maybe you should see the doctor. Maybe you're deficient in something.'

'Oh right. Well, hadn't thought about that. Don't think so, dear, just doing too much in the garden that's all.' Good lord, now her daughter thought she was losing her marbles. Well, maybe that was preferable to believing she was angry with her father.

'Well, it was just to say I was speaking to Dad this afternoon and he thought you might quite like the idea. I haven't really thought it all through yet but I've talked to Simon about going back to work and well of course that would mean the little munchkin going into nursery. And, well, it's just the *thought*. All these strange Latvian women and kids he doesn't know stealing his toys and hitting him for no good reason. Completely irrational, Simon says, but it's the sort of thing that's keeping me awake at night. Anyway, I just thought maybe you could take him for a couple of days. Then I'd know he was safe and happy for two days out the week at *least*.'

At *least*. At least Caitlin had spoken to her father that very afternoon which was more than Sheila had. He'd taken the time to break away from his precious work schedule to speak to their daughter.

'So, when did you speak to Dad exactly?'

'This afternoon. We popped to that coffee place round the corner from his office. Why? Is everything okay? You're sounding a bit funny, Mum.'

'Fine, fine. Milo – yes, well let me just think about it, Caitlin, will you? I mean I'm sure Simon's right. I don't think there's anything to worry about.' She reran Caitlin's pitch in her head. 'I don't really understand the thing about Latvian women. What's wrong with Latvian women?'

'Yes, but you're not doing anything are you? Dad didn't seem to think you'd made any plans yet.'

'No, well I don't know how he knows that really – we haven't spoken about it much at all. I mean, I've been thinking about some things. Just not really done much about them. It's just – two days is quite a big chunk out of my week.'

None of this was going right; none of it was going the way she'd wanted it to.

'Well, will you think about it, Mum? It would be a real help. But if it's too much trouble then just say.'

Was there a hint of bitterness in that last sentence?

'Yes, yes, of course I will. I'm sure we can work something.'

They said their goodbyes and Sheila gently placed the phone back into its sleek black cradle.

Her head suddenly felt very hot. She wanted to scream although she wasn't sure at who or what. Everything was spiralling out of control. This evening was really supposed to have been about one thing – a relaxed and happy dinner at home which, while carefully planned, would look as though it had been nonchalantly thrown together – something she could do at the drop of a hat. Instead there were conspiratorial meetings going on behind her back planning what she should be doing with the rest of her life.

She walked through to the kitchen to consider next steps for her culinary creation. She looked at the salad. The vinaigrette dressing, poured some forty minutes earlier, had completely doused the vibrancy of the crisp green salad leaves.

But then maybe she wasn't capable of creating anything new. Maybe John and Caitlin really believed that. Busy lives meant they'd all just got on with things before, rubbed along perfectly well. Her life, this 'new chapter', looked like it was to be written by her daughter and her husband. However the story was going to pan out, it looked like she would be lucky if she got to come up with a few footnotes.

Then, just as she was about to throw the salad away and start again, she heard the key in the door. She glanced up at the kitchen clock. It had just gone eight.

'Hi darling, it's me. Sorry I'm late. That shareholders' meeting went on forever.'

There were familiar noises of keys being thrown onto the hall table, the door to the cloakroom opening, and the clatter of wooden clothes hangers before John appeared at the kitchen door and stood rolling his sleeves up. 'Don't know why we bother with all these presentations – passenger numbers, expanded routes, staff turnover. God, all these people want to know is whether they're seeing a return for their buck.' He moved towards the fridge, opened it up, peered past the marinating chicken and chilled wines and went straight for a bottle of beer. 'I mean they don't care about how "green" or "socially responsible" we are. Know what I mean? Is there any of that pâté left?'

He pulled back from the fridge and went straight for the bottle opener in the cutlery drawer. Only after he'd taken a few slugs of cold beer did he seem to figure out that all was not well. 'What's wrong, what's happened?'

'Nothing, nothing's happened.'

He took another slug of his beer. 'Oh yes it has and I'm about to get it in the neck. Am I right?' He stared right at her.

She wanted to move or at least look away, but she couldn't. 'No. You just said you'd be home at seven that's all. I told you I was cooking.' She ran the tip of her tongue over her bottom lip. Lipstick was gone, all gone.

He glanced up at the clock. 'Okay. Well it's just gone eight. Can't be in the doghouse for being an hour late, surely?' Then he smiled, a jokey kind of smile. 'I mean how often have we managed to eat at the same time during the week? I can't remember the last time.'

'No, I know. But that was before – when I was working. Just thought I'd make a bit of an effort tonight.' The very thing she hadn't wanted it to look like.

'Well, I'm sorry. I hadn't picked up that you were going to a lot of trouble.' He walked over and kissed her lightly on the cheek. 'I'll just go up and change. Sure it will be lovely.'

She chopped, dressed, sliced, buttered and griddled while her husband took his time upstairs. Finally John came down just as aromatic smells began to fill the kitchen and the burning chillies were starting to make her eyes water. He made for the fridge again and pulled out the ice-cold white wine, tiny little droplets of tears running down the side of the bottle. He picked up the chequered tea towel and quickly dried the bottle off. 'Are you okay? You're not upset, are you?'

'No, no. It's just the chilli stinging my eyes. I was going to do gins before we ate but if you'd rather—'

'I've had my beer now. You should have said when I came in.'

For the first few minutes they ate in silence. She couldn't even summon up the energy to ask him about his conversation with Caitlin. She felt so tired all of a sudden that all she wanted to do was finish the meal and go to bed. But he wasn't going to let it go.

'Look if this is a new regime where we have planned meals at set times then you just need to let me know. But to be honest, I don't really see it working. I mean I don't always know what's happening day to day never mind week to week.' He wiped his mouth with one of the new lemon print napkins she'd bought for the occasion. 'This is lovely though. Really tasty.'

'No, it's fine. Honestly. You're right. No point during the week really.'

'But lovely at the weekend. You know if we're not at Jean's place or over at the kids'. Great then.'

'Yes.'

'Met Caitlin today. Did she tell you? About her plans I mean?'

'Yes, she rang.' Sheila picked up her wine. 'She's going back to work.'

She looked across at her husband, but she could tell he had exited the conversation. He quite often did that. Started something and then another thought, an idea would occur to him, something far more important.

'John.'

'Yes, sorry. Just thought about something – something someone asked tonight. Wasn't sure what he was getting at and think I might have waffled a bit. Hate when that happens. Hate when I'm not on top of things.' He looked sternly down at his empty plate then blinked and was suddenly back in the room. 'Sorry, what were you saying?'

'Caitlin. Does she often meet you for coffee?'

'Sometimes. If she's passing, she pops in. I'm not always there.' John pushed his seat back from the table and rested one ankle on the other knee. He cradled the glass of wine in his lap.

'It's just I never would have thought to disturb you at work like that.'

'Why?'

'Well, you're always so busy.'

'Not necessarily. Depends what I've got on. But you were busy at work too, remember. Can't imagine Colin or any of the others being too happy if you'd just swanned off in the middle of the afternoon.'

'No, I suppose not.' She started to fiddle nervously with her napkin. She didn't really know what she was trying to say. 'I just never knew, that's all.'

'Oh my lord. Scandal – Chief Executive of bus company has secret rendezvous with his daughter.' He shook his head and smiled. 'Well, we can meet for coffee or lunch if you want now. If I'm around, that is.'

'Yes, lovely.' She smiled at him, stood up and started to clear the table.

'Can I help?'

'No, it's fine. There's not much to do. I'll be through in a minute.'

She cleaned the plates of limp leaves and small pieces of burnt chicken before stacking the dishwasher. Soon they would return without a trace of food, gleaming like new, as though real griddled chilli chicken had never existed – just some imaginary perfect meal for some imaginary perfect couple.

She felt stupid for making a thing about the coffee. She hadn't really meant to. It was just John and Caitlin again – that was the thing really. What about all these mother-and-daughter lunches or coffees or shopping trips that other women she knew seemed to have in their lives? Why didn't she have that? No, it was just John and Caitlin and she wasn't factored in at all when it came to cosy little chats over coffee. Well, no that wasn't true. Not in the planning perhaps but, of course, she was factored in when it came to their conversations. Criticising her, laughing at her. She was tired of feeling ganged up on – tired and helpless. Helpless because suddenly it felt much too late to think about creating a whole new family dynamic.

She finished up in the kitchen and joined her husband in the lounge. He was sitting feet up on the tartan-clad footstool reading the newspaper.

She sat on her seat near the fireplace suddenly feeling uncomfortable in her crisp blouse and smart trousers. 'Caitlin said she'd spoken to you about me taking Milo a couple of days a week.'

He dropped the paper down to his lap. 'Yes. Well she doesn't seem too happy chucking him into the nursery five days. But then I've looked into it and it seems like just the ticket. Really good assessment ratings, empathetic staff, children seem to thrive. You know, all that modern day "wrap the child in cotton wool" guff. But there you go, that's our Caits.' He lifted the paper back up again.

What was he doing looking into what nursery Milo should go to? Surely that was the prerogative of the parent? Where was Simon in all of this? 'Well, I'm just not sure about committing myself to two days a week.'

The paper came down quickly this time and she could see his grip was tighter. 'Not sure about committing yourself? Well, I guess I can understand that. But is there anything else you've been thinking about? I mean plans for anything else? I just couldn't think of anything when Caits asked me.'

She looked down into her lap. What was she saying? How could she even suggest it might be a problem?

But then his voice softened and when she looked up, he was smiling at her.

'I know he can be a handful and God knows I wouldn't want to be stuck with him two days a week. I mean I love him to bits and all that, but I'd probably throttle him.' He leaned forward, looking right into her eyes. 'Look, no one's making you do this, Sheila. If you don't want to look after Milo, you really don't have to.'

And now she felt worse than ever.

CHAPTER 6

'This is amazing, Caits. Really tasty. Spicy but not too spicy. Just the way I like it.' Sheila's husband was waxing lyrical about – what he imagined to be – his daughter's culinary creation. It was Saturday night and Caitlin and Simon had invited Sheila and John round for dinner. It was a rare event and Sheila imagined that it was nothing to do with treating the parents – the whole evening was most probably designed to seal the deal on her potential childcaring responsibilities.

'Well, Simon does it all really. He's much more adventurous on the food front than me. You wouldn't think it but there we are.'

Simon looked up from his plate straight across at Sheila. His face was expressionless. She smiled at him and he smiled right back. 'John's right, Simon, it's lovely. We all have hidden depths, you know. Things we're good at – sometimes we don't even know we're good at them till we give them a go.'

'What's your thing then, Sheila?' Simon picked up her cue.

'Not sure I've any particular hidden talent but I do have interests in things. Things I'm going to follow up now

I've a bit more time.' She looked across at her daughter to see the expression change from relaxed indifference to one of emerging panic.

Caitlin put her knife and fork down rather clumsily. The clanking on the plate made everyone sit up. 'What sort of thing, Mum?'

'Well, I met Agnes and Sandra the other day and they're involved in so many things. Not all to my taste of course but still – there's so much out there for retired folk like me.'

'Okay.' Caitlin dragged out the second syllable as she slowly digested this new piece of information. 'And what about Milo? Are you still thinking that might work?'

Sheila smiled. Caitlin needed to lock this down and she couldn't wait a moment longer. Particularly now that other opportunities to bag her mother's time were beginning to emerge.

'Yes. Two days is fine. As long as they're fixed days.' Sheila was suddenly aware that everyone was looking at her. 'If that's okay?'

'Oh yes, that's great Mum, thanks. Honestly it's going to be a real help. I know I'm being silly, but I'll just feel better about the whole "going back to work" thing now.' Caitlin smiled. It felt to Sheila like a genuine, loving smile and it made her heart skip a beat. Of course it was the right thing to do. More than that, she realised right there and then, it was something she *wanted* to do.

The meal was over and Sheila was starting to clear the plates away when she noticed John slap Simon on the shoulder and then mutter something in his ear. Simon, who had been about to pick up a couple of serving dishes, looked apologetically across to his wife, set the dishes back down and walked off with his father-in-law, through the kitchen and out into the garden. The women, not unusually, were left to clear everything away and clip-clopped back and forth across the oak wood floors from the open plan lounge/dining room to the sleek white melamine kitchen that seemed, to Sheila, to house every integrated German-made appliance in existence.

The house wasn't really to Sheila's taste. It was part of a brand new and exclusive development on the outskirts of the city and the word 'exclusive' was constantly emphasised by her daughter when she spoke about where she lived. Why was exclusive better than inclusive? All these Council strategies on inclusion just never reached some parts. To be fair, it was in a lovely quiet location with a beautiful outlook, but Sheila always felt as though she was walking into a vast laboratory. Everything seemed inordinately clean, almost sterile.

'So what are these other things you might do, Mum?'

Sheila was handing her daughter the dishes and Caitlin was neatly stacking the spick-and-span washer.

'Well, I think I might look into one of these university short courses. Something to do with history. Nothing too academic, though. I really don't want to get bogged down with essays and assignments. Couldn't really be bothered with all of that.'

'Oh right. Didn't realise you were interested in that sort of thing. Come to think of it, Simon's old boss Harry is a bit of an amateur historian. I think he runs some sort of club or society. Started it off when he retired. Something like that anyway. You should ask Simon about it.' Caitlin stood up and turned towards her mother. 'You remember Harry, don't you? Came to a few drinks things we had when we were living in town.'

Sheila couldn't remember at all. But then she'd probably blanked out most of these 'drinks things' – both her own and her daughter's. Caitlin was so like her father in so many ways. 'Harry? I think I do. Not sure though – I've met so many people at these things.'

A little while later the four of them were sitting in the off-white lounge area drinking coffee. Caitlin and Simon sat on a pale beige two-seater couch and Sheila and John took up their places on each of the matching armchairs.

'What colour are these walls?' John asked.

'It's called Elephant's Breath. Supposed to be a sort of uplifting mid grey,' Caitlin replied quite matter-of-factly.

John nodded but said nothing. Sheila knew what he was thinking. There wasn't really anything terribly uplifting about mid grey. She looked across at Simon and asked, 'So what were you two talking about in the garden?' Simon shifted nervously in his seat but just as he was about to answer, John butted in.

'I was just talking to Simon about the wee lad's nursery fees. Thought it might be something we could help with.'

Sheila tried to remain expressionless. *Help with*, she thought to herself. Why on earth would a successful tax lawyer and hedge fund manager need any help with nursery fees for all of three days a week?

Caitlin merely smiled across at her father, but Sheila could see how uncomfortable Simon was at the proposal. 'It's very kind of you, John. Kind of you both, but really there's no need – honestly.'

'But darling if Daddy wants to, then I think we should let him. It's a lovely thing to do for Milo. It's just a gift.'

Simon wasn't going to back down. Sheila watched him shift in his seat and then in a much more forceful tone than she was used to from her son-in-law, 'Well, I think your parents have been extremely generous with the bank account they've set up for him so, really.' He turned and looked across at Sheila. 'I think that's more than enough – honestly.' His dark brown eyes, normally so kind and welcoming, suddenly had a sharp steeliness to them.

Sheila smiled and nodded but said nothing. Simon had stood his ground and Caitlin would just have to accept it. She turned to look at her husband, but John looked nonplussed at the rejection of his offer. He liked to make the grand gesture – its subsequent acceptance or rejection was of little consequence to him. Only Caitlin appeared to mutter something under her breath and then quickly put the matter out of her mind. She's probably thinking of bigger battles ahead, Sheila surmised. Battles that would be far more important to win. Caitlin stood up smartly, began gathering up the coffee cups and moved on to the subject of her mother's new-found interest in history.

'Mum's looking at taking a course in history and I told her about Harry. He's running something like that, isn't he?'

Before Simon could answer, the sound of whimpering came from the middle of the glass coffee table where a large wooden bowl sat filled with wooden apples, bananas and pears. Sheila quickly realised that a baby monitor was wedged in amongst the faux fruit.

'Oh, isn't he a sweetie, I'll just leave him for now. See if he goes back to sleep.' Caitlin sat back down again and looked lovingly at the ornamental display.

'Didn't realise you still used the monitor?' Sheila asked.

'Yes, well, best you should know now that you'll be looking after him.' Caitlin smiled at her mother. 'We don't really need to use it. I mean he does sleep through mostly. It's just we can't hear him when we're down here – he's so far away.'

'Yes, we didn't really need a house this size. Five bedrooms is a bit daft really.'

Once again Sheila could see that Caitlin did not appreciate Simon's intervention.

'Maybe not now, Simon, but we need an eye on the future. There could be more babies one day.'

Simon's eyes grew wider and Sheila found herself desperately hoping that they were both on the same page when it came to more children. It was a subject matter that she and John had never managed to completely reconcile. She looked across at her husband, but he was gazing out through the French windows, seemingly lost in a world of transport solutions and profit margins.

The fruit bowl fell silent and Simon picked up the conversation. 'Yes, he does something. It's like some sort of history club. Every session, he picks say half a dozen historical characters and leads some kind of study and discussion. If I remember, he also asks the group to nominate any character they might have a particular interest in. Anyway, he's been running it for a few years now – devotes nearly all his time to it now he's retired. I think they even go off for little jaunts round the country. All quite relaxed and informal, I think. He tried to get me interested but it's not really my bag and anyway I just haven't the time. Might be right up your street, Sheila.' Simon paused. 'It's just that Harry...'

'It's just that Harry what?' Sheila felt slightly alarmed at the way Simon's upbeat description had suddenly tailed off.

Caitlin decided to pitch in. 'Oh, I guess what Simon's trying to get at is that Harry just isn't everyone's cup of tea. He's a bit loud, bit over the top, but then he's just really enthusiastic about his little club. I mean one of our old neighbours used to go along before she popped her clogs. Remember Gladys upstairs from us?'

Sheila nodded.

'Well, she just loved him. Said his enthusiasm was infectious. She loved going along. Friday afternoons I think it is.'

Simon seemed to regain his positive view of Harry's History Club. 'Yes, of course I'd forgotten all about Gladys. I'm sure Caits is right. I'm sure you'd enjoy it. Well, you could always go along and see. No harm in that.'

No harm in that. Sheila wasn't entirely sure what Simon meant and really couldn't contemplate dealing with any more challenging men in her life. But she'd think about it. Simon was going to speak to Harry and get her a bit more information. Then she could decide. She didn't need to rush into anything, she didn't need to *do* anything. World was her oyster after all.

'John?' Her husband had been remarkably quiet throughout the evening but then she saw he was checking emails on his phone.

'Sorry. What?' He whipped his glasses off his face and stared intently at his wife. She knew he still wasn't back in the room.

'What did you think about me joining this history club?'

John sat for a minute clearly trying to recalibrate his thoughts. 'History club? Well if you'd like to. Don't see why not.' He blinked and returned to his phone. It hadn't even occurred to him to ask why his wife might want to take up studying history.

Later that evening John and Sheila took a taxi home. The cab raced back into town and, unusually for an Edinburgh taxi driver, there was no chat about roadworks or tram costs. The trams seemed to provoke an endless stream of bitterness and misery for the black cabs and she noticed how John had become quite adept at listening and concurring with every new 'fact' about overspends and poor design. Not once had she heard him rise to the bait or challenge even their most fantastical assertions. She began to feel tired and allowed her head to rest on John's shoulder while he continued to scroll down through his messages.

'Couldn't you leave that for just a minute, John? Honestly, you were at it all night tonight. Hardly joined in the conversation.'

'Sorry. It's just annoying me. I know I sent this bloody email but I'm damned if I can find it.'

'Well, it's looking like my week is starting to take shape. Caitlin will speak to the nursery but I'm going to have Milo Monday and Tuesday and then we'll see if this club works out on a Friday afternoon. That leaves me Wednesday and Thursday to be at home or see friends – even you, now that I know you can do lunch or coffee during the week.'

Suddenly, he stopped what he was doing and lifted his arm round the back of his wife's shoulders and pulled her in close to him. 'Well, that all sounds quite good then, doesn't it?'

'Yes, dear. That all sounds quite good.'

*

Both she and John had decided that they would set aside one of the spare rooms to be Milo's playroom so they didn't have to worry about the Colefax and Fowler wallpaper or the antique furniture in the rest of the house. They would also create a little bedroom for him, which Sheila was looking forward to decorating with Thomas and Friends wallpaper. John had already checked that it would be easy enough to remove when the time came – so everyone was happy.

As she was filling the new playroom with toys, Sheila began to think of their old house – a cosy detached 1930s bungalow. Happy times watching her little girl play with prams and dolls, all too quickly abandoned in favour of hockey and pony club and then finally the descent into

Goth-style grunting and blackness. That last phase never lasted. Caitlin was far too talkative, far too sociable, even in these difficult teenage years, to lock herself away for long. And then everything that had created a solid, comfortable home was abandoned for something much grander. Tall ceilings, beautiful cornices, ornate furniture.

She knew Caitlin had hated the move. Not because they'd talked about it but because Caitlin's friend Sophie Taylor, her only true friend to this day, had told her own mother. It was Margaret Taylor who'd mentioned the news to Sheila at an old neighbours' summer barbecue.

'Well, yes, you're right, Caitlin has found the move difficult and of course leaving here has been a wrench for everyone. But we're all agreed the new house is lovely, Caitlin does really like it and of course she's going off to university soon.'

What a load of nonsense. They'd never talked about any such thing. Maybe they *had* moved on too quickly. Maybe if they'd stayed where they were for just a little bit longer, Caitlin could have enjoyed the feeling of coming back home in the holidays. The home she grew up in, the home she was familiar with. But they'd moved on with their lives, shut the door on life as a family and Caitlin just had to follow suit. Talk to her friend, talk to her friend's mother. Talk to anyone except her own mother.

She told herself to snap out of it. Things were coming together for them all. They shared Milo now – perhaps that would bring them closer.

The first Monday with Milo proved to be a resounding success. He didn't appear to miss his mother at all and was excited to explore Granny's house unfettered by overprotective parents. He ate without fussing and played with new toys with a fierce abandon. He threw them about the room and then toddled off to pick them up and chuck them again from the other side. Sheila sat on the floor with him and enjoyed watching his antics, wondering what was going on in his little mind as he picked up something new, and turned it over in his sweaty little hand. Then suddenly his chubby little arm would snap back ready to launch Thomas the Tank Engine through the air. Even Caitlin was stunned when Sheila told her that he'd gone down for an afternoon nap without any fuss, happily cocooned under his Lego covers.

The same thing, unfortunately, could not be said for the Tuesday. He cried when his mother left, threw his food at Sheila and the playroom walls and downright refused to go down for any kind of nap. Sheila was beginning to despair. All the warm, almost maternal feelings from yesterday were quickly dissipating. What had she let herself in for? Was she going to start to dread having her grandson over? Good God, they were only two days in. Then she suddenly remembered – warm milk followed by the plastic dummy. She didn't remember Caitlin being quite this violent with her tantrums, but these were her 'go-to' remedies. She had heard her daughter calling them pacifiers which, she assumed, was another example of the creeping Americanisation of child-rearing. But for her they would always be dummies.

Suddenly the phone rang, just as she was about to execute her masterplan.

'Colin? What a surprise. How are you?'

'Oh, I'm fine, Sheila. All the better for hearing your voice. I just wanted to discuss a little proposition I've got for you. Are you free any time this week? I've taken the week off but not really doing too much so got plenty of spare time.'

A proposition? Sounded intriguing but also made Sheila feel slightly wary. She thought back briefly to the springtime drinks party and Colin's rather unsettling behaviour. 'Well, actually, I'm looking after Milo a few days a week, so I've not really got much time to spare.' Why did she say a few days, why not just tell him it was Monday and Tuesday? And then, just at that point, Milo began to wail as if to back up the whole childcare story.

'Oh my, sounds like you've got your hands full.'

Then a thought struck her. Why not kill two birds with one stone? Get Milo out in the stroller today to meet Colin. That might just send him off to sleep and she wouldn't have to use up one of the other precious free days to meet up with her old boss to discuss the mystery proposition.

'Might not be ideal, Colin, but I could meet you today with Milo. I know he sounds a bit of a nightmare, but he'll calm down when he's in the stroller,' she said in hope rather than in expectation.

'Oh, right. Okay, well, why don't you pop along for a bit of lunch? Say one o'clock?'

'Great. See you then.' Sheila felt slightly uncomfortable about going to Colin's house. She had been before, of course, but only with John. Always with John. She checked herself. There was no need to feel uncomfortable – that was being silly. It was just lunch and she was taking Milo. Sheila bent down to pick the little boy up, all ruddy-faced and now grinning from ear to ear. 'We'll have a nice lunch with Uncle Colin, won't we?' Milo's little body suddenly stiffened and it was all Sheila could do to get him strapped into his pushchair.

CHAPTER 7

As Sheila pushed the stroller along the busy main street down to the Water of Leith walkway, she began to notice people delivering parcels, serving coffee, emptying bins, washing windows. All of them caught up in their own pressing world of work – the world she'd left behind. You didn't really notice it when you were in it, she thought. There was an urgency about these men and women – targets to be met, appointments to keep, customers to be served and they all seemed to move with the same sense of purpose. Sheila used to move with a sense of purpose but not so much anymore. No more smart, sharp paces. Walking tended towards meandering and strolling – just as she was doing now with her grandson. A whole new gait appeared to have been adopted, a whole new pace to her movement. A pace she would just need to get used to.

Colin lived in an old stone lodge house set back from the Water of Leith – away from the path, away from people. Although situated just yards from main roads and cycle paths, Sheila felt like she was stepping into another world when she visited Beech Lodge. She wondered how Milo would react to the dark, austere house – all nooks and crannies and little odd-shaped rooms, quite unlike anything he'd experienced in his short little life. In truth, she was hoping he'd be asleep by the time they got there and would awake happy and refreshed. Again, it was more a triumph of hope over expectation.

She opened the creaky iron gate and walked up the narrow uneven path to the house. Either side of her, rhododendron bushes grew wild among the oak and copper beech. Gnarled and twisted vine-like trunks, obliterating light, sucking up all the moisture and letting little else grow. Their compensatory gift was a canopy of outrageously bright pink flowers. It was an impressive display and Sheila liked that the blooms countered the cold, dark tones of the house.

Milo was staring at her from inside the stroller as they approached the front door. He was tucked in cosily, had relaxed his taut little limbs and now prepared for the onset of sleep. Sheila knew it was going to happen any minute. The wide-eyed stare was the giveaway. The little boy was in the last throes of fighting sleep and every immature muscle behind his shining eyes was straining to do its job. Suddenly there was a slow, heavy blink, then another one. No sound came, his chin sank into the rolls of fat round his little neck and he was gone.

Ideal, Sheila thought as she walked into the large stone-clad vestibule and pressed the front doorbell.

The door opened quickly and there stood Colin, in a checked shirt and tie – the only concession to time away from work being the rolling up of his sleeves. 'Lovely, lovely, come in you two. Sorry about all the bird droppings, I've got house martins nesting up there.' He pointed to a small dark construction perched perilously under the sloping roof of the vestibule.

'Oh, that's fine. It's always lovely to see house martins.' Sheila glanced upwards and then tiptoed round the mess, pushing the stroller into the dark wood-panelled hall. 'I think I might leave him in this – he's only just now gone off to sleep.'

'That's fine,' Colin whispered. 'Just wheel him into the lounge.'

Sheila did as instructed: took her coat off, sat down and pulled the stroller closer to her so she could keep an eye on Milo. Colin was standing in the middle of the room looking down at her. He was, as ever, very smart but Sheila thought there was something vaguely unclean about him. Not really the Chief Executive she was accustomed to. Everything he wore looked like it needed a good dry-clean and his house a good steam-clean. Everything very ordered, lots of nice features but just a bit grimy – man and house. She tried not to breathe through her mouth. She didn't want to taste the bad smells.

'Not too early for a gin and tonic?' he asked.

'Well, it probably is for me and I am, after all, the responsible grandmother,' she replied jokingly, nodding to Milo.

'Oh nonsense, we'll just have a swift one before lunch. Relax you a bit, Sheila. You're taking these grandparenting responsibilities awfully seriously.'

She forced a smile, as he about-turned and left the room, not really knowing what else to do. Was Colin not a grandparent? He did have children, she knew that. One down south and one in Australia. How sad if he was, she thought, and never saw his grandchildren. The thought prompted a surge of affection for the little boy sleeping soundly in front of her.

The gin and tonic arrived slightly chilled but not ice-cold – not the way she liked it. There was a sliver of lemon and one small cube of ice slowly melting as it floated miserably around the glass.

'I've just got some quiche and salad. Hope that's okay? Not much of a cook really and since Patricia – well, I really haven't had the inclination. You're a good cook aren't you, Sheila?'

'I try. I like to make an effort at weekends but during the week there just isn't time. John and I – well we're like ships that pass in the night.'

'Not anymore, Sheila.' Colin stood almost directly above her looking down. She felt hemmed in. The stroller at one side and this tall, slightly musty-smelling man on the other, blocking out the light from the small picture window.

Suddenly he moved aside, the light shone back through into the room, and he sat down beside her. She put one hand on the stroller and turned to check on Milo who was fast sleep, oblivious to all around him. Sheila had caught the faint whiff of stale alcohol as he'd taken up position on the couch, but Colin, really? He wasn't a drinker, not a serious one. Nothing like the permanently slightly inebriated Clive Johnston – Colin's predecessor Chief Executive. But then how much did she know about his life outside work?

'So, are you and John making big plans?'

God, why was everyone else so interested in their future? It was their business, no one else's.

'Not really. He'll be working for a year or two before he retires but that's fine. I've got plenty to keep me occupied.'

'Ah, well that's what I wanted to talk to you about.' He seemed to be pressing his thigh up against her leg, but she wasn't altogether sure. Maybe it was just the way he was sitting wedged into the corner of the sofa. 'You see, we've got a big town twinning event coming up. Italian this time so that's the Florence lot. Italian Consulate's been in touch and, well, there's so much to organise.' He looked at her almost pleadingly. 'I can't leave it all to Janet. She just doesn't know how to deal with people. Important people, I mean. Don't get me wrong, she's competent enough at all the admin but it's the people skills – they're not there.' He placed his hand over hers. 'She's just not you, Sheila.'

She sat frozen to the spot. She could feel her heart beating. 'I don't know, Colin. I've got Milo now and there are other things I'm looking into.' She slid her hand away.

'Yes, yes of course. Silly of me to think you might want to come back. Obviously it would just be a short-term contract, say three months. Just want to make sure we're giving it our best shot, that's all.' Suddenly he looked like her boss again. Sitting upright, his voice assumed its calm, controlled tone once more. 'Look at me, trying to soft-soap you. Should have known that would never work.' He stood up suddenly. 'Right, enough of work talk. As I said, it's only quiche and salad – that's as much as my culinary skills will stretch to. Hope that's okay?'

'Great, fine,' she replied, following him through to the kitchen.

Everything relaxed – her shoulders, her cheekbones, her heart rate. So it had just been a tactic to get her to manage this silly twinning event. What had she been thinking? And now that the proposition began to settle in her mind, Sheila couldn't help but think how much she would really enjoy getting stuck into all the organising. Shrinking Council budgets would mean nothing too extravagant, but she could work within tight constraints – she had in the past. The key was making sure that no one would think that money was an issue. That was the trick; that was the skill. Put on something that looked polished and professional. It was nothing to do with cost, it was about a quality programme – keeping everything tight and focussed and not a penny overspent. Show the Italians what Edinburgh had to offer, make the right cultural and business connections. There was so much crossover – she'd need to speak to the galleries, libraries, museums as well as the Chamber of Commerce, of course.

She was lost in her own train of thought and had finished the warm bacon quiche before she knew it. She pulled herself away from the stream of scattered thoughts and looked up at Colin, who was staring intently at her. He knew exactly where her mind had been.

*

Sheila was standing at the kitchen door as her husband sat on the garden seat and carefully cleaned his golf clubs.

Soft cloths and some sort of cleaning solution were being applied. She watched as he carefully, almost tenderly, drew the edge of a cloth down between the thin grooves of his carbon-shafted three iron. She knew it was carbon shafted and she knew it was a three iron because she'd had to buy the thing for his Christmas present. She stood transfixed as he traced, with his thumb, the path of the cloth softly brushing away any specks of dirt left behind until finally he gently caressed the face of the club with his hand. It stirred something until she shocked herself back to reality.

Her thoughts drifted to the enjoyment she could gain from watching him actually *play* golf. Not the tediousness of following him round a golf course, but rather just watching him address, and then hit, a golf ball. Something about the way he stood, feet firmly planted into the ground; the muscles on his legs tensing up until he rotated his upper body and then whipped it back again, fully loaded; finally unleashing a searing amount of power. All to crush a small, white ball.

Was it his stature, the pose he adopted? Was it the power? Was it the strength he carried through every part of his body until that moment of final release? Sometimes she had physically ached for him going through his moves. Strange, given it really didn't resonate that much with the reality of their physical relationship these days. Functional more than passionate.

He carried on with his carefully ordered cleansing ritual, oblivious to his wife standing just yards away. She knew some people regarded John as insanely driven and self-obsessed. But they didn't really know him. For her it had never just been the physical attraction. That had been there from the very outset and had never changed and, of course, there was drive and ambition. But it had been more than all of that.

John had fallen in love with Sheila long before she had fallen in love with him. It had been an uncompromising love, an overwhelming love like nothing she'd ever felt before. He had once told her that he knew he wouldn't always be the easiest man to live with but the thing that she had to remember was that, for him, there would always be 'a consistency of feeling'. And that, he explained, was what love was all about. 'A consistency of feeling.' To some people that would have sounded cold and detached, businesslike, even. But because his love had filled every crevice, because it made her feel complete and because it made her feel safe, Sheila had known that she would be with him always. Remembering and reliving those words, those times, suddenly brought an overwhelming sense of calm. She smiled and walked up behind him, put her hands on his shoulders and gently kissed the top of his head.

He turned with a start. 'Christ, Sheila – what are you playing at sneaking up like that? Oh God, think I've twisted my neck.' As he turned and put his hand up to his neck, she could see him wince. 'Better be all right for foursomes tomorrow. Bloody hell, Sheila.'

She began to gently massage his shoulders and he relaxed back into her. 'Ah, that's better. Just keep doing that till I tell you to stop.' He reached back and patted her hand.

'So you're off tomorrow?'

'Well, not really. Company golf outing. I've managed to hook up with Roger and Martin, but old Albert Sneddon from Accounts is making up the numbers. God knows how he's going to walk eighteen holes. Anyway, how's your day been? What have you been up to?'

Her kneading of his muscles intensified. 'Well, Simon's not long away. Just picked up Milo. The wee soul wasn't in such good fettle today, but I took him round to Colin's. He rang this morning and asked me over for lunch.'

'Oh, I see. The old boy thinks he can make a move now you're at home and I'm at work all day. I'll need to have words.' He laughed at the creation of what he clearly thought was a ridiculous scenario.

'Hardly.' She stopped massaging John's shoulders and thought back to the warm gin, tepid quiche and the gloomily oppressive house. Colin's leg pressing up against hers, his hand on top of hers. The stale, sweaty, vaguely unclean smells.

'Hey. I thought I was going to tell you when to stop.'

She dragged herself away from all thoughts of Beech Lodge and once again picked up the rhythmic kneading of muscle. 'Anyway, he asked me if I'd like to go back for a short while just to help them out with a big twinning event.'

'Seriously? How are you going to fit all that in?' He'd turned again too quickly and winced in pain.

She moved to sit beside him on the garden bench and John carefully moved the precious golf clubs to one side. 'I don't know. It's too much really, I know it is, but I would love to be involved in some way. Just not sure how, not sure what would work for everyone.'

'Do you want me to talk to Caits? I don't mind. Might be easier coming from me. I said to you before, the lad will be absolutely fine at that nursery. Absolutely fine.'

That was the thing about John. He didn't really delve too deeply, didn't think about the potential repercussions of picking apart arrangements that had been barely formulated. There was a problem to sort and he would sort it. But Sheila worried that just as she was beginning to get closer to Caitlin, all might be lost in one fell swoop.

Sheila rested her head on his shoulder. 'No dear, thank you. I can't let Caitlin down like that.'

'Mind you, thinking about it, I'm not all that sure about you being dragged back to that place, Sheila. They'll get their pound of flesh that's for sure – and just when you were starting to think about new things.' He looked down at his feet. 'Is it because of the other night? The meal and everything?'

Sheila lifted her head and looked at him. Not the successful businessman, just her husband who looked a little bit unsure about the twists and turns their lives seemed to be taking. 'No, no, of course not. That was just a silly misunderstanding.' She squeezed his arm to reinforce the point. 'I don't know, maybe my vanity got the better of me. You know the fact that he doesn't think they could really put this on successfully without me. Maybe I just got carried away with the thought. I mean once Colin mentioned the twinning event, my mind started to race and I started thinking about all the things that would need to happen *now* never mind a few weeks down the track. But really, I can't let Caitlin down.'

'Maybe you could do something, just not full-time. Why not have a chat to Colin about what you could do, realistically. And are you still thinking about following up this history class?'

'I was actually. Simon gave me some more details and the new session's kicking off in a couple of weeks' time. But that's just a Friday afternoon and it's happening in the church hall along the road. Oh, and Sandra and Agnes have both said they'd quite like to come along to that.'

A look of derision swept over John's face. 'Really? I mean Agnes is fine. But Sandra? God, she'll never keep her mouth shut. Probably tell the poor bloke she knows far more than he does.'

'No, she's fine really. She'll just be glad to get away from Brian for a few hours.'

They sat quietly for a few minutes.

'And is that what you want to do? Get away from me for a few hours?'

'Oh John, for goodness' sake. You're not even here, you'll be working.' He really was overplaying the pity hand now.

He smiled. 'Okay, well, why not have another chat with Colin. Just see what might work for both of you. He's a decent sort. Dull as dishwater but he's a good guy. I mean I guess you should be flattered that they can't run the thing without you and I'm sure he'll happily take whatever assistance you can offer.' John slapped her on the thigh and stood up, hands on hips, then turned to look down at his wife. 'Sorted?'

She wanted to say, 'Not really,' but that wasn't what he wanted to hear. 'Sorted,' she replied.

CHAPTER 8

It was Wednesday afternoon and Sheila was getting ready to go round to Sandra's for afternoon tea. It was a beautiful sunny day. A beautiful *Edinburgh* sunny day that was. The sky was a sharp clean blue but as Sheila had stepped out into the garden earlier she'd walked straight into a chilling breeze. *This is Edinburgh's take on summer*, she thought. It looks the part from the outside but step right into the middle of it and you get a harsh cold slap across the face. Sheila had put Colin to the back of her mind and concentrated on structuring her post-retirement life. Caring for Milo; work project; history club. All of which meant juggling of course – she'd be back to juggling. But that was all right, that's what she enjoyed. Everything was perfectly manageable if it was organised properly.

She'd take a jacket and a brolly just in case. You needed to be prepared venturing out in this city. Everything could change in a moment – suddenly and without warning.

Sheila arrived at Sandra's smart little bungalow just after two and walked up the weedless driveway to the front door. She glanced at the front lawn, which seemed to hold no more than a tenuous link to nature. Certainly bore little similarity to grass as she knew it. Luminescent green, uniformly cut and clipped. Nothing growing from it – no daisies, no dandelions, no clover.

Suddenly, a body emerged from the rose bushes at the corner of the house. 'Ah, Sheila, how are you?'

Brian, Sandra's husband, was wearing a large wide-brimmed hat, kneepads strapped to his trousers and was holding a hoe aloft.

'Great, Brian, thanks. Just admiring the garden. It's looking lovely.'

'Never-ending Sheila, never-ending. I could spend every waking minute in here, I really could. But then that would be bordering on the obsessive. I've got other interests, of course. Otherwise you know – you just start to get tunnel vision. Must always broaden your horizons, don't you think?' He was squinting at her in the sun, or was it smirking? She wasn't quite sure.

'Yes, yes. Well, I'll just—'

'They're already in the garden. Just go round the side. Gate's open.'

Brian returned quickly to the array of pale pink roses spaced carefully along the garden wall. Sheila was about to say something else complimentary about the garden until she realised she'd lost him. He'd immersed himself once more in a joyful little existence of his own creation. Didn't really matter a hoot what she thought of his garden.

She turned the corner and saw the ladies already sitting out in chairs on the patio suntrap. Sandra shot up as soon as her friend rounded the corner. 'Lovely, lovely.' Sandra approached, arms outstretched, a vision in salmon pink today. 'We're having a gin. Perk us up before I get the tea on the go.'

Sheila nodded approvingly. It was a relief to be with her friends. Relaxing out in the sunshine on a weekday, drinking proper gin and tonics with great cubes of ice clinking against the glass. It felt almost decadent and a world away from yesterday's oppressive atmosphere – the musty, slightly nauseating odours, lukewarm food and tepid drinks.

'So, Harry Stuart's history club on a Friday afternoon. Looks like we're all keen to join. But are you sure you can fit everything in, Sheila?' Sandra was beginning to look uncomfortably hot in this sheltered little corner. Tight fringe curls were damp with sweat, sticking to her forehead, and little beads of sweat were forming along her top lip.

'Yes, all fine. I like a bit of structure to my week. And I'm having to rethink the going back to work thing anyway.' She'd told Sandra about the offer from Colin that morning on the phone, but her friend had just sounded incredulous that anyone would want to plan their time to that extent.

'Well, they'd be lucky to have you.' Agnes smiled across at her.

'It's just…' Should she say something about Colin? She felt as though she might but then what to say? Whatever was beginning to formulate in her mind suddenly vanished.

'Just what?' Sandra looked concerned.

'Oh nothing, I think Colin just wants more of a commitment than I can give.'

'Well, as I said to you on the phone, you've always got on well with him. I'm sure you can talk it through.'

Sheila smiled but said nothing more. That was enough. Time to move the conversation back to the topic in hand.

'And you're good with our new little venture, Ag?' Sandra duly obliged.

'I think so. I'm not a great history buff, though. Not sure how much I'll be able to contribute.' Agnes always dressed for comfort, today's ensemble being loose-fitting brown linen trousers and a short-sleeved cream tee shirt. She would never match her friend in the fashion stakes, but she always won out on comfort.

Sandra finally accepted defeat, took off the salmon silk scarf that draped over her bosom and undid her top buttons, presumably to allow her cleavage some air.

Sheila sought to assure Agnes. 'Well, I'm not sure we need to know that much. He seems to be happy to allow people to contribute if they want to and it might be fun learning a bit more about Scotland's history.' She sat somewhere in between her friends, both in terms of vocal enthusiasm for the club and in a fashion sense, preferring cool pastel shades to bright pinks or dull browns. It would never do if they were all the same. Everyone needed to show a little bit of individuality – put his or her own stamp on the world. 'We can always go along and see if we like it. The tutor, lecturer, whatever he calls himself, is supposed to be quite fun.'

'Ideal.' Sandra slugged back the last of her gin. 'Could do with a bit of *quite fun*.'

*

'You know what these things are like, Sheila. You commit to a few hours a week and then the whole thing starts to take over. Before you know it, you'll be bringing work home, doing nights, weekends.' John had voiced his concerns without really pressing the issue.

He had a point. She knew that, but her excitement at the prospect of getting her teeth into something again was overriding everything. John used to say if you really enjoyed something, chances were you'd be quite good at it. It was probably something to do with golf, but Sheila understood the sentiment. She knew she was at her best at work, maybe even better than in the home – as a wife, as a mother. Was that awful? Was that an outrageous thing to even think? Yes, it was – so time to just park that somewhere very, very far away too. There was absolutely no harm in talking things through with Colin – just to see what the options were. She looked at the clock on the mantelpiece. John wouldn't be home for at least another hour. Best to have the conversation when he wasn't hovering at her shoulder, putting in his twopenn'orth. She took a deep breath, picked up the phone and pressed the speed dial for Colin M.

'Oh Colin, you are there. I was just about to hang up.' Sheila had decided to get back to Colin with her own proposal. Take the initiative and cast aside any negativity. She'd talked it through with John but he was only worried that she'd be pushed into doing far more hours than intended. She hadn't bothered him with all the uncomfortable stuff, real or imagined.

'Sheila, lovely. How are you? I was just sorting things out downstairs when I heard the phone. Got a lot of stuff stored down in that old cellar but it's not the best place – just a bit too damp, I think. Showed it to John last year – remember? He thought I could really do something with the space but, well, I don't need it for anything special. Just like to keep my files, folders, stuff like that down there.'

'Well, no, I don't think you should be keeping anything very important in the cellar, Colin. I mean you know, the damp, the mildew. Things could start to rot.'

'No, there's nothing critical, nothing financial or anything like that. Just stuff that's of interest to *me*, I suppose. But I've got plans. Definite plans.'

Sheila didn't know what else to say. It really was of no concern to her what Colin Meikle kept in his cellar. Time to move onto things that really did concern her. 'I've been thinking about your proposal – for me coming back to work for a while.'

'Oh, that's great, Sheila. I knew once I laid it all out there, you'd be hard-pushed to turn the job down.'

'Well, actually, I'm not really in a position to accept things as they stand, but I could perhaps oversee things for you. Come in on a Thursday, for example. I could design a work schedule, allocate tasks to everyone, check on their progress. What do you think?'

She had no real idea how this was going down, but she assumed not well. There was silence at the end of the line.

'Shame, that. I really thought I was giving you something on a plate there, Sheila. To be honest I thought you'd bite my hand off to get back to doing something worthwhile.'

'Giving me something? Sorry, I thought you needed someone to manage things – oversee the visit, that sort of thing. I'm sorry, I didn't expect you to *give* me anything.' She could feel her heart beating.

'No, no. Wrong words. Didn't mean *give* you something. Just I thought I was helping you out and, well, this sort of thing is right up your street, isn't it? I thought you'd be grateful.' Suddenly he stopped talking. Sheila searched for something else to say but then he started up again. 'So difficult having this sort of discussion over the phone, don't you think? Why don't you come along to the house and we can talk it through properly?'

She didn't want to go anywhere. He was just doing her a favour, felt sorry for her even. He didn't need anyone for his stupid twinning event.

'I don't think so, Colin. I don't think *I'm* really what you're looking for. I thought I could do a job for you – even if it was just for a few hours a week – but I can see you need much more than that. Not to worry, these things happen. I probably just got a bit carried away thinking about it, to be honest. Anyway, good luck with it all – I'm sure Janet will have everything under control.'

She put the phone down sharply. That was rude, she thought, not even to let him say his goodbyes. Rude and childish. But tears were stinging her eyes now and all she could think was how humiliating it was to have been so roundly rejected. She had always sorted things for him but to Colin Meikle CBE, she had merely become a charity case.

I'm still capable, professional, organised, she thought to herself as she looked down, blinking through the tears, at the notes she'd quickly cobbled together – ideas, plans. Clearly she was supposed to be grateful. Maybe even a charity case that would be willing to give a little something in return.

Her mind went back to the feeling of his warm sweaty hand and the hard pressure of his thigh against her leg. What was wrong with her? What was wrong with all of this? Work had been so straightforward; there was never any of this nonsense to contend with. There were rules, behaviours. Everyone knew their place, what was expected of them. But this was some blurry place between work and real life where normal rules didn't seem to apply and it was a place she didn't like. The balance was all wrong.

She picked up her notes and began to tear them into little pieces.

The following day, John came in and launched into a tirade about work. Sheila was strangely glad to be back into the normal way of things and happy that he'd forgotten about her possible return to the world of local government. His mind was filled with launching the latest eco bus model, a golf handicap that remained resolutely stuck at an unacceptable level and the forthcoming Chamber of Commerce summer lecture series. He certainly knew how his wife spent the first part of her week given the number of odd pieces of Lego that were scattered about the house on Mondays and Tuesdays but it occurred to her that, having dispensed his advice about work, he really wasn't that much interested in what happened next. He talked about Caitlin, Milo and exhaust emissions and then suddenly brought out the Chamber of Commerce lecture programme. 'You'll never guess who's on next week. Think you should come along, darling.'

There were times when she was happy that John could be completely indifferent to what was happening around him and this was one of them. She really didn't want to talk about twinning events and so with a new-found enthusiasm for the Chamber of Commerce, asked her husband who it was they were going to hear speak.

'Colin Meikle? *My* Colin?'

'Yes, dear. *Your* Colin. Don't sound so surprised. We get all the Council Chief Executives along to talk about economic growth, regeneration plans, integrated transport – that kind of stuff. It's Colin's turn now. We had the West Lothian woman along last month. Pretty good actually. Could teach the likes of Colin a thing or two about dynamic leadership that's for sure.' John brought his newspaper down and peered at her over the top of his glasses. 'I know what you're thinking. You're waiting for me to say "pretty good for a woman" aren't you? Well, I'm not going to. She's just the sort local government needs.'

She just smiled and shook her head. No, that wasn't what she was thinking at all.

*

Sandra had taken up the cudgels as far as the Harry Stuart history club was concerned.

'He sounds so nice.' Sandra had called, excited to be escaping Brian for an afternoon every week. 'Not anything like your normal academic type.' Sheila wasn't sure how many academic types Sandra had come across in her life but, no matter, her friend was raring to go. 'Hard to tell how old he might be just from his voice, but he sounds quite young. Can't wait to meet the three of us. Says he hopes we'll enjoy ourselves but something about getting out as much as we put in. Don't really know what he means by that, but anyway we're all signed up for Friday afternoons.'

'He can't be that young. He's retired.' Sheila was now intrigued to meet the enigmatic Mr Stuart. Charming, enthusiastic but could be a bit much, bit over the top. That's how Simon had described him wasn't it?

'Well, anyway, we'll find out soon enough. Says we should give some thought to characters we might want to study ourselves. I really haven't a clue, Sheila; I'm just fancying the idea of the little jaunts around the country. Any ideas?'

'Well actually I had started a list. It's a bit all over the place though. I'm not sure what periods he'll be covering. Is it the usual suspects? Is he looking for characters that might be a little less obvious? I don't know, Sandra, I really don't know.'

'Well, throw a dog a bone, Sheila. I'll just tag along with whatever you come up with. Usual suspects or not.'

*

The friends had agreed to meet for coffee an hour before the club was due to meet, in one of the new Scandinavian coffee-shops-come-bakeries that were sprouting up all over the city. Hard pine seats, cardamom buns and Americanos so strong, Sheila felt her skin tingle and her brain snap ready for whatever Harry Stuart had to throw at it.

'God, this is strong stuff.' Sandra stared wide-eyed as she drained the last of the coffee from her mug. Sheila wondered if her pupils should be looking quite that dilated. 'Okay, so who's on your list, Ag?'

'Oh, I couldn't think. I'll just go along with whatever Sheila comes up with.'

'Oh, hell, that was my trick. So what have you come up with then?' The disconcerting eyes were now boring into Sheila.

'Bit of a mixed bag to be honest. I've got Mary Queen of Scots, Walter Scott and, well, Elsie Inglis.'

'What, the hospital?'

'Well, yes, but there's so much more to her life. I mean really what that woman achieved is absolutely incredible and here we are in her home city and all anyone seems to know about her is a hospital in her name that closed years ago. I mean there should be statues, scholarships, medical bursaries. But there's nothing. Absolutely nothing.' Sheila always spoke passionately about Elsie Inglis. A woman who could easily have spent her days passively learning and doing nothing meaningful with the knowledge gained. And at a time when women were expected to be content with making homes and looking after husbands, she was putting her surgical skills to use out on the front line of a devastating war. Railing against a system that would have seen her ambition thwarted and her sense of worth dismissed out of hand. It was a cause Sheila had championed since reading a little-known account of her life some years ago. But no one else – friend or family – seemed to feel the same sense of injustice.

'Well, I don't know if she fits the bill to be honest, Sheila. I mean I get Mary and Scott, of course, but Elsie Inglis – she's not *that* historical and really her life's confined to Edinburgh and a clapped-out old hospital – not what you'd call a great *Scottish* figure, is she?'

Sheila felt her hackles rise but she didn't want to argue the toss with her friend in a coffee shop. If Sandra only knew the half of it. Elsie Inglis had succeeded in the male world of Edinburgh medicine at the beginning of the twentieth century but it was her doggedness and bravery during the First World War that had really grabbed Sheila's attention. Rebuffed by the British War office she had set up field hospitals in France, Belgium and Serbia, a country that hailed her as a national hero. Sheila liked to hear of women striving against the odds, seeing no obstacles in their path, driven to do the right thing. But that was all too much for today – she could argue the toss with Harry Stuart if needs be.

The three women picked up their coats and bags ready to embark on their new adventure. Well, it was coats for Sheila and Agnes. Sandra had thrown on a tartan cape, which she clearly felt befitted the occasion. The other two women merely exchanged knowing looks and followed the stout Miss Marple lookalike out the door. Whatever

– it was going to be an interesting afternoon and, most important of all, thoughts of twinning events and chief executives had all but disappeared from her mind.

They walked down the driveway, which led to the old ivy-clad parish church on the left and the utilitarian church hall on the right. It had always seemed like a temporary construct to Sheila. Long, rectangular in shape with a grey tiled roof that looked like it had just been placed on top, after all the Lego bricks had been firmly locked in place. Sheila pulled the big metal handle of the heavy-duty door to let the other two ladies through. They made their way, uncertainly, into the main hall. The cleaning smells, the highly polished floor all reminded Sheila of her school gymnasium. It was one vast echoing chamber and the voices – talking and laughing – mixed with the scraping of chairs from one side of the room to the other, sent little shivers up her spine. And then suddenly a tall man broke free from the small crowd and bounded towards them. She first noticed the red-and-grey streaked hair that was swept back from his face down to the nape of his neck, a neat little ginger goatee beard, set off by a bright red tartan waistcoat. The man smiled a dazzling smile on approach and as he was drawing closer, Sheila could just make out the glint of a small silver earring in his right ear. So this must be Harry Stuart.

CHAPTER 9

They were an odd little band. Harry made a quick round of introductions before sitting them down in a circle. Just chairs, nothing else. No books, no desks. *More support group than history class*, Sheila thought, looking around.

They were seven in all. Quite a nice number, he said. Not too big for anyone to feel lost and not too small to feel awkward or exposed. Magda from Lithuania smiled at everyone and every now and again clapped when Harry spoke. Paddy (Sheila was unsure if this was his real name or an off-the-cuff racial slur that the long-limbed, languid Irishman couldn't bother correcting) looked down at the floor throughout and Leonard, a retired history professor from the University of Edinburgh, bore a look that Sheila could only describe as one of pained contempt.

Introductions made, Harry sat back and looked round at his students, naturally taking more time to assess the three newbies. Sheila felt her cheeks flush slightly. His look was lingering as though trying to nail something on each of them. 'Look, this isn't your run-of-the mill history class. I don't pretend to be overly academic; I'm not going to drown you in reference books or exam papers. Yes, we'll look at texts, *important* texts but it's more than that.' He paused. 'I want you to *feel* history. I want you to live inside these people's souls.' His eyes narrowed. 'And so why are we here? This motley band of complete strangers. I have to assume that you all love history, of course.' He dragged his hand through his hair, and then leant forward resting his arms on his knees. 'Look, why do we speak about these people? Why are we interested?'

Sheila glanced round, wondering if they were expected to say something in reply.

'Why have they endured? What is it about their lives that we find so fascinating? What are they saying to us now? Now, right here in the twenty-first century, what is it that they're trying to tell us?' Questions fired out like a spring-loaded Gatling gun.

Sheila could feel Sandra's eyes boring into her left temple, but she wasn't going to look round. Sandra would be looking for some of sort of affirmation. Something that said, 'This is way off beam for me.' But it wasn't for Sheila. It wasn't at all.

'We started looking at Bruce last session, didn't we Paddy?'

The Irishman nodded his agreement.

'Bruce?' Sandra asked.

Oh God, Sheila thought. *She doesn't even know Robert the Bruce.*

'Robert the Bruce.' Harry smiled at Sandra and she smiled back.

Well, there you go. No embarrassment and not a hint of a reprimand from Mr Stuart. Sandra had been won over by a simple smile.

'Not the well-known stories, none of that. No caves, no spiders – but what made the man. What made him tick?' He suddenly slapped his hands down on his thighs. 'I want you to think carefully about what I'm going to tell you. Think about it and get into the mind of the man.

'As the others will remember, a Scottish nobleman handed William Wallace over to the English King, Edward Longshanks. Bruce asked the man to switch allegiance. The nobleman, John Monteith, refused, saying he'd already sworn his allegiance and couldn't serve two masters. Bruce made a choice then – he didn't kill the nobleman but chose to hold him captive. Bruce was called a traitor but some months later, when the English King died, Monteith immediately swore his allegiance to Bruce.'

Harry sat back again, put his hands behind his head and crossed legs at his ankles. 'So what does that tell us about Bruce, the man?'

Paddy was about to say something when Harry looked at him and raised a finger to his lips. 'What about the new members?'

He'd spoken quickly, sharply, intently and Sheila was drawn in. Engaged, interested. Thinking, turning over Harry's words in her mind, piecing together a response. 'Well I guess he would have seen some short-term gain in killing Monteith. Would have earned respect from his soldiers, his peers – maybe even his enemies. But Bruce was clearly looking at the big picture – how this man could be useful to him in the future.'

'Exactly, Sheila. Bruce valued the man's honesty and his principled stance above any perceived short-term gain.

He could see ahead, he played the long game.' Harry leant forward again looking straight into her eyes. 'Strategic thinking, Sheila. The facts as they present themselves can often provoke an instant reaction. But it might not be the *right* reaction. Monteith wasn't trying to deceive Bruce – and Bruce could see that. He could be patient and wait for the big prize. And what was that prize? Unflinching, unwavering loyalty. He could wait for that. He was prepared to wait for that.'

Harry spoke with authority, but his delivery wasn't overbearing. Not the way Simon had described. He was calm and resolute. As she watched him, Sheila felt as though something quite insightful had been passed on to her. It was difficult to know what that something was. More than a history lesson, perhaps, but quite what, she couldn't put her finger on. Harry broke off at that point to speak about more mundane issues – something about the scheduling of classes. Diverted now from his gaze, Sheila relaxed back into her seat. She thought about trying to fix the accent, but it was difficult to pin down the voice. It was the most Scottish voice she'd ever heard. An absurd deduction to make but she couldn't describe it any other way. There was no West Coast singsong, definitely not Edinburgh, perhaps there was a bit of a Highland lilt in there. Whatever, she had enjoyed letting the warm, deep tones gently lap over her. To be truthful she could have happily shut her eyes throughout but there was nowhere to hide and she couldn't risk appearing rude and disinterested.

'Right ladies, any thoughts about characters you might want to look at this session?'

Sheila was jolted out of her pleasant, meandering thoughts. She turned to her friends. Agnes looked terrified, her pleading stare passing between the ladies. Sheila smiled, nodded and was just about to offer up number one of her carefully selected choices when Sandra suddenly blurted out, 'Elsie Inglis?'

Harry sat back and nodded approvingly. 'Well, Elsie Inglis. What a great choice. A forgotten Edinburgh hero. Bit modern-day for me but no, that's great Sandra. Inspired even.' Harry smiled, his piercing blue eyes shining at the quality of his new pupil's contribution. Sandra blushed and her bosom heaved.

Sheila couldn't believe it. *Elsie bloody Inglis was my first choice*, she thought. Harry turned to her, but before he could ask his question, she shouted 'Mary Queen of Scots.'

*

Classic FM was on faintly in the background – not quite loud enough to drown out the soporific call of the woodpigeon. A small bowl of fresh fruit; a cafetière of coffee; a jug of orange juice; croissants and toast with assorted condiments, all covered the dining table. Sheila and John were taking time over breakfast. Unusually for a Saturday morning her husband wasn't off golfing and Sheila had been enjoying the quiet and unfussy domesticity that a rare leisurely breakfast could offer. It was a novelty and a pleasant one.

'So what did Colin have to say for himself?' All too suddenly the spell was broken and she was remembering the cold damp lodge house and the awkward conversation with her old boss.

'Oh, I don't think it's really going to work out. Think he pretty much needs someone there full-time.' She picked out another slice of wholemeal toast from the rack and began to slather it with marmalade.

'Sure the old fool doesn't know what he wants. We can try and pin him down next week at the Chamber of Commerce thingy.' John spoke from behind his newspaper and so thankfully couldn't see Sheila's gloomy expression.

Why can't he go back to being only vaguely interested in anything I'm doing? she thought. 'Oh right, so we're both actually going to that then, are we?' The tension was back and she was ripping at the toast with every bite. Even her teeth were on edge.

The newspaper came down. 'Well, yes. I thought we'd decided that one. Look a few of the wives are going and some of our more successful female entrepreneurs. Give you a chance to catch up with the likes of Carol Stoddart, Jenny Blyth-Hume. Now there's a smart cookie.' And after a quick wink across the table, the newspaper went back up.

The doorbell rang. There was no movement at all from behind the newspaper, so Sheila got up and went to the door. And there they were. Caitlin, Simon and Milo.

'There you go, Milo, there's Granny.' Caitlin unclasped her hand from her little boy's and manoeuvred him towards his startled grandmother.

'Well, hello there. I didn't know you were coming round. Should have called, I'd have made breakfast for you.' Milo was standing arms outstretched. Having been offloaded from one adult he was keen to get into the arms of another.

'Oh, it was just a bit spur of the moment. I said to Simon, what would settle our wee munchkin down today do you think? And before he could answer I thought, *Granny of course*.'

Simon stood behind his wife offering Sheila an apologetic look. She smiled back but could only think how quickly her bite-sized version of a domestic idyll had all but disappeared over the space of two hours. But that was wrong, that was just plain wrong, so she quickly switched focus to the little boy in front of her, swept him up in her arms and marched ahead through to the kitchen.

The newspaper quickly came down; John swiped off his glasses, his whole demeanour energised at the sight of his daughter. It happened quickly like that. The disengaged, almost absent husband turned into sociable and attentive father. Still shocked her, though, still made her feel uncomfortably envious.

'Hello, Caits, this is a lovely surprise.' John enveloped his daughter in a heartfelt hug at the same time stretching out his hand to Simon. 'So, to what do we owe this pleasure?'

'Just thought it would be nice to see you. You sit down, Mum; I'll put the kettle on. Coffee darling?' Caitlin turned to her husband.

'Yes, coffee good.' Sheila knew that Simon easily saw the differing reactions from his in-laws to his wife's intrusions, but he never seemed to judge.

'So how are things going with you two? How are you filling your days, Mum?'

Caitlin had her back to her mother, arranging mugs, grinding coffee beans.

How am I filling my days? Quite a chunk of them are taken up looking after the 'wee munchkin', she thought but said nothing. And right on cue Milo picked up a piece of cold, leathery toast, the middle of which had sunk under the weight of thick-cut marmalade. She watched, unsure what was going to happen next, until suddenly he slapped the soggy mess onto her mouth.

John laughed, Milo squealed and even Simon smiled. Caitlin turned to see her mother's face dripping slivers of glutinous orange peel. 'Oh Mum, he does adore you.' Sheila quickly picked up a napkin, wiped her face and looked down at her grandson smiling and smacking his lips. The feeling was entirely mutual.

An hour or so later, Milo had exhausted himself and was lying flat out on the couch, his rosebud lips pushing out tiny air bubbles.

'So what had you guys planned for the rest of the day? Whatever it is we'll happily tag along.'

'Oh, I don't know. We hadn't really talked about it. I thought I'd pop along and see your granddad.'

'And I was going to hit a few balls at the driving range. Club's getting a bit stuck behind, Simon, you know.' John stood up and did something rather unsettling with his hips.

Sheila was fairly sure Simon didn't know but he nodded anyway. Caitlin just looked confused and turned to her husband for guidance.

'Why don't we go with your mum? We can take Milo. Sure your granddad would love to see him. He's never met his great-grandson, Caits.'

Horrified anguish was the best description Sheila could come up with. Her poor daughter was so stunned at Simon's suggestion that she couldn't get any words out and quite frankly, she didn't need to. Her face said it all.

And then out it came. 'But these *people*, Simon…'

Even John raised his eyebrows at that one.

'These people include your bloody grandfather, Caitlin.' Sheila could sense a weary resignation in his voice.

'Okay, okay.' Caitlin shuffled uncomfortably in her seat. 'Just let's all keep an eye on the munchkin though. Don't want him wandering off with any of the crazies.'

Simon shook his head as his wife stood up and wandered off to the kitchen. 'I'm sorry, Sheila. It's just that—'

'Oh, Simon. Don't worry about it.'

Simon let out a resigned sigh and then quickly changed the subject. 'Meant to ask. Did you get in touch with Harry Stuart?'

'Who's Harry Stuart?' John looked quizzical.

Caitlin was suddenly back in the room and picking up Milo. 'Oh Dad, we talked about his history club last time you were over. Mum was thinking of joining.' Caitlin smiled across at her father. 'What are you like?'

John's brow furrowed. He clearly had no recollection of any such conversation, so he just shrugged and returned to his newspaper.

'Yes, well Sandra got in touch actually and the three of us – me, Sandra and Agnes –went along yesterday.'

'Did you? You didn't say.' Sheila desperately wished that if John was going to show interest in anything she said or did, he could at least stick with it for the duration of the conversation.

'I must say he's a very interesting man. Bit out there, mind you. Not sure if the ladies took to him quite as much as I did.' She glanced at her husband, but he'd clocked out again.

'I know he's a bit over the top but what do you mean *out there*?' Caitlin screwed her face up, same way she had as a child when she didn't quite understand what was being said. It really was an off-putting look. Sheila had often said that to her growing up. But that was a time when she felt obligated to influence her daughter. When at least she should have tried to hold the balance of power in their relationship. Needless to say the scales had slowly shifted over the years.

'Well it's not like a traditional history class. He's really trying to get under the skin of these famous people. What drove them to become the people they were? I guess looking for what makes them different from lesser mortals. What were their passions, their motivations, that kind of thing. It's just very different, that's all.'

'So who are you going to look at this session?' Simon asked.

'Well, Elsie Inglis. She was my first choice actually, but wouldn't you know it? Sandra got in with her name before I had a chance to say anything.'

'Bloody typical.' The voice from behind the newspaper boomed forth.

Sheila ignored the intervention. 'Anyway, I came up with Mary Queen of Scots. That's the funny thing though. As soon as I said the name, Harry kind of glowered at me. It's the only way I could describe the look on his face. It was really quite disconcerting and then – I don't know if he thought he was making me uncomfortable – he suddenly just broke into a huge smile, laughed aloud. Kind of a forced laugh, mind you, and said, "Great choice, Sheila, first-rate choice. Fascinating woman." Then it was something like, "Yes, she was a queen so one could assume she had greatness thrust upon her but still questions of motivation, drive." Funny, he sort of sat back and asked me whether I thought she was a woman of principle or was there something else at play? Had I really thought about her character? I could feel his eyes boring into me again. All very odd, but, I have to say, I find it really very stimulating.'

John's newspaper came down for good at this point and he looked at her quizzically.

'Did he tell you anything about his supposed family connection?' Simon again.

'No, nothing at all. What do you mean?'

'Oh, it's all nonsense, Mum.' Caitlin sat with her arm firmly placed round her husband's shoulder. He looked trapped. 'Says he can trace his line back to Lord Darnley. You know, Mary's husband – the one she was supposed to have had killed.'

'Really?' Sheila looked towards her son-in-law for confirmation.

'Yes.' Simon shuffled about in his seat, loosening Caitlin's hold slightly. 'Whether it's true or not we don't know. And of course that was Darnley's name. Well, Henry Stuart anyway. God knows if that's Harry's real name or not.'

'Oh, I'm sure it isn't,' Caitlin pronounced. 'Just typically affected behaviour I would say.' She stood up quickly, walked over to the scattered mess of the breakfast table and wolfed down the last croissant.

CHAPTER 10

The little boy pressed his small hands into the old man's knees. Pressing down and pushing up, using the spindly limbs as ballast.

Alex felt the pressure, the weight being exerted, but he didn't know what it meant. He didn't recognise the form in front of him. A small person, perhaps. Maybe he knew him, maybe he didn't. The desperate desire to recognise no longer existed. No more pressure in his head. Thoughts now were like gentle waves; gentle brainwaves that ebbed and flowed. Sometimes there were moments of panic, moments of fear like jagged rock protruding from the lapping water. But not today, not right now.

He was unsure if his legs could keep rigid for much longer. They might buckle under the pressure but it didn't bother him. The small form might crumple, fall and then what would happen? He remembered falling over a small table as a young boy. There were tears, crashing sounds. The grown-ups rushed towards him, tidied up the mess, got everything back into its right place.

There was no running now – hardly any moving. Not doing anything very much at all. He didn't much concern himself with reactions or consequences anymore. There was something though. Nothing logical, rational, of course, but there was a feeling of warmth, of contentment. He liked the fact that this little person was close, this little boy wanted to be close – to him.

'Milo. For God's sake, Simon, I told you to watch him.'

Did he recognise the voice? Maybe. It seemed vaguely familiar, but he didn't really want to try to place it. What did it matter? And suddenly, there they all were. The monstrous cacophony of sound. Bodies huddled round, lifting the tiny hands away from him. Predictable – so utterly and painfully predictable.

*

'He's not exactly brilliant at this sort of thing, is he?' John leaned into Sheila, whispering loudly enough into her left ear. It was causing her a modicum of discomfort, but Sheila stared straight ahead and nodded. John was right. This wasn't Colin's thing. Standing up being the showman, heralding the Council's lofty ambitions to the wider business community. The theme of the talk was something about Edinburgh as an economic powerhouse, but the poor man could barely operate PowerPoint. *Just not his forte*, Sheila thought to herself. She knew what he was good at, where his strengths lay or at least she'd thought she did. Now she wasn't so sure.

There was polite applause when he'd finished and the chairman moved across the stage to shake Colin's hand and then turned to ask the audience for any questions. There was an uncomfortable silence until John shot his right arm up and waved. Sheila looked down at her feet as the microphone made its inexorable way down and along the row of chairs until it was grabbed from the hand of the nervous young assistant by her husband. When she raised her eyes, she could see Colin had fixed his sights on the unwelcome inquisitor and the woman, guilty by association, who was sitting beside him. *Oh, how uncomfortable this all was*, Sheila thought. Colin was looking slightly flushed as he peered out into the assembled throng.

'That was great, Colin, thanks but I'm still not sure what *your* vision is for an integrated transport system for Edinburgh. I mean, I think we can all agree with you that it's important to have one but really – what's the vision?'

Oh no, really? Why do this? Why do it now in front of all these people? Couldn't he have just had a chat with Colin at the drinks thing afterwards? Why embarrass the man? Things were difficult enough.

Colin now dropped his gaze to the lectern in front of him and started to nervously thumb through his notes. He cleared his throat, took a drink of water and stumbled slightly as he began some meandering explanation that referenced trams, buses, trains and planes. Sheila left behind integrated transport and could hear the voice in her head singing 'trains and boats and planes', but who was it? There was a gentle rhythmic feel to the melody and the voice singing in her head had a kind of aching quality to it. Dionne Warwick. That's who it was.

Sheila had managed to completely skip Colin's reply but there was nothing she could do about that. Dionne Warwick was filling the thought space. She was glad, until she could feel John start to tense up next to her. He was going to ask another bloody question. Burt Bacharach's lyrics quickly dissolved and she gave her husband a quick kick to the ankle.

Finally, the torture was at an end and a low thrum filled the room as people stood up and made their way to the back of the hall where drinks and cheese straws were being served. She was glad to be disappearing into the anonymity of the crowd as she followed her husband. But relief soon turned to frustration as John stopped abruptly in his tracks, only halfway to sanctuary, to check in with somebody or other. Then just as she spied the white-covered trestle tables and smiling, spotty young people in ill-fitting waiting clothes ready to pour white or red, Sheila felt a hand on her shoulder.

Heart racing, she turned. Thank God, it was Jenny Blyth-Hume. She towered over Sheila in her impossibly high stilettos. Short cropped dyed blonde hair swept back from a face that had either been lifted or syringed to eradicate every wrinkle from its surface. Only the brown crinkled neck gave her away. Sheila never understood it herself. The remoulding of the face only drew attention to the bits left untouched by needle or scalpel.

'Sheila, how lovely. Where have you been hiding yourself? It's been ages since John managed to drag you out to one of these dos. Not that I blame you, mind you. That was dry as dust.' A dawning realisation crept over Jenny's face. Nothing much moved mind you, but Sheila could see it in her eyes. 'Oh God, I forgot he's your old boss.'

'Oh no really, don't worry…' Her voice trailed off as John turned and Jenny immediately diverted her attention away from Sheila.

'Oh John, great question. You were quite right trying to pin him down like that. Honestly, the Council really does need to buck its ideas up.' Jenny stood at almost equal height to John. Sheila noticed she had her arms folded but leant right into him. So it was okay to invade his personal space as long as a defensive pose was adopted. Clever. Sheila wondered if Jenny noticed her husband wince slightly. He couldn't stand overpowering perfume and Jenny had drenched herself in some deep, dark heavy scent. Her nostrils filled with aromas of cedarwood and coffee.

'Actually he's not a bad operator, just lacks a bit of dynamism that's all.'

Sheila stood at the periphery of this little scene and observed her husband's expression. He was interested and engaging but there was no reaction to Jenny's seductive look and tone. She wasn't even sure he recognised it as anything more than polite discourse. After a few more exchanges, Jenny pulled back. Perhaps she felt there was no point in pushing things with the wife standing just feet away. But then Sheila wondered if she was just simply seeing things that weren't there. Suddenly she felt her husband's hand at her back and the tension began to ease. But it quickly kicked in again as he motioned with his other hand towards Colin who was standing in the corner of the room with some Council colleagues. Sheila recognised the behaviour pattern. Colin felt exposed, ripe for criticism. Best to surround himself with a coterie of faithful guards until sufficient time passed to allow for a swift, unnoticed exit.

'Hey Colin, over here.' John's arm beckoned. Colin politely shook his head and nodded towards the door. John beckoned again with two quick 'towards me' motions that apparently left the Chief Executive of the City Council no option other than to do as he was bid. Sheila recognised the uncomfortable look. It matched the uncomfortable feeling in the pit of her stomach.

'That was great, Colin, just what we needed.' John didn't skip a beat. 'Sorry about the question but it's something we all need to be focussing on, don't you think? Why don't you give me a call next week sometime and I'll share some of my thinking.'

Colin's expression seemed to relax at that point, shifting towards impassive, but Sheila could see a flicker of anger in his eyes. She remembered that look from her days in the office. He was normally a placid character but if some poor soul undermined him, merely challenged him even, then the look would start to form. A flicker could turn into full-blown anger. Not in his words, not in his tone, just his eyes.

'Yes, of course, John. Will do. But really, I must dash now. Got a lot to catch up on.' Colin smiled a forced smile and turned his gaze to Sheila. 'Big twinning event coming up.'

'Ah yes, of course. Well that's why we wanted a word actually.'

We, Sheila screamed inside her head.

John looked quickly at Sheila and then back to Colin. Back to her and again to Colin. Sheila wished he would stop. Just let it be.

'I'm sure you two could sort something out. You're keen, Sheila, aren't you? To do something I mean.'

God she wanted to kill him. Right there and then. Just kill him quickly, cleanly so he couldn't utter another word.

Colin smiled again, the same smile. 'I just thought you didn't have the time for it, Sheila, that was all.'

'Well, it was just the afternoon. Thursday afternoon. That's all I could do.' She rushed the words, desperately wanting this exchange to be over and then looked down at her feet. Felt absurd that she could do no more than offer her old boss a half day out of her busy week.

'But that's fine, Sheila. Of course it is. I'll take whatever you can offer – you know I will.'

She didn't know what to say. Over the phone he'd made her feel so ungrateful for rejecting his offer of full-time work and had completely dismissed her counterproposal. What the hell was he playing at?

'Well there you go then. Knew we'd get that all sorted out. You were probably just talking at cross purposes.' John slapped Colin on the back. 'Difficult sometimes to sort business out over the phone. Prefer face to face myself. You don't get these misunderstandings.' He turned to Sheila and put his arm round her shoulder. 'Okay darling, you can both sort out the details later. Better let you go then, Colin.' He looked so pleased with himself but Sheila just didn't know what to say. Control of the situation had all been wrested from her once again. Far from being on top of things, planning out her week on her terms, it was all being *sorted* for her.

They said their goodbyes and Sheila and John finally headed towards the smiling teenagers holding a bottle of red and a bottle of white in each hand. God did she need alcohol.

'Glad we got that sorted out then.' Happy with his work, John planted a firm kiss on the top of his wife's head.

*

'Doesn't sound like much of a retirement to me.' Sandra was talking into the oven. Agnes and Sheila were sitting in her kitchen breathing in the aromas of freshly baked scones. Cinnamon and raisin, cheese and chive.

They were four weeks into Sheila's new routine and finally she felt as though everything was back onto an even keel. Colin was back to being Chief Executive. No more difficult conversations – normal behaviours had been restored and she had slotted right back into Executive PA mode. She'd worried about resentment from some of the staff given she was just parachuting in for a half day a week but there hadn't been any. Nothing that she could detect at least. In fact they actively looked to her for guidance, direction, and everything seemed to fit again. Just as it had when she put her Jean Muir suit back on for the first time since leaving work.

'It's good. Look, my Wednesdays and Thursday and Friday mornings are all free. And looking after Milo is great fun.' That wasn't strictly true. She loved being with her grandson but had forgotten how exhausting toddlers could be. It was non-stop. But strangely enough when he went down for a nap Sheila was energised again. Checking her schedule management plan for the Florence event or delving into her reading material from the history class. Time well managed encouraged focus. There was no drifting, no letting hours or minutes pass unproductively. Sheila could account for every hour of every day – except Wednesdays. And this sort of lazing about chatting, drinking and eating still felt wonderfully decadent.

'Well I don't know where you get your energy from.' Sandra was red-faced from all the baking activity and her chunky yellow teardrop necklace was stuck firmly to her chest.

'My life needs to move at a very sedate pace. I've only just come to realise that.' Agnes was very slowly and precisely cutting her warm scone in half. 'Think Harry Stuart's made me realise that. Everything at a hundred miles an hour. Honestly, my brain just doesn't work at that speed. It's all too much.' She started to spread butter at an even thickness right up to the edges of each half. 'Not sure I really want to go back.'

'Oh come on, Ag.' Sandra was brooking no nonsense from her friend. 'I'm really looking forward to the field trips. Once we get you out in the fresh air you'll be fine.' She ladled strawberry jam onto her two scone halves. 'Magda's looking forward to them too. Now there's a lovely lady. She's got a degree and everything, did you know? I know it sounds terrible but the only Eastern European women I've come across are cleaning or waitressing.'

Sheila felt herself blush. What kind of insular world did these women, her friends for God's sake, inhabit? 'She told me about her degree. It's in engineering.'

Sandra stopped eating. 'Yes. Isn't that a funny thing? Anyway, she says her English has improved tenfold since coming along to Harry's class.'

'Well, that's all well and good.' Last word from Agnes. 'But we're all different, that's the thing. Some of us search for new adventures, new meaning in our lives. I'm honestly quite content with where I am. Just a very slight expansion of my horizons would suit perfectly.' She looked at Sheila and smiled. 'But if some of us want more from life then I don't think anything or anyone should hold us back.'

That Friday they were back in the church hall, drinking coffee with the other club members and waiting for Harry. He was late. Only fifteen minutes, and Sheila was enjoying chatting to her classmates.

She found herself standing next to Leonard, the retired history professor. 'I'm interested Leonard in what attracts you to something like this. I mean you're a history professor after all. Can't be much you don't know about all of this.'

He was a small man. Bald on top but with straggly grey hair that wafted down to his collar. He wore the same clothes very week – three-piece tweed suit, shirt and tie and polished brown brogues. 'I need something to stimulate the mind, Sheila. Gets me out the house too. I've been a widower for a long time now and work – well, work was my sanctuary.'

'Don't you have any family?'

I have a son, but I don't really see him.' Leonard pursed his lips and looked down at his feet. 'Anyway, thing is I didn't want to take up with any formal educational course. Been there, done that. I'd heard a lot about Harry Stuart. Colleagues seemed to know something about him and I wanted to see for myself.' He gave Sheila a knowing wink. 'Real thing or charlatan?'

Sheila raised her eyebrows. 'And?'

'Let's just say the jury's still out.' Leonard drained the last remnants of coffee from his cup. 'I can't quite work out his angle. I've always loved sharing knowledge. I enjoyed watching my students immerse themselves in history. I wanted them to appreciate how understanding our past aids understanding of our present. Gives us the tools to shape our future. But with Harry I don't know. He wants to understand psychology, motivation at a far deeper level than I think we're able to.' He smiled at Sheila. 'I may be completely wrong of course.'

Sheila smiled back. *What an interesting man*, she thought. *Gentle. A gentleman.* She moved off to refill her coffee cup when Sandra came bounding up beside her. Leonard sat back down with the others.

'Saw you talking to the professor there,' Sandra whispered loudly, almost caressing Sheila's ear with her mouth.

'Yes. He's a nice man.' *Hidden stories, dramas*, she thought. We don't know what goes on in other people's lives. Not really. She watched the old man chatting amiably to Magda. *We all struggle with something*, she thought. The scale might be different but when it's our struggle, when we're right in the middle of it, we don't see what's around us. She thought of Colin and his awkwardness. John and his desperate need for affirmation and now Leonard. There was gentleness but also sadness. A son that he didn't see. Caitlin often tested Sheila's patience but she could never imagine not seeing her. How awful for him.

Suddenly the doors swung open and in flew Harry. 'Sorry guys, really sorry I'm late. Just back from the Serbian Consulate. Wow, that Elsie Inglis was quite a woman. Heroine of her time. Thinking we need to start campaigning for a statue or something.' He winked at Sandra who blushed like a teenager. Blushing was now her default setting around Harry.

Harry. A man who didn't seem to struggle with very much at all.

CHAPTER 11

'He hit himself with a brick.' Sheila was sitting on the makeshift playroom floor, explaining to her daughter why a small dark purple patch had appeared just above Milo's right eyebrow.

'What do you mean a brick?' Caitlin peered at the little boy who was now sucking on the offending article, seemingly unconcerned by the raised tone of his mother's voice.

'Well, a toy brick, of course. The one he's got in his mouth now. He just caught the edge that's all.'

'Weren't you watching him?' Caitlin yanked the wooden brick from Milo's hand and turned to look incredulously at her mother.

'Of course I was watching him. Not every second though, Caitlin, that's absurd.'

Milo started to cry.

'Now see.' Caitlin looked on the verge of tears herself as she picked Milo up. The little boy matched the escalating behaviour of his mother with a full-blown kicking and screaming tantrum. 'Christ, this is the reason I didn't want him going into nursery full-time. Trying to minimise the opportunities for reckless injuries.'

Sheila couldn't help herself. The ridiculousness of the situation forced out a little laugh.

'Good God, Mum, that bruise is getting bigger and all you can do is sit there and laugh.'

She got up quickly and put her arm round the distraught twosome. 'Look, he's fine. He's a little boy and little boys are going to get hurt occasionally.' She felt her daughter wince under her embrace.

'Just little boys. Not little girls. You don't remember me tripping and hitting my head on the door handle and the bruise I got from that.'

'Of course I do. It was just a turn of phrase.' Sheila stepped back knowing her overtures were falling flat.

Caitlin looked round for Milo's coat and hat. 'Well, I don't know. Maybe I'll just need to keep him in nursery full-time – they are professionals after all. Or maybe I'll work reduced hours.' She swung round in a full circle, her free arm flailing like an out-of-control spinning top.

Sheila softened her tone. 'This is ridiculous, Caitlin. I'll get his things – they're upstairs.' Her steps were heavy. She ached to see the pain and anguish that such a small incident could cause. So often as a child and now as a mother, Caitlin's reactions to everyday crises seemed extraordinary to her. Simon knew, seemingly understanding and accepting, but it always struck Sheila that her daughter was very often on the verge of something. It could be an unexpected bout of happiness but was more likely to be an over-the-top angry outburst.

She knew more words were futile and so she silently fetched Milo's outdoor clothes. She helped Caitlin dress the crying little boy and then watched as they hurried down the path to Caitlin's car for the drive back to the safety and security of the sterile white house. She had no idea if this apparently disastrous turn of events signalled the end of her time with Milo or indeed what it meant for her fractious relationship with her daughter. She sighed with sadness and went back inside.

*

Sheila had secreted herself away inside the Dean of Guild Court Room. It was one of the smaller meeting rooms in the City Chambers but stood shoulder to shoulder with its bigger cousins in terms of grandeur. The dark red of the mahogany walls and tables matched the plush dark mulberry carpet; oil paintings of old city worthies took their place at each end of the room. Tables were set in a horseshoe style and Sheila sat herself down at the apex of the curve, spreading all her papers either side making sure she didn't topple the interconnected microphone system. She loved the smells of these rooms. It was probably layers of beeswax rubbed and buffed over decades into the contours of the wood.

And of course the silence was wonderful.

The small team assembled to administer the twinning event were, for the most part, young and enthusiastic – eager to get stuck into something interesting. But with young and enthusiastic came noise. They talked at warp speed and even when they'd fallen silent to concentrate on the task in hand every movement seemed to create unnecessary sound. Sheila enjoyed their company but occasionally she needed to escape. She'd never had to endure open-plan working during her career and, for her at least, occasional spells of solitary confinement were absolute requirements for producing accurate, high-quality work. The necessary oasis of calm was right here in the Dean of Guild Court Room – space for clarity of thought and quiet contemplation.

After an hour or so, she heard the click of the handle and the creak of the hinges as the heavy wooden door at the far end of the room opened just enough for Colin to pop his head round. 'Ah, there you are. Wondered where you'd got to. The team thought you'd popped off for a bit of peace and quiet.' He walked in and let the door shut loudly behind him.

'Yes, well I just wanted to have a final look at the programme and make sure we hadn't missed anything.' She breathed a heavy sigh knowing that Colin was far enough away not to notice.

He ambled up towards her, hands in pockets. He looked relaxed, back to normal. No more stale aromas – sweat or alcohol. 'It's amazing what you're able to achieve with just a half day a week in the office. Although I'll bet you've been taking work home. Am I right?'

'Oh, I don't mind. I love it and when Milo's down for his nap I've managed to just catch up, that's all really.'

Colin pulled up a seat next to her, sliding her work plans, notes, and folders to one side.

They were there for a reason, she thought to herself. *There, in that order. For a reason.*

'Well, I'm very impressed with what you've managed to pull off in such a short space of time. Above and beyond, I would say.' He patted her hand, but his touch didn't linger. Not like before. 'Anyway I think you should come along to the welcome reception. A thank you for all your efforts. It would certainly make me more comfortable knowing you were there.'

Just like the old days. *That would be quite nice*, she thought.

'Great, yes. Is the whole team going to be there?'

'Oh no. Hospitality budget won't quite run to that, but you'll know the Provost and the Leader of the Council of course.' Colin stood up. 'Be good to have you by my side again, Sheila.'

He smiled and turned towards the door, leaving her to reorganise a scattered pile of folders and plans. Sheila sighed. Where was the running order? Where was the guest list from the Consulate? Typical Colin, messing everything up.

*

Sheila heard John's key turn in the lock just as she was cutting the lemon for their gins. She glanced at the clock. He was on time for a change. Said he'd be home at six and he was. She opened the fridge, pulled out two small cans of tonic and walked back to her G&T workstation. She was just about to pull back one of the ring pulls when it occurred to her that the normal clattering sounds associated with John's arrival home were completely missing. There was silence. She waited, hand poised to release the effervescence of the tonic. She wasn't sure what she was waiting for until suddenly John appeared in the doorway of the kitchen. She couldn't make out his expression at all. His brow was slightly furrowed suggesting either brooding anger or confusion. He held a white envelope in his right hand and stood smacking it into the palm of his left.

'Hi darling. You made good time. Traffic not too bad tonight?'

John looked at her but said nothing. His expression didn't change. He looked at her over the top of his glasses and started to blink. Sheila knew at once that something big was happening. She'd discovered the formula herself sometime in the early nineties – the direct correlation between speed of blinking and severity of problem.

'John? What's wrong?'

He let out a big sigh and moved towards her still slapping down the envelope.

'I got this today. In the office. In the post.'

Sheila looked down at the offending object, but it was plain and white, and she could see nothing that might give a hint as to her husband's state of mind.

'Scottish Business Awards. I'm the Scottish Business Leader of the Year. Apparently.' He looked straight ahead, almost over her head and continued blinking.

'Oh John, that's wonderful.' She laid the tonic down on the worktop and moved to hug her husband. At last, somebody had recognised all his hard work. Appreciated his talents. She held him tightly for a while, finally pulling away and taking his face in her hands. 'See, I told you. You're good at what you do. Really good and it's just taken a little time for others to see that.'

'Yes, well. There you go.' He gently lifted her hands away from his face and kissed her. 'Probably somebody decided they'd better give the old guy something. Shut him up.'

Sheila shook her head. He didn't know what to do with it. Recognition, reward and acclaim from his peers. They were all alien concepts to John. The establishment he railed against had finally accepted him into the fold and now he was one of them. No more looking in from the outside. Only she knew what it meant – the journey from a tenement in Leith to this and he just didn't know what to do with it.

'Why don't we tell Caitlin and Simon? Invite them out to dinner to celebrate at Café Jardin.' Sheila squeezed his hand. 'Saturday night. How about it?'

'Really? Not going a bit overboard then?'

'No, not at all. It's a great reason to celebrate. Caits will be thrilled.' She also saw an opportunity to try to normalise relations with her daughter. Milo had been returned to Granny the following week without any fuss but there was an undercurrent of tension and she wanted to try to make things better.

John's face relaxed into a smile. The prospect of familiar dining territory was enough to turn him back into brash, confident John. His vulnerable side wasn't often on view but just then, just before she'd opened her mouth, she'd held it close for a few precious moments. A few brief, intimate moments and then she'd let go. No one's fault but her own. He'd looked lost and uncomfortable and because that look pained her, she'd jolted him back with the promise of a little piece of theatre that he could choreograph all on his own.

He hugged her enthusiastically. Her ribs concertinaed together and she struggled for breath momentarily. He let go suddenly and she could see things start to settle in his mind. The whole exterior persona thing didn't *really* matter to her. She firmly believed that she was the only person who really knew John and that was enough for her. They both knew. Like the inner workings of a fibre optic cable, the connection ran the length of their very existence as a couple. Strong and durable on the outside covering discreet bundles of complex, interconnected strands.

That evening they celebrated, just the two of them, with a light supper and a half-bottle of champagne from the stash that John kept for unexpected celebrations. She enjoyed her husband seemingly being at peace with himself. He zoned out from their conversation from time to time and just smiled. *Perhaps he's playing out his acceptance speech or anticipating the reaction from some of his colleagues*, she thought. Whatever it was, she only prayed that this could be the end of his all-consuming ambition and painfully uncomfortable social climbing.

After breaking the news to Caitlin the following morning, John seemed to relax more into his newly exalted status. Caitlin had apparently screamed in delight over the phone, couldn't wait to celebrate on Saturday and most importantly couldn't wait to tell work colleagues and the other toddlers' mothers. John lapped it up.

'Think Caits is more excited about this daft award than I am,' he beamed after putting the phone down.

Sheila immediately thought of her daughter basking in John's reflected glory but it was an uncharitable thought that she quickly pushed to the back of her mind. At least Caitlin would be in a good mood.

'Just proud of you, darling. We all are.'

John grabbed his briefcase in the hallway and made his way to the front door. He certainly had a spring in his step. 'See you tonight, love. Got your history thing today?'

'Yes. See you tonight.' They kissed. Not just the usual perfunctory workday kiss but something a little more sensuous.

'Couldn't have done any of this without you, you know.'

And there he'd done it again. Sheila's eyes filled with tears. She couldn't say anything but gently stroked his cheek.

'Right, let's see what the Chairman thinks of my little piece of news then.' He turned away from her, unlocked the front door, swung it open and marched confidently down the path.

*

Friday afternoon's history club was on a bit of a day out. They trooped off on the number 29 bus to the Surgeons' Hall Museum to learn about Dr Elsie Inglis. They heard all about her pioneering work at the beginning of the twentieth century, improving conditions for the poorer residents of Edinburgh, particularly women and children. Sheila and Magda conscientiously took notes while the others just sat back and listened to their enthusiastic guide. All except Sandra who was whispering loudly into Agnes's left ear. Finally Agnes turned to her friend and put a finger to her lips. *Good*, Sheila thought. Mild-mannered Agnes was a little hacked off and wasn't just going to let it pass. About time.

After a brief tour, the little group happily set off to the Dean Cemetery to have a look at her final resting place and pay their respects. Given everything they were learning about this remarkable woman it occurred to Sheila that Elsie Inglis's gravestone really was quite an unassuming memorial. Just a simple Celtic cross with a few inscriptions. *Shipping merchants and industrialists boasted far more prestigious monuments*, she thought. But then that was all about the growth of Empire and the generation of wealth. Championing the poor and dispossessed didn't really warrant much of a tribute. The injustice of it all grated with Sheila and her comrades. They muttered amongst themselves as Harry gave them some more details of her good works.

The previous week they had listened to a passionate oration from the Serbian Consul General on Dr Inglis's establishment of a Red Cross Hospital in Serbia during the First World War. 'The noblest warrior for the good of humanity' was how she had been characterised in *his* country. The first woman to be decorated with Serbia's highest order. Commemorative stamps and memorial arches and so it went on. The little band of enthusiastic amateur historians had all sat feeling suitably chastised at the lack of recognition in Inglis's own country. They nodded and shook their heads, all seemingly willing to take on the burden of guilt on behalf of a whole city, perhaps even a whole country.

Today's outing, however, had been a much less sombre affair. No longer doom-laden, the motley band had adopted quite a breezy air about them as they traversed the city. They ambled at assorted speeds and Sheila noticed that Paddy tended to hang at the back, keeping Leonard company and making sure he didn't lag behind.

Harry had promised coffee and cake in the café at the Gallery of Modern Art after their day's activities and so they finally made their way up from the cemetery and through the landscaped gardens till they reached the entrance. Sheila waited for Paddy and Leonard and watched as the old man suddenly stopped to look up at the grand pillars of the imposing neoclassical building.

'Used to be a school for fatherless children,' he said. Sheila looked at him and was sure she saw a tear in his eye.

'I didn't know that. How interesting.' She took the old man's arm and led him into the entrance hall following the group as they trundled down the stairs into the bowels of the gallery. Sandra and Agnes were out on their feet and Leonard too had clearly found the pace challenging. Sheila let go of his arm and he sank down with the others into a corner of the bright little café. Even Paddy stretched out his long limbs and yawned.

'Well, looks like Sheila and me are the only ones keeping up the pace.' Harry looked down affectionately at his faithful followers. Only when Harry spoke did Sheila notice they were the only ones standing. It reminded her a bit of guide camp. Harry and she had assumed the role of patrol leaders and began to gather in everyone's orders. When they returned the group had broken into two little subsets. Agnes, Sandra and Magda were chatting and laughing and Paddy and Leonard were engaged in what appeared to be a very sombre discussion. Coffees and cakes were passed around; there was some general chit-chat around the group as a whole and then the subsets reformed. Harry and Sheila sat down next to each other at a separate table. They were on their own.

'Was Elsie Inglis really Sandra's idea?' Harry broke off a piece of flapjack and looked straight ahead.

Sheila blushed. He knew. 'Well, it was a joint thing really.'

'You're close, aren't you? Sandra, Agnes, you.'

'Not that close really. But we've been friends a long time. Just seeing a lot more of each other now I've retired.'

'Important to have good friends, Sheila. People you can trust around you. That's important. Remember Bruce? It was important to him.'

'Yes, I suppose it is.' Sheila was struggling to pitch Sandra and Agnes into the same character analysis as Robert the Bruce.

Harry lifted his head back and suddenly adopted a lighter tone. 'So what drew you to Elsie Inglis?'

She thought for a second. 'Well, not so much the medical stuff or even the First World War hospitals. She was quite a leading light in the suffragette movement up here and I think that's what drew me to her. She was so frustrated that, as a woman, she had so many barriers placed in front of her. I remember reading that she said something about how a pigeon with a tumour in one part of its brain walked round and round in circles. And when a nation used only one part of its brain it was apt to walk round in circles too.' She let out a little laugh. 'I quite liked that.'

'Ah, I see. Men just walk round in circles like demented pigeons unless women are allowed to exert their influence.' Harry's eyes narrowed.

'No, not quite.' It wasn't really the response she was expecting from him. 'Just why not use what's at your disposal? Why be the demented pigeon when you don't need to be?'

'Sorry, of course.'

He started to play with the crumbs on his plate. 'Just seems to me sometimes that women think men aren't capable of displaying any kind of sane, rational behaviours without their input. Or that men couldn't possibly have the intelligence needed to successfully run a business or country. Never mind that they've been doing it rather well for years now.'

He looked at her intently. 'Somehow it's women who are being groomed for success now. Men can just look after themselves. Although you're probably going to tell me they can't do that either. Either that or women are considered the great moderators of our time, aren't they? Needed to smooth down the sharp edges, curb the excessive behaviours of the male of the species. Am I wrong?'

She didn't know what to say, where to begin and so she stumbled over her words. 'Well, it's just I think that women have a lot to offer. I mean, most people think that – don't they? Most rational people anyway.'

They sat in silence for what seemed like an age. Sheila could feel anger welling up. 'How can you say all that, Harry, when we've spent the last few weeks studying a woman who excelled at so much and has never been given due recognition? I thought we'd all agreed about that – never mind thinking about any modern-day examples.'

Harry smiled and laid a hand on top of hers. Men seemed to be doing a lot of that lately. 'Quite right, Sheila. Quite right.' His eyes widened again and he smiled gently at her. 'I was only trying to provoke a reaction. The right reaction. Took a little while there but I think it's fair to say I just got it. Wouldn't you?'

CHAPTER 12

Café Jardin was buzzing as Sheila walked in with her family. Saturday night and chairs were clattering, glasses clinking. She was immediately hit with the familiar heady aromas of bubbling shellfish, grilled meats and hot garlic butter.

'My friends. How are you? Where have you been?' Jean strode across the restaurant and shook John's hand vigorously. John was beaming as though he'd just caught sight of a long-lost love.

'Oh, I know, Jean. We've just not had the time. But we'll be back into our Saturday routine from now on, won't we, darling?' He turned to look at Sheila.

'Absolutely.' And she knew they would. The Saturday night ritual had fallen by the wayside for a few weeks. Not deliberately perhaps but it just hadn't seemed to fit her new life. The release that came at the weekend after a punishing work schedule just hadn't been there. Somehow she couldn't equate caring for her grandson with the same sense of purpose she got from work. Was that a terrible thing? Did Milo rate lower in terms of her sense of achievement? It was just different, that was all. She was happy spending the time with him, of course she was. And of course she would need to be watching him like a hawk from now on. But with work she was putting the hours in and there were projects and plans that had to be delivered. Throw in a bit of historical research and Sheila felt her Saturday night indulgence had been earned. She was back in synch with her fellow diners.

'Ah and we have all the family tonight,' Jean bellowed.

He moved past Sheila and John, shook hands vigorously with Simon and then lifted Caitlin's hand to his lips. It was a faux kiss. A show of Gallic chivalry but one that didn't overstep the mark.

Jean showed them to a table tucked into a corner of the restaurant. Sheila liked this table. It looked down onto the dark cobbled square below. A square enclosed by dark and brooding buildings with arched entrances. She imagined black cloaks billowing in the wind as nineteenth-century dwellers hurried to their clerking jobs. Edinburgh did that with her mind. The streets and the structures laying out a canvas for her imagination to fill.

They all settled down into their seats. 'Shall I bring the wine list?' Jean asked. 'Or is it just the usual?' He winked at John.

'Oh, Daddy, I think we need something special, don't we?' Caitlin grinned and turned to her husband. 'And of course it's on us, isn't it Simon?'

Simon replied with a yes, but Sheila couldn't be sure if it was an affirmative statement or a question.

Caitlin looked up at Jean. 'Daddy is an absolute star, Jean. He's the Business Leader of the Year.' She turned to look at Sheila.

Why the almost pleading expression? Sheila thought. 'Of course he is, Caitlin. With or without a business award.' All was fine. Caitlin was back in familiar territory, idolising her father.

'Well, Scottish Business Leader. Not that important really, Jean. Not anything you'd have heard of.' John was starting to look uncomfortable again, shuffling about in his seat.

'Well, that's very impressive, Monsieur John. I knew you were an important man. I said to all the staff. That man there, he's very important. Didn't I say that? Didn't I say that, Jakub?'

He turned to the pale, blonde waiter hovering at his shoulder who smiled at the foursome in the corner. A weary smile. A smile that said I don't really care whether you're important or not. I'm on minimum wage and I've got another four hours of feeding you and clearing up your mess. 'Yes, yes you did, Jean.' Sheila wished it would all stop now. She could see John meet the eyes of the young waiter and she knew he could see the emptiness too.

'Champagne, champagne on the house,' Jean declared with a flurry of his right hand. He turned and marched off with young Jakub trailing in his wake.

'It is wonderful, though, Daddy. It really is. We're so proud of you.' Caitlin's loud voice followed on from Jean's bellowing tones. 'Aren't we, Mum?'

Sheila, who up to now had felt like a bit part in the Jean and Caitlin tribute show, was just about to speak when John interrupted.

'Well, thank you, both of you.' He smiled gently at his daughter and her husband. 'Let's look at the menu now, shall we?' He slid his hand along the edge of the table searching for his wife. Sheila gently took his hand in hers and held it until she could feel the tension ebb.

Their frenzied little corner of the restaurant calmed down and the foursome relaxed into their dining. *This is better*, Sheila thought. People had stopped staring. Caitlin was regaling her father with tales of Milo, happily leaving out the brick incident, and Sheila and Simon were talking about Harry.

'So why did he retire early, Simon?'

'He was just one of those guys, Sheila. It was his way or no way. Never wanted to try anything different. Liked to stick to what he knew. To be honest I think he was just scared. Anything out of his comfort zone and he didn't know what to do with it. But fund management is a competitive world. You can't afford to be left behind. And then if any of us pushed back at him – well, he just didn't like it.'

'No, no. I can see that.' She could see it all too well.

Simon sat back savouring a mouthful of food. 'This swordfish is bloody good, don't you think?'

After the meal, they made their way across the restaurant to the stairs that led them out through the bar below. They all trooped down with John bringing up the rear. Sheila felt warm and comfortable. A few little anxious moments but it had been a lovely little celebration with the people she loved best in the world. As they gathered at the restaurant's entrance Sheila looked behind to see

John talking to the waiter called Jakub. She watched as he handed the young man a business card and quietly shook his hand.

*

Sheila stood in the corner of the European Room in the City Chambers, watching anxiously. Of all the things to forget. The job had been assigned. It was there on the project sheet. The sheet she gripped in her right hand. But looking at it and seeing the names attached to the action point wasn't going to make it suddenly happen. Of all the things.

The waiters were waiting. Waiting, mingling, chatting. They couldn't see it was missing, why would they? They wouldn't even know what it was. Suddenly the heavy double doors swung open and in came Ryan and Josh with the large painted emblem. The red lily on a white background. The fleur-de-lis of Florence. The emblem of Florence. Looked more like an iris than a lily Sheila had thought when they'd been discussing its hanging, but that detail wasn't important right now. What was important was getting the bloody thing up next to the City of Edinburgh's coat of arms. Should have been done that afternoon. Why hadn't it been done? She asked them both – Ryan and Josh. Trying hard not to be accusatorial but genuinely curious. Genuinely curious as to why a perfectly reasonable instruction had not been carried out in accordance with the project plan. At the time stipulated in the project plan. It hadn't been raised as a problem at the time so when did it suddenly become a problem? And if it had become a problem why had no one told her?

Ryan, the older of the two, looked at his comrade hopefully. But Josh just stared down at his shoes. Ryan was clearly at a loss and not quite sharp enough to come up with a plausible, even if entirely false, explanation. 'Yeah, sorry about that, Sheila. Don't know how we missed it. Took ages getting the right chairs and tables in here.' Then a light-bulb moment. 'Maybe that was it. Maybe we just got bogged down in tasks…' He strained to read Sheila's sheet upside down. 'Yeah, three and four. Tasks three and four. Just never made it to five.' He looked pleased with himself. Figured it all out just like that.

Sheila was caught between just getting on with things now and mulling over the futility of the project plan. The explanation from Ryan made it all sound faintly ridiculous. 'Well, let's just get the thing up now. We've still got time.' She quickly folded up the plan and slid it into the pocket of her black tailored trousers.

The boys set to work. A Lord Provost from yesteryear was swiftly removed from his vaulted position and the bold, simple beauty of the flag of Florence was hung in his place. Sheila's eyes widened as she stared at the vibrant symbol. Simple but still flamboyant, its redness seemed to fill the room. She looked over at the Edinburgh coat of arms. Busy. Castle, anchor, young woman showing a bit of leg and a prancing deer. Just didn't have the same impact.

The door opened again and this time it was Colin. He wore a crumpled brown suit. The very suit she'd prayed he wouldn't wear. *You can't wear brown to an evening reception*, she thought as he rushed towards her. What had happened to him? Sheila had been so busy during the day she hadn't had time to touch base but then there hadn't been any need. They'd gone over everything the day before.

'Everything okay, Sheila?' He looked flustered, sheets of paper in his right hand. 'I'm just going to run over my opening remarks again. Do you want to hear?'

'Well, if it's what we agreed yesterday then I don't think there's any need. Unless you've changed anything?' She wasn't sure if she'd adequately masked the anxiety in her voice.

'Just a bit. Added in a couple of things. Nothing important of course.'

He looked up at her, apologetically, and Sheila noticed the slightly glazed eyes and the stale smell of alcohol again.

'I was going to go home. Have a shower, get changed but then that planning appeal came in. Remember the one?' He looked down again at the sheets of paper slowly being crumpled by the grip of his sweaty hand. Beads of sweat appeared on his worried brow. 'Well, the developers got their way. Committee went with them, against Malcolm's advice, mind you. What a bollocks we've made of this I tell you.'

Of course she didn't remember any bloody planning appeal. It was nothing to do with her, nothing to do with this event now. Here and now. 'No, Colin, no I don't.' She prised the papers from his grip and gently squeezed his arm. The situation could be recovered but she would need to be calm and gentle. 'Let's just focus on the reception for now, shall we? I'll copy these papers so you've got a clean set to work with. Why not just nip out to your private bathroom and freshen up a bit? Just clear your head for a minute.'

Colin headed out of the small side door behind her just as the double doors at the far end of the room swung open again. It was the Lord Provost, swaggering towards her with the heavy gold chain of office covering his broad chest. No ermine today, in fact, she wasn't sure the last time she'd seen the Provost wear ermine. Must surely be unacceptable to wear dead animals in public now but for as long as she could remember it was part of the garb. *I am an important dignitary and you know I am because I wear dead animal fur.* Gordon Johnstone was a big man with a fighter's swollen knuckles. Knuckles that bulged like eruptions from the craggy surface of his boulder-like hands. Hands that shook those of the Queen every July when she stayed for a week at the palace. Hands that were entrusted with the keys of the city. It wasn't right. Hands like that could snap fingers and break keys.

'All right, Sheila? Where's our lad got to then? Hear there's been a right old balls-up in the Planning Committee. Thought I'd have a word before the Tallies get here.' He winked at her. A lot of his sentences ended with a wink.

Sheila's head gave an involuntary shudder. The derogatory wartime description of Italian immigrants, synonymous with the cafes and fish and chip shops that had sprung up across the city during the thirties and forties, was still part of this Edinburgh so-called dignitary's everyday language. She hoped that was it out now, never to be repeated. But she couldn't be sure. She could never be sure just how any of the city's democratically elected representatives were going to behave at functions like this.

'He's just freshening up, Gordon. Shouldn't be long. You've got your words of welcome?' Just cut through the nonsense and get straight to the job in hand. Sheila had been dealing with these men, and they were almost always men, for years now. Don't let them wander off at a tangent. Just keep their attention span fixed on the task in front of them.

'Aye. I've not got much to say by the looks of things. Just a couple of sentences.'

Sheila smiled. 'Yes, and then just hand straight to Colin. You can relax and enjoy the evening after that.'

Gordon winked the inevitable wink.

After a few more minutes of nodding and smiling, checking on wine supplies and seating arrangements, she felt herself start to relax. After all, what did it really matter if Colin stumbled over his words? After tonight she'd be out of here. It suddenly struck her that, much as she'd enjoyed the experience, she really was looking forward to getting back to her new relaxed pace of life. John seemed more at ease with himself, she enjoyed her time with Milo and she'd met new and interesting people at the history club. If only she could just let go of the thought that she was somehow undeserving of a bit of downtime.

She suddenly noticed the side door edge open and in came Colin. This time in a black lounge suit. So much better.

Sheila bounded up to him. 'Feeling better? You look so much better. Where did that suit come from?'

Colin smiled, looking pleased with himself. 'Yes, found it hanging behind the door of the bathroom. Must have worn it to that awards ceremony last week and forgot all about it. He looked down at himself, brushing his hands over the front of his jacket. 'So I've scrubbed up quite well then, have I?'

Sheila grabbed his arm. She meant to move him across the room towards the Lord Provost. 'Scrubbed up very well, I'd say.'

She quickly realised they weren't actually going anywhere as Colin stood fixed to the spot and quickly placed his hand on top of hers.

'Thanks, Sheila. Thanks for everything.'

She pulled her hand away quickly, but it was too late. She'd thought she was in control and suddenly she wasn't. Her gesture had been misinterpreted. Once again, Sheila felt Colin's hand at her back gently pushing her towards the far end of the room.

By the time they'd joined the Provost, Colin had removed his hand and she could relax. But still she felt the imprint. It made her shiver and sweat at the same time. Drinks were being handed round, but Sheila stuck to orange juice. At that moment, she felt she might gag on anything stronger. He stood next to her but was in deep conversation with the little coterie of councillors who'd buttonholed him about the planning appeal. She could breathe again, until, that was, she stepped back. Just a bit, really just changing leg position.

It was his arm up at her back, barely grazing her soft silk blouse. He'd kept it there all the while. No pressure against her skin but just something that said, 'I'm here, always, always by your side.' John often did that when they were at receptions, functions and it had made her feel safe. But this wasn't the same thing at all, not at all.

The double doors swung open again and Sheila was shaken from her feeling of loathing. Now, the image in front of her eyes transported her immediately to the Palazzo Vecchio in Florence. The dour Protestantism of the old city fathers was overwhelmed by the grand flamboyance of the Medici. Two young courtiers held the doors open as the Mayor of Florence, followed by two more attendants, walked diagonally towards them. There were no sweeping overcoats overlaid with scarlet, but there was the same air of peacockery. The twenty-first-century overcoat was smart, tailored, probably Armani and it sat firmly upon the shoulders of its host. Mayor Mazzi stopped in front of them performing some elaborate gesture with his right hand before proffering it to the Provost. Sheila was astounded to see that the overcoat didn't move an inch. Big Gordon, a man unused to elaborate gestures of any kind, stumbled uncertainly towards the Italian, offering him a bone-crushing handshake.

'A very warm welcome to Edinburgh, Señor Mazzi.'

Oh God, he was using Spanish. Sheila despaired as she watched Gordon's big knuckles wrap themselves round the Italian's slimline versions. Their brief Italian language lesson had clearly been in vain.

'Signore Johnstone, a pleasure,' came the reply in impeccable English followed by a brief bow of the head.

Sheila eased herself out of the grouping. Not really appropriate for her to be included. It was a status thing, much beloved by local government. She didn't really mind as it gave her the ideal opportunity to cast an eye round the room and make sure everything was in its rightful place. She stood on the periphery making small talk with some of the Mayor's entourage while mentally running down her checklist. Lectern – tick. Emblems – tick. Subdued lighting – tick. Wine and canapés – tick. It was all going so well until Colin's voice interrupted the flow.

'Oh and of course this is Sheila. My right-hand woman. Well, she was till she retired but we managed to entice her back. Couldn't have organised this visit at all without her skills and know-how.' Colin ushered her back into the fold and she once more felt his hand press into her back.

The Mayor stretched out his hand in greeting and again performed his little bow. 'Signora. Delighted.'

'Welcome, Signore Mazzi. I hope you will enjoy your visit and of course the programme of events we've put together.'

'I am sure I will, Signora, I am sure I will. In fact, just this afternoon, Antonio and I, we sneaked in…' The Mayor turned in search of Antonio, who broke free from the other courtiers and stepped over to be by his master's side.

'Si Signore?' asked the young man, looking eager to please.

'Sneaked? Is that the correct English word? Did we *sneak*?'

'Si, Signore. We sneaked.' Happy that he'd provided the necessary assurances to his master, Antonio returned to his colleagues.

'Yes, we *sneaked* into the National Gallery to look upon the Raeburns.' He smiled at Sheila. 'Sir Henry Raeburn, he makes my heart sing, Signora. I am sorry I could not resist.'

Sheila didn't flinch. There was a whole tour arranged for the following afternoon focussing on the Canalettos with the director of the gallery, the Italian Consul General and a string quartet from Venice, who happened to be touring Scotland. She kept smiling, determined that the Mayor's wayward excursion would in no way impact upon her meticulously planned schedule. True enough, mind you. Why would he want to stand and stare at numerous Canalettos? Florence was dripping in them. But then again, just as before, it occurred to her that it didn't matter a jot if the Mayor chose to spend the remainder of his visit staring at the Canalettos or the Raeburns. Didn't matter to her one tiny bit.

'Well, you just get double the enjoyment.'

The Mayor laughed, his deep brown eyes widening, drinking her in. A little spark of connection, a moment to bond over old masterpieces. Whatever it was, Sheila relaxed and laughed with him. Big Gordon winked at her. A 'job well done' wink, while all the time she was aware of Colin hovering at her side, silently building up a little wall of tension.

'I must say this, Signore Johnstone. The rubbish in your city. It is not good.' The Mayor wagged his finger, moving swiftly from enthusiastic tourist back to civic dignitary. 'And all around your magnificent buildings too. Outside your galleries and on the steps of your churches. It is not good, Signore Johnstone.' Mayor Mazzi placed a hand on big Gordon's shoulder. 'In Florence we have our workers take the water and…' He looked around again for Antonio who bounded up once more to his master's side. The Mayor held his arms out as though gripping some imaginary sword. 'What do we do with the water, Antonio?'

'We hose down the steps, Mayor Mazzi. With water coming down through the hose. Very fast. The water covers the steps. Makes them very wet. Far too wet for sitting.'

'Yes.' The Mayor nodded at Antonio and began brandishing a pretend hose from side to side like a light sabre. Antonio took his cue and sidled off, nodding gently as he went. *Looked like it had been a good day for Antonio*, Sheila thought. 'The steps. Very wet. Then the tourists can't sit and leave all the rubbish. We don't want people making litter on our beautiful buildings. You agree, Gordon?'

'Absolutely, Signor Mazzi.'

'Pietro, please.'

'Don't know why we haven't thought of that, Pietro.' Wink. 'Colin, why haven't we thought of that?'

All eyes turned to Colin. He was struggling to respond. 'Well, I suppose it's something we could look into.'

'The beauty of our cities is very important, Signore. Yes?' The Mayor was speaking to Colin like he was one of his own and Colin wasn't enjoying the experience. He didn't say anything but Sheila could see the anger in his eyes, as if he had a sudden contempt for all things Italian. The Mayor stared him down. A Florence master playing imaginary swordfights.

After all the speeches were over and the reception passed without a hitch, Sheila stood in earshot of Big Gordon having a word with Colin. 'Think the Tallie got you there, Colin,' Big Gordon bellowed. 'Why don't we ever come up with good ideas like that? We need people with a bit of imagination, Colin. Don't you think? What do they call it? Thinking out the box. That's what we need. You need to start thinking out the box.'

Colin said nothing and so Sheila turned to join them. Just to try to smooth the waters – somehow. One last time, smoothing the waters. But just as she turned, Gordon waddled off leaving Colin alone. Alone and brooding.

'Well, that all went very well.' It was the best she could do in the circumstances.

'What does he know about Edinburgh? Bloody Italians are just desperate sods who couldn't make a living in their own country. Come here and open up fish and chip shops. Some contribution to the life of the city that is.' He spat out the words.

'Colin! What utter rubbish you're talking. Insulting rubbish.'

He leant right into her brushing her hair with his lips.

'That's the type of man that impresses you, Sheila, is it?'

Pathetic, she thought. But she didn't say anything. He didn't make her feel anything any more. He was a lonely, pathetic man. The respect that had built up slowly over the years was all gone now and none of it mattered.

She picked up the plastic envelope file with invites, schedules and guest lists from the table behind her and thrust it into his body. 'Goodbye, Colin.'

CHAPTER 13

A rim of bright light framed the heavy jacquard curtains. Was there ever really such a thing as blackout lining? The dawn light always managed to spill through into their bedroom. Sheila lay with one eye barely open. Lid slowly lifting, brain starting to engage but her body remained perfectly still. Cocooned, safe, cosy, she didn't want to move. She turned her head slowly to see John lying in his customary position. With his back to her, he was sleeping soundly. She wanted to lift her hand, stroke his hair, even nuzzle into his neck, but she knew that was a risky manoeuvre. It might signal a desire for sex and sex wasn't what she wanted. Not now. Not at this moment. She felt him move slightly and then, like synchronised parts of an intricate timepiece, he turned into her, linking his body with hers, and followed her move from sleep to wakefulness. He opened his eyes and smiled.

'Well, I'm glad that's over. You're sure it was okay? I didn't go on too much?' He rubbed his eyes, dragging his knuckles into the creases either side.

'No, it was fine. Everyone said. What a great speech.'

Then he yawned and a hint of stale whisky breath wafted over her. 'I just wanted to strike the right note. I mean I wanted to sound surprised, pleased – honoured even.' Finally, he lifted one arm and stretched. 'But I don't want the bastards to think I'm one of them now.'

'One of them. What does that mean?'

'I'm just not one of them. That's all.' John suddenly threw back the duvet and left the marital bed for the sanctuary of the en suite. Just like that. She knew he was irritated with her but probably more so with himself. He didn't really know what being 'one of them' meant but it suited his narrative.

Last night he had gracefully accepted the Scottish Business Leader of the Year award at a reception and dinner at the Balmoral Hotel. It had all been very swanky. He'd looked very distinguished in his dinner suit and Sheila had bought herself a new dress from one of the more fashionable boutiques in Edinburgh's West End. They made quite the couple, she'd thought, as they made their entrance up the red-carpeted stairs. And *of course* he was part of it now, a fully paid-up member of the Edinburgh business establishment. A position he craved and despised all at the same time.

She shouted at him through the bathroom door. 'Look it was a great night. You were funny, charming. I felt really proud of you.' But it seemed there was nothing more to be said and, as though to confirm the fact, she heard the power shower drowning out the possibility of any more words.

They sat in silence over the breakfast table. Sheila watched as he scraped a thin layer of butter over his toast. Short sharp bursts of scraping. The sound was rough and harsh.

'Do you want any more tea?' She couldn't bear the grating noise any longer.

'Yes, thank you.' He looked up from his newspaper and lifted his cup toward her. 'Thought there might be something in this rag this morning. Can't see anything though.'

John had stopped buying *The Scotsman* some years ago. It had been the staple daily news diet for the Edinburgh middle classes for generations, but circulation had been steadily falling and, as with so many other middle-class institutions, 'standards', according to John, had fallen too. But today he'd rushed down to the newsagent just in case anyone was reporting on his accolade.

After all these years he was still an enigma to her.

'Who was that with the camera last night? Thought someone was snapping us for the papers.'

Okay. So he wasn't 'one of them' but still wanted to be feted by them.

'I heard someone say it was *Edinburgh Life*. You know that magazine I sometimes buy from Waitrose.'

'Really? Never heard of it.'

'It has society pages at the back. Probably be in there. Be a few weeks before it's out mind you.' Sheila drained the last dregs of tea and made to clear the table. She couldn't massage his ego any more today. She had things to be getting on with.

'*Society* pages. I don't want anything to do with society pages. I want to be in the business pages.'

Sheila turned and walked away desperately trying to stifle a laugh. Only when she was in the sanctity of the kitchen did she allow the absurdity of the whole morning's conversation to make its full impact. She laughed quietly to herself.

Later that day, they both sat opposite each other in their matching chintz-covered armchairs, drinking coffee. John had spent the rest of the morning honing his skills at the driving range and Sheila had spent a very pleasant couple of hours catching up on her historical reading. Mary Queen of Scots now. A woman, it seemed, plagued by bad decision-making. John had resumed reading the paper and Sheila sat with the journal of the Marie Stuart Society in her lap. It had been a spur-of-the-moment decision to join the society. She hadn't really intended going to meetings or joining them on their various trips, but the journal was a good source of information and all held together in a nice compact form. Ideal for any amateur historian.

'Meant to say. How did the Italian thing go the other night? You didn't say much when you got in.' John spoke from behind the newspaper, his words slightly muffled.

'Well, you were asleep when I got in.'

The newspaper came down. 'Was I?'

'Yes, there on the couch. I just left you to it and went to have a bath. God knows what time you came up.'

'Must stop doing that. It's not good. Always feel crap in the morning when I've done that. You shouldn't let me do that, dear. Wake me next time.' The newspaper went back up.

She made a mental note to add that to the list of things she should stop him doing.

'Anyway, there's a picture in here of the Florence mayor with our esteemed Lord Provost. Pietro Mazzi and Big Gordon – chalk and cheese.'

'Yes, bit of a clash of cultures I think.'

There was a snort from behind the paper. 'Oh and there's our Colin hovering in the background. God he looks miserable.' Paper down again. 'But it went well? You were happy with it?'

She put down her journal and looked straight at him. 'Yes, it went well. But I'm not in any hurry to do anything like it again.'

'Really? I thought you'd missed the buzz of the workplace. Bet Colin was glad to have you back.'

'Yes, well, I don't know about Colin. He's changed. And it just wasn't the same.'

'Same as what?'

'Same as before. When I was working for him. Properly, I mean. I don't know, John; he's just become all bitter and twisted. And I think he's drinking too much. I just didn't like being around him, that's all.' She turned back to her journal.

'He's just a bit of a sad old man, Sheila. And what with his wife and then you leaving—'

'How can you lump my retiral in with his wife's death? I'm not responsible for him for God's sake. He's nothing to do with me. Nothing at all.'

'Okay, okay.' John carefully folded his newspaper, placed it on the small lamp table at the side of the fireplace, walked over and sat on the arm of her chair. 'Of course you're not responsible for him. Just he's probably feeling a bit lost. Maybe he's just having one too many now and again and losing the rag with people he wouldn't normally bark at.' He kissed the top of her head. 'I mean if I didn't have you with me...'

She looked up at him. 'Can't you see that's different, John? Completely different. I just don't want to be around him, that's all.' She pulled herself up out the seat and walked off to the kitchen. How could she explain how she felt? How he'd made her feel. The actions, the words in themselves just sounded awkward and pathetic. It was how it all made her feel that was the issue. But how could she even begin to tell him? She might inadvertently end up embellishing for effect – just to get her point over. And she didn't want to do that, she didn't want to provoke any kind of reaction from John that might mean reprisals or anything else that would make this thing bigger than it needed to be.

'Okay.' Suddenly he was right there beside her.

She turned round to see the worry begin to take shape. He looked concerned and a little bit scared. A little bit scared about what she might say now perhaps or unsure about where his line of questioning should go next. She put her hand up to his face. 'It's fine, darling, honest. I just didn't really enjoy it as much as I thought I would. And now – well I've got so much to be going on with, it really doesn't matter.'

John gently stroked her hand and she watched the worry disappear. A few words spoken in the right tone. That's all it took. A few words to make everything right for him and to let the rest of the day open up, untrammelled by thoughts of sad and bitter old men.

She locked up the depressing and uncomfortable thoughts and slid them well out of sight. She took a deep breath, let it all go and smiled. 'Come on,' she said. 'We've got Caitlin's party to think about. It'll be lovely. I won't have to think about cooking and *we* can just relax and enjoy ourselves.'

*

John was buttoning up his pale blue Ralph Lauren shirt in front of the full-length mirror in their bedroom. Shirt tucked into grey slacks, all to be topped off by a navy blue blazer currently hanging over the bedpost. He was making an assessment of the overall presentation and appeared to like what he saw. 'What's this party for?'

'Oh, I think it's a number of things.' Sheila had gone with dark grey tailored trousers and light blue blouse but was beginning to feel a slightly uncomfortable 'match' for her husband. She added a floral scarf and long silver drop earrings to ensure a sufficient level of distinctiveness. 'Caitlin will obviously want to show you off to her friends, you know what she's like. It's also Simon's birthday in case you'd forgotten.'

'Don't know how you can forget something you knew nothing about in the first place.' John was now slapping on his aftershave balm a bit too liberally for Sheila's taste.

'So, it's a few of Simon's friends and Harry's going to be there too.'

'Harry who?'

Sheila nudged him out the way while she applied her lipstick. 'My history club guy. Old colleague of Simon's, remember?'

'Oh, yes.'

She doubted he remembered at all, but she didn't want to prolong the discussion. They were running late and Caitlin could not abide anyone being late for one of her parties. She picked up her jacket, keys and birthday present and followed John down the stairs.

He stopped abruptly on the bottom stair, causing her to quickly grab the bannister to avoid careering into him. He turned to look at her. 'What do you mean she wants to "show me off"? Show me off to who?'

'Never mind that now. We're late.'

She pushed John into the taxi, too harassed to deal with his worries.

Sheila kept checking her watch, but the taxi driver was on a mission to speed through all the side streets across Edinburgh and make good their escape to the city limits and beyond. It really took them no time at all.

As they drew up to the driveway of Caitlin and Simon's house, she reckoned they were only fifteen minutes later than originally planned. John paid the driver and winked at him as if to acknowledge the man's brilliantly intricate knowledge of Edinburgh's lesser-known road network.

Sheila left them to it and walked quickly up to the front door, pressing the bell three times. Short, sharp bursts.

Simon opened the door and welcomed his in-laws with a smile, laced with mild concern.

'Great. You're here.' He ushered them quickly into the vast, bright hallway. 'Caits is having a bit of a meltdown in the kitchen.'

'Why, what's wrong? What's happened?' She immediately took off her coat and made ready to face the impending disaster. John on the other hand was still in the vestibule eyeing up Simon's golf clubs. *Probably best*, Sheila thought. *If he wades in with his size tens he might just make matters worse.* She made her way quickly to the back of their house with Simon trailing in her wake. As she turned to go into the kitchen, she saw her daughter down on all fours staring into the oven.

'What's wrong?'

Caitlin looked up, tears streaming down her face. 'Oh, here you are. Finally. I thought you were going to be here earlier to help. I've been here all on my own trying to get everything ready.' She stayed down on all fours, hung her head and started to sob. Even her shoulders shook.

'I've been here too.' Simon said the words softly.

Sheila got down on all fours beside her daughter and started to pull her hair back away from her face. It reminded her of when Caitlin had been sick as a child and wanted her mother to pull back her hair and rub her back. 'What's wrong, Caits?'

Caitlin replied through sobs and tears. 'It's the oven. It's not working and I can't do anything with my pavlova.'

'Pavlova? What are you doing with a pavlova, darling? It's a drinks party. You didn't need to make a pavlova.'

Caitlin pulled herself together and slowly got to her feet. Sheila stayed where she was. She could feel an explosion building and being close to the ground felt like the safest place to be.

'Well, people like my bloody pavlova. Without that, all we've got are shitty little crostini and some cold cuts.' And with that she marched out the kitchen, brushing past her father and made for the stairs.

'Bloody hell. People are going to start arriving soon.' Simon stood looking helpless.

'What's happening?' John asked. Sheila didn't know where to begin with either of them and so just smiled at Simon and squeezed her husband's arm as she went after her daughter. She climbed the stairs and followed the sound of crying to the nursery and to Caitlin sitting at the side of Milo's cot.

'Come on, darling, you're going to wake him. Look, he's sleeping soundly. You don't want to wake him. Let's go into the guest room.' It took all her strength but she pulled her daughter up and through to the room across the hall. They both collapsed, somewhat precariously, onto the large bed and its soft thick duvet.

Caitlin sat bolt upright. 'Of course I didn't want to wake him. I mean you only have to look at him, Mum, to see how completely perfect he is. And how precious. Totally and completely precious.' And then she was off again, sobbing.

Sheila got herself up onto her elbows. 'But of course he's precious. What's this all about?' She looked around for tissues, anything really that might stem the flow. Then she spotted a pile of clean baby towels on the chest of drawers in the corner of the room so she got up and grabbed one.

She handed it to her daughter and Caitlin quickly buried her face in the soft and fluffy fabric. After a few moments, she emerged with eyes red and weepy. Small indentations from the towel were imprinted on her cheeks.

Caitlin turned to her mother. 'I just don't think I can do it all. I don't want to do it all.' She started to scrunch the towel up in her hand. 'Not anymore.'

Sheila gently covered Caitlin's hand with her own in an attempt to stop all the rapid movements. Trying to slow everything down – thoughts, speech, heart rate.

'You don't have to do everything.'

'But people do. Everyone I know does. All the women in the office, they all manage to juggle home and work. And I've worked so hard to get where I am, you know I have. It's just there's no let-up. It's not just the ten-hour days, it's all the other stuff. Taking calls in the evenings, weekends even.'

She looked at her daughter. It hadn't been the same for Sheila – she knew it hadn't. There hadn't really been the same pressures with her job at the Council – certainly not compared to Caitlin's highly pressurised tax lawyer position – and she'd never really struggled to maintain a balance. And now when she thought about the choices she'd made, she wondered how she could have done it, with no hint of regret or remorse. Leaving Caitlin at nursery had never really been a wrench. So maybe it was fair enough that she should accept responsibility for some of Caitlin's apparent coldness. But the struggle that was emerging right in front of her eyes was nothing to do with her. This was all Caitlin – her feelings, her needs, her family's needs. And watching all of this unfold, she felt glad, relieved even, that her daughter had reached this point.

'Oh, Mum. It just doesn't matter to me anymore. I thought I wanted it, but I don't. I just want Milo and Simon. I just want my family.' Caitlin started crying again.

'Right, that's enough. Stop right now.' She took her daughter by the shoulders. 'It's absolutely fine to want to be with your son. Absolutely fine. These years are really important.' It suddenly crossed her mind that this might be the time for Caitlin to question her own mother's child-rearing choices but if it did occur to Caitlin, she said nothing. Maybe it just wasn't the time or place.

'Look, why not talk to them about a career break. Employers are far more open to that sort of thing nowadays. And if they can't keep the job open for you – well, just walk away, Caits. You're lucky, really lucky, that you can live very well on Simon's salary and we're always here to help. You know that. Then maybe when Milo's at school you can think about work again.'

Caitlin's whole body seemed to let go. The tension began to ebb away.

'You just don't know which way to go. But once you've made the decision your head will clear and you can start thinking more positively about things. A new kind of life, Caits, but still a good kind of life. Just different, that's all.'

Caitlin smiled and rested her head on her mother's shoulder. Sheila couldn't remember when they'd last felt this close but then maybe they never had been. It felt like a good place to be.

CHAPTER 14

Sheila left her daughter quietly drying her eyes and reapplying make-up. She turned her thoughts to the impending party and moved quickly downstairs to join the men in the kitchen. When she reached the bottom of the stairs, she stopped in front of the large framed black-and-white portrait photograph hanging on the wall opposite. A happy, smiling little family. Caitlin, Simon and Milo lounging on a pristine white floor, clad in matching black trousers and white shirts. She'd passed it a hundred times before but had never paid too much attention. It had always struck her as slightly ostentatious to put your family on show like that and John had agreed.

But now she stopped and looked and saw – perhaps for the first time. The bonds, the connections that made a family. Her daughter's family.

The moment of quiet contemplation was quickly over and she made her way to the kitchen to organise things before the first guests arrived. The sight that greeted her was unexpected, to say the least. John had rolled up his sleeves and was dropping spoonfuls of cream cheese onto small Melba toasts. His brow was furrowed and his tongue was edging out at the side of his mouth, signalling extraordinary levels of concentration.

'What are you doing, dear?'

He didn't look up. 'Simon told me that this stuff goes on here and then I have to tear up some smoked salmon and swirl it about a bit on the top.'

'Where's Simon?'

'Getting the champagne. I could have done that. More my thing.'

'Will I help?'

'No. I'm on a roll now; don't want to break the rhythm. Speak to Simon. He'll give you your orders. We've to do something with crostini, whatever that is.'

So the world had completely turned on its axis.

'Caits. How is she? Have you sorted it? Is it all sorted?' He still didn't look up.

'Yes, it's sorted.'

John smiled. That was all he needed to know. Simon came back in with the champagne and looked at Sheila, concern written all over his face.

'You go to her, Simon. She needs you now.' He dropped the crate rather heavily on to the worktop, causing the bottles to shake erratically, and headed upstairs.

An hour or so later, a sense of calm had descended over the household. Harry Stuart had been one of the early arrivals to the party but Sheila had been far too busy for meet and greet and so she had despatched Caitlin and Simon to welcome guests. She watched them hold hands as they walked towards the front door. Everything that had fallen apart appeared to have been quietly put back together.

Before long, a satisfying thrum of low-level noise was filling the spacious lounge/diner as the party got into full swing. She surveyed the scene from the hall. Caitlin was wandering about, talking to small groups of her guests. There was a serenity about her now. Relaxed, smiling and every so often searching out her husband, placing her hand on his back or slipping her hand into his. Sheila thought back to her uncomfortable encounters with Colin. Funny that the same small acts could be performed with completely differing intent. Here, there was familiarity but, more than that, there was safety and security.

She watched John appearing to be entirely content in the company of Simon's colleagues. Men he'd met before and who were happy to talk golf swings and handicaps. As she made her way further into the room, she noticed him eye up a canapé and nod in her direction. *For God's sake*, she thought. *He needs positive strokes just for making up a few sodding party bites.* But truth be told, the culinary element of the party appeared to be passing off with little fuss. It had really just comprised whatever the three musketeers had managed to summon up from the fridge. Anything that entailed a minimal amount of construction and, of course, absolutely no heating in an oven.

None of it really mattered, in the scheme of things. People were at the party to enjoy the company and no doubt the excellent champagne but more importantly to celebrate Simon's birthday. And to Sheila's surprise, Caitlin appeared to have foregone any natural urge to impress. There was certainly no shouting from the rooftops about John's award and she wasn't engaging in her normal practice of plucking people out of one group to thrust them into another. Making sure the right people were making the right connections. No, there was none of that. And so a completely unforeseen and relaxed evening was unfolding in front of them.

Sheila spotted Harry in the corner of the lounge, surrounded by a group of men and women, old and young, transfixed as he regaled them with his entertaining stories. As she strained to listen above the general din, Sheila could only pick up broken snippets. There was something about travelling in France, Italy. He was extolling the beauty of these countries, the richness of their cultures. *Interesting*, Sheila thought. She'd never heard him talk like that before.

Simon was then suddenly beside her, arm draped around her shoulder and swaying slightly.

'Well, Sheila. Three hours ago, I could never have imagined that all *this* would be happening.' He gave her a kiss on the cheek. 'Thanks. Not sure what you said to Caits – but thanks.'

She smiled up at her son-in-law. 'She's fine, Simon. She's going to be just fine. It all got too much for her, that's all. Needing to be the best at everything. Nobody can be the best at *everything*. Well, I don't think they can. She'll be okay now she's able to think a bit more clearly.'

'You, dear mother-in-law, are a star.'

They laughed and clinked glasses. Sheila nodded across to the far side of the lounge. 'Look at Harry, Simon. He's got that lot enthralled with his stories. He's just like that at the history club you know. I don't know if it's his voice, his delivery or just his interesting stories.' She sighed. 'Such an engaging character.'

'Yes, well, he's always been able to do that. Hold people in the palm of his hand.'

'But you'd think that would have counted for something at work. You know, the fact that he could take people with him.'

'Well, yes, up to a point. But ask him to construct a position with his team, Sheila, and he'd give you forty reasons why his way of thinking was the right one and another forty why it wasn't worth taking on board anyone else's point of view.'

He planted another kiss, this time on the top of her head and headed off to join his mates. As he did so, Sheila spotted John and Caitlin on the small sofa near the entrance to the kitchen. As she made a move towards them, she noticed that father and daughter appeared to be engaged in a very earnest conversation. She had no idea what it was all about but the one thing she did know was that she really couldn't be bothered with anything terribly earnest. Not now, not after all the preceding drama. But she was genuinely pleased to see them talking, alone, together. It occurred to her, then, that all the pieces of her life were starting to fall into place. Her life with John, with Caitlin, Simon and Milo and with her new-found passion for history.

Whether as a result of that minor epiphany or because she felt strangely liberated after the Caitlin crisis, Sheila was suddenly more than ready to enter into the party spirit, have a few laughs and drink champagne. Lots of it. With those heady thoughts filling her mind, she made for Harry and his jovial little band.

'Ah, Sheila. Make way everyone for my star pupil and mother-in-law of the birthday boy.'

Sheila could feel herself blush as the little group suddenly split apart paving the way for her entrance into its centre. It felt very biblical, akin to the arrival of the Queen of Sheba. Some of the group she knew, some she didn't, but they all smiled and nodded. With all eyes fixed on her, she walked straight up to Harry, standing resplendent in bright green tartan trousers and red waistcoat. His hair was red-and-silver streaked and gleaming in the twinkling light from the mix of tea lights and LEDs strewn over the mantelpiece.

'Now don't exaggerate. Has everyone got enough champagne?' Everyone nodded at her.

And so she joined him, as he entertained his audience with tales from the history club. At times the two of them spoke in unison and she was conscious and slightly embarrassed by the fact that they occasionally finished each other's sentences. She hadn't felt this relaxed in anyone's company, not even John's, for years. They seemed to pick up on each other's sense of humour and she found herself going along with his occasional embellishments.

Unfortunately the tight-fitting, crisp cotton shirt was beginning to knock her mood a bit. Everything she was wearing suddenly felt uncomfortably hard and formal and she was starting to wish she'd worn something a bit less businesslike, looser fitting, more flowing, a bit brighter perhaps. But not to worry, none of that was going to stop her let rip a little bit. Just this once.

Champagne glasses were mysteriously being topped up, but she wasn't altogether sure from where. A glass was quickly downed only for her to find it filled to the brim again. Her cheeks felt flushed, but it wasn't embarrassment this time. This time it was the work of bright little bubbles slipping down the back of her throat and working their way effortlessly into her bloodstream. The good feeling rushed through her, pumping its way round her body.

Harry's eyes continued to sparkle as he spoke and at one point, he put his arm round her shoulder and drew her closer, just for a moment. A strong hand gripping the top of her arm, pulling her into his burly chest. But she didn't feel threatened, didn't feel threatened at all. On the contrary, it was a warm, friendly gesture.

*

The party was over and Sheila and John had said their goodbyes. So many emotions in one evening. Pain at her daughter's distress had turned to feelings of warmth and empathy. A short period of settled contentment as the party got into full flow had been broken by raucous laughter and quick-fire chatter. And now? Now, there was just overwhelming exhaustion.

'Well, that was some party.' John gave his summation of the evening as they headed for home in a taxi. He was half sitting, half lying on the seat, long legs stretched out in front of him.

'I thought it went very well, considering.'

'Suppose so. As you say. All things considered.' He turned and put his arm round her shoulder. 'We really stepped up to the plate for our Caits there, don't you think?'

Yes, Sheila thought. *John had been way out of his comfort zone in the kitchen but at least he'd mucked in.*

'Did you manage one of these things I made? The crusty whatsits?'

She turned and smiled. 'Crostini, dear. Yes. They were delicious.'

'You sound exhausted.' He laughed, a short, sharp little laugh. 'Ten minutes ago you were getting carried away with Harry what's-his-name. Laughing at all his jokes. He's a bit over the top. Don't you think?'

'No, not really.' She suddenly felt embarrassed. Had she been laughing at all his jokes? And what did John mean by getting carried away?

'Looks like he's completely drained you. You did really well there, though, I have to say. The man's so bloody full of himself.' He squeezed the top of her shoulder – hard. 'Definitely hats off to you there, darling. Think you went above and beyond putting up with him all night.'

Yes, drained. That's exactly how she felt. But it was nothing to do with 'putting up with him' as John so kindly put it. Nothing at all to do with that. Quite the opposite in fact. She was exhausted because she'd been having so much fun. Adrenalin had been coursing through her veins, she'd laughed until she hurt and the champagne had seemed to heighten all her senses. No, it was nothing to do with Harry being obnoxious and everything to do with her just enjoying herself – in his company. It was only when the champagne had stopped flowing and the guests began to drift off, that she'd felt the heavy clunk of a throbbing headache begin to work its way to the bony ridges above her eyes. The adrenalin had simply washed away and the after-effects of domestic drama, followed by slightly excessive partying, were taking their toll.

'I enjoy him, actually.' There it was again. Maybe John's comments were irking her; maybe it was the tiredness, but she felt compelled to set the record straight.

John struggled to sit upright. 'Seriously?'

She just looked at him. The lines on his face. The lines around his eyes, across his forehead. There seemed to be more of them now. Maybe the years of striving, climbing, reaching for something left a physical mark, like indentations on a rock face. Would they go when he got there? Reached that point, that pinnacle. Would he even know when he'd made it?

Her thoughts were wandering and tiredness was overwhelming her. She could almost sense the cocooning warmth of her thick duvet, surely just a few hundred metres away now. Still she kept the conversation going.

'Yes, seriously.'

'Look at the state of him. What's that hair about for a start? Man of his age. Could do with seeing a decent barber.'

She knew she was beginning to annoy him. Consciously beginning to annoy him and she could feel the tension in his tone and in his body. Languid had turned into animated. Her lack of response just seemed to make things worse.

John was now looking and sounding incredulous. 'You do agree he talks drivel, don't you? All that stuff about being descended from Lord Darnley. You can't believe that nonsense surely, Sheila?'

She just shrugged. Were they ever going to get home? Why was it that the taxi ride home seemed to be taking so much longer? If he would only stop having a go at her friend, at someone she liked, then there wouldn't be this need to jump to Harry's defence. No need at all.

'Simon thinks he's an arse.'

'Hardly, John. He wouldn't have invited him to his birthday party if he'd thought that.'

The taxi made its final approach towards the sanctuary of her bed, trundling over the narrow cobbles of their street and coming to an abrupt halt at the entrance to their home.

'You don't find him attractive, do you?' He threw his head back and laughed. 'Oh my God. You can't really be serious.' Then he slapped his thighs. 'Oh, that's hilarious, Sheila. Absolutely hilarious.'

*

Her father was sitting in his usual seat in the far corner of the common room. It seemed to Sheila that his head was permanently angled, looking out at the manicured lawn and its surrounding neatly clipped bushes. She often wondered if he knew what he was looking at. Was it a world he wanted to escape into? A solitary hide, deep among the leaves and the thorns, deadening the sounds of confusion and anguish.

She had decided to take homemade Scotch broth into the care home. She'd been doing it for months now, ever since he started to refuse food. The episodes were few and far between, but the lovely Carole had relaxed the regulations for such emergencies and allowed her to heat soup up in the microwave. Sometimes she had to spoon-feed him and today was one of those days. It never felt right, feeding her father. He would never have wanted that, but then at the same time, she'd never felt closer to him. Feeding him, sustaining him, seemed like such a basic act of kindness. Something she could do for him after all he'd done for her.

She tucked the bright red napkin into his shirt and then she noticed. That wasn't his shirt. They must have got the washing mixed up again. She thought to mention it, but it had happened before and she never liked to. They were all so busy and really trying to do their best. It was a shirt, it fitted him and, to be perfectly frank, her dad wouldn't have known if he was sitting in a pink dress or a black tuxedo. She'd mentioned clothes mix-ups once to John. He'd been going to write a letter of complaint to the trustees, but he soon forgot all about that, thank God.

'Oh Dad, sorry that was me. It's too hot for you, isn't it?' Her father screwed up his face as he swallowed the first mouthful of thick broth, almost wincing in pain before opening his mouth for the next spoonful. She could feel her own pain as the burning liquid travelled down his gullet. It was too hot and hurt him, but he still wanted his soup. Scotch broth had always been his favourite and maybe he was scared it would be taken away if he didn't eat.

She lifted up the napkin and gently wiped the corners of his mouth. 'There you are, Dad. We'll just let this cool down for a minute.'

He stared straight ahead, blinking his watery eyes until beads of moisture fell down his cheeks. Were they crying tears, or was it the heat from the soup? She didn't know. But he opened his mouth again and a soulful cry escaped. He wanted more.

'Oh Dad, don't. Look I'll just blow on the soup, then it won't burn so much.' He waited patiently while she blew on the hot liquid and wafted her hands over its surface. The soup-feeding then continued peacefully and without further incident.

When there was no broth left, a young assistant in a mustard coverall cleared the empty plate away and Sheila sat with her father, stroking his hand.

'It was Simon's birthday, Dad. Saturday night. There was a party. Think I had a bit too much to drink.'

She let out a little laugh.

'Well, at least John says I did. Got overly friendly with my history tutor apparently. At my age, Dad. Can you believe it? No, neither can I.' She looked down, wiping away imaginary crumbs from her front. 'Lot of nonsense on John's part, to be honest. I'm just enjoying meeting new people. Interesting people. Nothing wrong with that is there? And who the hell would look at *me*? Not that I want anyone to look at me.'

She knew she was looking pleadingly at him. What was she doing sharing this nonsense with him at all? He'd never liked John, so he was probably thinking he was being a bit of an overbearing idiot. Is he thinking that? Or maybe he's actually thinking what John's thinking and she was just making a fool of herself, getting carried away with somebody or something that made her feel different. What did she think she was doing? Maybe John was right to pull her up about it.

No. Her dad wouldn't think any of that. He wouldn't think badly of her at all.

'I wasn't chatting anyone up, Dad. You know I wasn't. That's just a ridiculous thing to think.'

She moved her hand up towards the slightly frayed cuff of his emerald green shirt. Not his colour, but then not his shirt. She clung on regardless.

'Everything's good with Caitlin now. She's going to give up work to look after Milo full-time. Think she'll enjoy it actually. Funny, there we were all thinking that she was the high-flying career girl when all she wanted to do was build her little family and look after them.'

She looked down at the mass of veins and loose skin that covered her dad's fragile bones. And then she looked up to watch for any hint of recognition but there was nothing. Her father just sat staring straight ahead and blinking.

'Remember Milo, Dad? Caitlin's little boy? We brought him in not long ago and he was scrambling all over you. He really liked you.' She paused. 'And you really liked him. Didn't you?'

She wanted to say this was no life, no existence if he couldn't even feel a child's joy. Milo's unbridled happiness. The need to touch and stroke and just feel the world around him. But she said nothing and went on, stroking her father's hand and looking into his tear-filled eyes.

CHAPTER 15

Caitlin saw out the remaining weeks of her career in tax law and transferred seamlessly into the role of full-time mother. Sheila had worried that there might be some signs of regret at the decision to give up the high-flyer status and lucrative pay cheque, but she needn't have worried. The move was meticulously planned and executed with very little attendant emotion. She really shouldn't have expected anything less.

It had been agreed that part of this new arrangement would involve Caitlin and Milo spending one day a week at Sheila's house. Milo had been used to being at Granny's for the first two days of every week and Caitlin was keen that there should be as little disruption on that front as possible. The specified day was a Monday – 'Although of course, we can always change that, if you give me a reasonable amount of notice, Mum.'

Sheila had sat perched on the edge of her Napoleon chair listening to Caitlin as the proposal was made. The emotional frailty that had been so in evidence a few short weeks ago had been replaced by a kind of determined efficiency. But that was fine. It was how Caitlin generally managed her way through life and she happily acquiesced.

At the same time, she had grown to love her time with Milo and was more than a little relieved at the Monday proposal. Of course, the dynamic would need to shift, she understood that. She would need to tread carefully with this new set-up and allow Caitlin to exercise full motherly rein. But it was all manageable. All perfectly manageable.

'It's a bit tedious this, isn't it?' It was the first day of the new regime and Caitlin was sitting on the floor of the playroom filling a little wooden trolley with bricks. She was wearing jogging bottoms and a zip-up sweatshirt. She had never seen her daughter in jogging bottoms before. Must have been the designated playtime uniform.

Milo watched her every move and when the trolley was full, he promptly picked up each brightly coloured block and handed them back to her.

'Its just the age he's at. They go through a phase of filling things up and emptying them. Sure it signifies something, not sure what.' Sheila smiled down at her grandson.

'Just doesn't seem much point to it, that's all. Simon and I like to have a bit of structure around his play activity.'

'Well, there's not always an obvious point to a lot of child's play.' She was trying not to sound too censorious. But it occurred to Sheila that perhaps her own child had never just played for the sake of it, without there needing to be an attainable objective at the end. Strange she'd never seen that in Caitlin but you couldn't go back over everything. What was the point in that? 'Anyway, he seems happy enough. That's the main thing.'

Caitlin looked at her quizzically but said nothing more on the subject.

Sheila went off to make lunch for Milo and shortly came back into the room with a plateful of banana sandwiches. Little squares of white bread, butter and squashed banana. The sight of Milo savouring all that tasty mush as he squeezed the squares through his chubby little fingers and into his sweet little mouth proved too much of a temptation. Twenty minutes later all three of them were sitting around the plastic red table eating banana sandwiches. Broccoli quiche and salad for the adults had been guiltily abandoned.

'So how's old Harry and his history club?' Caitlin relaxed back against the wall.

'Great, yes. Although we're on a break for a couple of weeks. Harry's off on holiday somewhere.' She felt her cheeks flush slightly. Ever since the party, she'd felt just a tad self-conscious whenever the subject of Harry came up. She kept telling herself it was stupid to feel like that. She'd done nothing wrong. Harry had done nothing wrong. They'd had a very enjoyable evening. Yes, maybe she had drunk a bit more than was normal for her but God, when you thought of it. It had been a pretty stressful evening all round. No wonder she'd wanted to just let go a bit.

But it was this feeling, whatever it was. She just wished it would leave her.

'Where's he away to?' Caitlin was using baby wipes to clean Milo's hands. Pointless, really. The little boy was still eating.

'I've no idea. He didn't even mention it in class. We all just got an email.'

'Actually, come to think of it, he and his wife never go abroad. They always go up to Pitlochry or somewhere round there. Milo! I've just cleaned those hands. Somewhere like Pitlochry, I mean. Might not be the exact place. I hate Pitlochry, don't you? Always seems stuck in a time warp. Full of very dull people all wearing the same clothes and sad little restaurants that still serve tinned pineapple. That's when you know somewhere is really stuck in the past. Like in the seventies or something. Anywhere that still serves tinned pineapple. Don't you think?'

A wife. There was a wife. She tried to shake the thought from her mind. Why wouldn't there be? And what on earth difference did it make in any case? It was a bit of a shock, that was all. Maybe because he'd never mentioned his home life. But then why would he? What on earth difference did it make to *her*? Strange the wife hadn't been at Simon's birthday party, though. She ignored the slight flip in her stomach knowing that her daughter waited patiently in expectation of a response about tinned pineapple.

She quickly refocussed her mind to Caitlin's bizarre take on a respectable little town in Highland Perthshire, minding its own business. Where did Caitlin get all this nonsense from? Pitlochry was a perfectly lovely place.

'Well, there's the Festival Theatre and lots of lovely walking in the area. Your dad and I have been up that way a few times. Maybe that's the sort of thing they like to do.'

'Really? I didn't know that.'

'Well, I don't know what they like to do either.' She shifted her focus on to Milo, wishing they'd never opened up the discussion about Harry.

'I don't mean *them*, Mum. Couldn't care less why they go to Pitlochry. If they do go there I mean. No, I meant you and Dad. I didn't know you and *Dad* liked going up there.'

Oh yes, of course. Mum and Dad. Sheila and John. Nothing to do with Harry.

*

A couple of weeks passed and Sheila was some way through a newly purchased pile of history books. Naturally, Mary Queen of Scots was first on the reading list. She had declined coffee invitations from Agnes and Sandra to give herself the space and time to try to fathom what it might have been like to live in the sixteenth century. For a *woman*, a woman of power to live and rule in that world. It was dark and dangerous. You lived on your wits, never really knowing who was friend or foe.

She picked out a heavyweight book on embroideries and marvelled at the subtle and often not-so-subtle messages Mary tried to convey in her tapestries. Studying the intricate detail of pattern and colour, she slowly turned each page.

The cat alongside the mouse as Elizabeth persecuted Mary. The tortoise climbing the crowned palm tree depicting Darnley's marriage to Mary and his desperate pursuit of the 'crown matrimonial' and finally the rising of the phoenix. *In the end is my beginning*. Mary's famous final words.

Why was she so entranced by all of this? A woman's pain – rights denied and demonised. Once treated so royally and then months, years of incarceration. Humiliating to think that you are destined to live life as a supreme being – only to be treated in death like a criminal.

And Darnley. What of Darnley? The handsome suitor. The perfect consort who had turned into nothing more than a drunken, unfaithful layabout, craving royal status. Thoughts again turned to Harry. The Harry she enjoyed and admired, supposedly descended from such a debauched character. And proud of it too. What did he see in Darnley that everyone else had missed? The wronged man perhaps.

Sheila sat back. Where was she going with all of this? She quickly turned the pages and landed on less turbulent descriptions of well-worn fabrics, colour palettes and stitching. But suddenly her mind flicked back.

Was that it? Maybe Harry's wife was a strong, striking woman who didn't put up with any of his nonsense. Her mind began to drift: *I wonder what she is like? What she looks like.*

A quiet thought. So quiet, no one else would ever know she'd thought it.

Sheila closed the book abruptly and looked at the clock on the mantelpiece. John would be home soon. It was time to wrench herself out of the sixteenth century and get some twenty-first-century gin and tonics on the go.

She stood up, smoothed down her tweed skirt and walked over to the other side of the room. No jogging bottoms for her. She took the gin from the sideboard cupboard and walked into the kitchen. She removed two small cans of tonic from inside the fridge door and placed everything on the worktop. Two Edinburgh Crystal glasses sat side by side waiting to be filled. Now for the lemon. Slicing neatly, thinly, she winced slightly as a drop of the biting acid caught the skin at the bottom right corner of her nail. A tiny crevice that she'd been picking at all afternoon. She looked up at the clock in the kitchen.

As she turned her attention back to the task in hand, she closed her eyes. Suddenly she could smell her husband. She could feel his lips caressing her neck, her breasts. She thought of his tongue exploring her mouth.

Right, enough of that. She hadn't thought about John in that way for years.

She moved to the freezer, pulled out the ice tray and ran it under the hot tap until the frozen blocks were warm enough to drop into the sink. She scooped them up and dropped them, two in each glass. She watched them swirl round the bottom, the icy edges beginning to melt.

A familiar noise. It was John's key in the lock. Then she heard the hall cupboard opening and closing and some muffled rant about gridlock at the West End. She watched and waited until he appeared at the doorway to the kitchen. He wasn't happy, she could tell. His face was screwed up as he continued with his tale of traffic woes, all the while loosening his tie and struggling to undo his top button. 'They need to look again at traffic flow round Charlotte Square. They've just not got it right.'

She didn't hear any of it but walked straight up to him, lifted his shirt out of his trousers and ran her hands up his body, sinking her mouth into his neck. He stumbled backwards slightly, holding her head to steady himself. She pulled her hands down to undo his belt and wrenched the navy blue pinstripe trousers down to his knees. Just for a moment he looked shocked, confused but it didn't last – they weren't subtle signals after all. The shock turned to desire and it didn't take him long to start pulling at the buttons on her blouse.

*

It felt cold as they lay there, side by side on the hall carpet. Sheila could feel a draught coming in from under the door or around the frame. Was that normal? Wasn't there a draught excluder fitted to the bottom of the door or was it the door itself that didn't fit the frame properly?

'Jesus, Sheila. Where did that come from?'

She stopped thinking about the door and turned to look at him. 'I don't know. It's okay though, isn't it?'

He spoke gently, quietly. 'Of course it is.'

The passion had ebbed away, now that her desire had been happily satiated. She looked down at the unaccustomed messiness and then across at her husband. They were just a pair of semi-clad and wrinkled bodies trying to regain a bit of dignity. She pulled at her tights but only managed to stick a nail through the left leg.

'Bugger.'

He laughed. 'Look at the state of us.'

Bits of clothing lay discarded in the hallway, her bra had been pulled up, her underwear pulled down and he still had his socks and shoes on. How could it be that something that felt so natural and instinctive only moments earlier, suddenly seemed so absurd. She rearranged what she could and then shoved him in the ribs. 'Come on, get up. Someone might come to the door or look through the letterbox.'

'What? Who does that? Why would anyone look through the letterbox?' He was still laughing as he pulled his trousers up. She picked up her blouse and ran upstairs to the bathroom.

She locked the door and looked in the mirror. What had come over her? In all their married life she had never once instigated sex. Not once. So why now? She was sixty for God's sake and all urges had been steadily receding for some time now. What on earth had possessed her? She splashed her face, wiped it gently with the facecloth and then brushed her teeth. Her heart was still racing. She moved in to look more closely; to spot clues; to see signs; something that might tell her what was going on. There was a definite brightness, a sharp vitality. Okay, cheeks were flushed from the unusual level of physical exertion, but it was more than that. She looked different, she felt different. Like someone had flicked a switch.

She splashed her face again and rubbed it hard with the cotton hand towel. Wanting him and needing him had felt good.

When she came back down John had poured the gin and tonics with sparkling new ice cubes floating to the surface. They both started to prepare dinner. He couldn't stop touching her, caressing her neck, nuzzling into the back of her head. It felt new, different and she revelled in it. But of course it wasn't new. There were glimpses from decades earlier when touching and intimacy had seemed like second nature, long before the structure of marital norms had begun to take shape.

Dinner was relaxed. Salmon wrapped in prosciutto, new potatoes and broccoli. Quick and simple. They sat with trays on their knees and laughed at themselves. This was the casual dining she'd been striving for. It felt like peeling back years of staid routine and discovering a young couple again, starting out in their first flat – without the gilt-edged mirrors and French-style furniture. She'd loved that flat. John had refused all help from her father to buy it, insisting on scraping together the deposit and buying their furniture from discount warehouses.

But then the norms slotted back into shape and they suddenly stepped forward into the constraints of the present. Stacking the dishwasher seemed to do it. John suddenly started to talk about bus driver training. Driver training, for God's sake. And that was it. Door closed on those blissfully happy days of a life that they couldn't wait to start together.

Later that evening they were both sitting in their customary armchairs, either side of the fireplace. John read his paper while Sheila flicked through the *Scottish Field*. After a while she began to feel his eyes on her.

'What? Why are you looking at me like that?'

He dropped the paper at the side of his chair. 'Just wondering where all that came from.'

She didn't want to think about it, analyse it, and so she got up and sat on his lap. Now there was another thing she hadn't done in years. She ran her fingers through his hair and pulled him in close, resting her head on top of his. Just like she used to when they were first married and could only afford one chair to match their two-seater sofa.

'I don't know. I just needed you, that's all.'

CHAPTER 16

Hello everyone. Very sorry about this but history club is cancelled for the next two weeks. Unforeseen circumstances. Sorry about that. See you all Friday 31 August.
　Best,
　Harry

She looked at the email again. History club cancelled for the next two weeks. That was it. No explanation other than some blanket reference to unforeseen circumstances.

They'd already been at the mercy of Harry's two-week holiday to Pitlochry, land of the tinned pineapple. And now after spending that time immersed in researching the life of Mary Queen of Scots, she was going to have to set aside her newly acquired knowledge for another fortnight. Maybe even longer. She'd be able to make the 31st August meeting but after that, John and she were off to France. How annoying.

She sat back staring at the computer screen. Yes, she was disappointed, but it was the timing and tone that really irked her. She picked up her mug of coffee from the desktop and held it firmly in both hands.

This lack of structure, of proper organisation, was really annoying. She liked to see what the weeks ahead looked like and really didn't have much truck for people who cancelled last minute.

She replaced the untouched coffee and took her Letts diary out of the drawer at the front of the desk and proceeded to score through the entries for the next couple of Fridays. But then maybe she was being unfair. Maybe he was ill. Maybe his wife was ill. She spoke the words from the email out loud – twice. No, not really the words of a disconsolate or weary man. The message was a bit too brusque, a bit too jaunty to suggest anyone was hovering at death's door.

Maybe she'd be better doing an Open University course, she thought to herself. There would be proper coursework, deadlines, tutorials, maybe even some residential weekends. She mulled over the prospect in her head. Space was again opening up in her once-crammed week so maybe now was the time.

Sandra and Agnes. *I'll talk it over with Sandra and Agnes*, she decided.

*

Sheila arranged coffee at home with her friends on what turned out to be a properly dreich Edinburgh morning. She watched at the study window as the two women marched up the path to the front door, heads bent to keep the incessant drizzle out of their eyes. Once inside, raincoats and hats were discarded and Sheila ushered Sandra and Agnes into the warmth of the lounge. On days like these, the grey mist never seemed to lift, shrouding every edifice in a cloak of gloom.

'What a day.' Sandra shook her head like a waterlogged dog. 'It's the kind of rain that just seeps into you. Every bit of you.'

'I did say we should have driven here.' Agnes looked sternly at her friend, but Sandra had moved on.

'Well, we're here now.'

'I'll just put on some lights I think.' Sheila walked round the room switching on her small table lamps. The soft lights accentuated the darkness outside, making everything inside feel warm and welcoming.

'What colour is this again?' Sandra walked the length of the lounge, all the while wiping down the dampness that was clinging to her face with a white handkerchief. She stopped at the far end of the room.

'Oh, it's one of the old Farrow and Ball blues. Not sure they do it anymore. Came from one of these stately homes down south. Something they had in the boudoir.'

'Oh my – *boudoir*. What are you two like.' Sandra spun round almost knocking over the small plaster cast replica statue of the Rape of the Sabines, brought back from Florence many moons ago. It was tourist tat really and didn't match their more expensive *objets d'art*, but Sheila liked it. She sighed with relief to see that it had avoided the sweep of her friend's hips. Satisfied that all was well she went off to the kitchen to make coffee.

When she returned, Sandra dropped into John's armchair. She sounded exasperated. 'Well, that's a bugger about our little history club, isn't it? Not that I'd done much recommended reading but still it filled a Friday and it was good to be out and about with our eclectic little group.'

Sheila handed round mugs of freshly brewed coffee and a plate of still-warm buttered cheese scones.

Sandra took a large bite and the crumbs fell down the front of her lilac polo. Sheila noticed how some of them stuck to the thick hoops in the yellow gold necklace that was covering her large bosom.

'Yes. Well, I suppose things will be up and running again in a couple of weeks' time. Mind you if we don't know what the "unforeseen circumstances" are they might continue for a wee while yet. And then of course John and I are off to France. I just don't know. It's all a bit unstructured and feels a bit haphazard somehow.' She paused for a moment. 'I'm thinking I might give it up and apply to the Open University to do a Scottish History course.'

Sandra almost choked on her scone. 'Oh no. You can't do that. You must stick with. Ag and I would be lost without you. Wouldn't we, Ag? And so would Harry, for that matter. You're his star pupil.'

'Oh good grief, I don't think so. It's just, I seem to know where he's coming from a lot of the time. And he challenges me I suppose. Makes me stop and think – I like that.'

She turned away from the inquiring eyes to pour her own coffee. It was slightly unnerving that Agnes had chosen to remain silent on the topic – she must have an opinion, after all.

'Ag? Don't you think? We need Sheila there.' Sandra had read her mind.

'I'm not sure I much mind whether we go back or not.' Agnes set her coffee mug down, quite forcefully. 'He gets awfully aggressive. Well, maybe not aggressive, but he's certainly combative. He likes to provoke an argument, get people contradicting each other. All this *challenging people*. Why? Why not let people have their own ideas, come to their own views? Tell us what you know, give us the benefit of your expertise and then let us make up our own minds. You know we can all look at the same set of facts and quite legitimately come to different conclusions about *why* things happened the way they did. I mean I know we can't be playing around with historical facts but we're talking about the human character here, the human psyche – what drives people. Well, I think we can all bring our own experiences, our own motivations, to that sort of analysis.' Agnes picked up her coffee again. 'That's what I think anyway. It's exhausting being *challenged* all the time. I would just quite like people to listen to what I have to say. And quite frankly you can all take it or leave it after that.'

Sheila looked across at Sandra who looked confused, unsettled. Neither of them had really heard Agnes speak at length on anything before. She was a kind, amiable woman who up until now had never offered up much of an opinion about anything.

Sandra boomed forth. 'But you never say anything, Ag. When we're there I mean. In class. You hardly open your trap.'

'Well, I don't like to.' And with that Agnes took a large bite out of her scone.

Sheila didn't quite know what to make of it all and the friends parted later that afternoon without having resolved the question of whether or not to continue with history club. All very unsatisfactory.

Later that evening after a meal eaten mostly in silence, John and Sheila were reading again in the lounge. The long silences had barely been noticeable when she was working. The focus had always been on getting food on the table, often haphazardly, often at differing points in the evening. But when they did connect there always seemed to be so much to chat about. There were times, of course, when they were both overly preoccupied with something work-related. When that happened, everyday chat became an unwanted guest at the dinner table. But they'd always seemed to pick up on each other's vibe in these circumstances and just let the other one *be*.

Now it felt like there was a distance opening up between them. The odd episode of impromptu sex was all very lovely, but it wasn't the answer, not for her. It felt, for the most part, like they were living out quite separate lives. But maybe they always had, maybe she just hadn't noticed until now.

'Everything okay?' she asked him.

John put down a large wad of papers and looked at her over his reading glasses. 'Just frustrating. Getting to grips with the tram project. I mean, we've got the thing back on the rails.' He missed the pun entirely. 'But I'm not sure about meeting the commencement deadline. It's going to be tight.' Papers went back up. He could have been talking to anybody. Project manager, users' group, politicians. He wouldn't want to be found wanting, she knew that. The tram project was a personal coup, but it also meant that his reputation was at stake. Sheila could never understand this kind of vainglorious approach to matters that may well prove disastrous due to unforeseen, or more importantly underestimated, risks. Bit like going to war but without the inevitable destruction of human life. It was high profile, public statements had been made, commitments given and of course he'd lapped up the ensuing praise. A damaged reputation was not something he could best handle. John did not wear the non-stick veneer of a career politician.

She turned back to her Mary Queen of Scots journal and away from project deadlines. Interesting. A bronze statue of Mary was to be unveiled at her birthplace of Linlithgow Palace. All society members were welcome and friends' attendance could be accommodated if adequate notice was given to the branch chair. She thought for a moment. Well, that would be a nice outing for their little club and even if Harry was indisposed, she was sure they could organise the trip themselves. In fact, she would be very happy to organise it.

The following morning, she phoned Sandra. 'What do you think? We could make a real day of it. Have lunch and then a tour of the Palace.'

'What – without Harry? What would he think of that? Shouldn't we wait till he's back into circulation?'

'Why would we do that? I know he's supposed to resurface on the 31st but I mean, *unforeseen circumstances*. Goodness knows how long *unforeseen circumstances* can go on for. And in any case the unveiling is next week. We'd miss all the pomp and ceremony.'

'Is there going to be much pomp and ceremony?'

'Oh good grief, Sandra. I don't know. We don't even have to organise it as an official club trip. Could just be a bunch of friends wanting to go on a wee outing.'

'But what about travel? Harry normally drives the minibus.'

'Well, we could take a couple of cars or even get the train. I don't know – hadn't thought that far ahead.' This was proving much harder work than she'd anticipated.

After an awkward period of silence Sandra's tone suddenly changed. 'Well, why not. It'll be fun – and what's he going to do about it anyway?'

It hadn't occurred to Sheila that Harry would *do* anything about it. Why would he? So they ended their conversation with Sheila agreeing to send a quick email round the club members to gauge interest. She had of course included Harry in the circulation list but on second thoughts she decided to leave his name off the list and send him something a bit more personal. A letter. She would send him a letter. If there was an ego to be massaged that might just do the trick.

Dear Harry,

I do hope all is well with you and yours. I know we're all looking forward to getting back to our club meetings starting on the 31 August, although I'm afraid I won't be around for much of September as John and I will be off to France.

(Decisions about Open University courses could wait for now, she decided.)

Thought I would let you know that the Marie Stuart Society is unveiling a life-sized bronze statue to Mary at Linlithgow Palace next Thursday and I thought it would be lovely if we all made the trip. I (as I think I may have told you) am a member of the Society and am sure I can get us all in on the celebrations, assuming I speak to the Branch Chair in the next day or so. Would be great if you could join us but I understand if you have other things going on at the moment. Do let me know what you think.
With all good wishes,
Sheila

She printed off the letter, signed her name, folded it carefully and placed it in an envelope. All good and well but she'd forgotten one crucial detail. She didn't know Harry's address. She decided to phone Caitlin.

'Hi Caitlin, it's Mum. How's things?'

'Oh great. I've found this playgroup on Wednesday mornings. It's just along Heriot Row. Simon said that's Robert Louis Stevenson territory. Not sure what difference that makes but Milo loves it and I think they really are a step up in their approach to child development, their social interactions.'

'But that's miles away from you. Isn't there anything closer?'

'Oh yes of course but the owners seem to have good solid ideas about intelligent play. But actually, it's the kind of mothers that are going along that really swung it for us. They're the kind of girls I grew up with.'

There was a short pause.

'I'm just not so sure about some of the ladies in our neighbourhood. Not really getting a feeling for their hinterland if you know what I mean. Whereas these girls – oh and by the way it is all girls – well, they're our sort, Mum. I feel comfortable with them; I know the schools they went to, that sort of thing. You know where I'm coming from, don't you, Mummy?'

It wasn't that she thought she'd created a monster or anything like that. It was just she couldn't always fathom where Caitlin's thinking came from. How had this kind of value system been built? Had she, as her mother, helped create it or had the Edinburgh establishment formed it? It often made her wince but at the same time she couldn't help but admire the certainty with which Caitlin espoused her views.

'Well, yes. It has to feel right for you and Simon – oh and Milo. Of course it does.'

'Anyway, what's happening with you?'

Sheila was pleased to be moving away from good parental choices and told her daughter all about the history club hiatus and her idea to invite everyone along to Linlithgow Palace.

'Well, sounds like a lovely day out.' Caitlin sounded less than enthused but Sheila let it pass.

'Anyway, thing is, I was going to ask Harry along. I doubt he'll be able to make it given he's cancelled the club meetings for another two weeks. But I thought I should at least invite him. So anyway, I wrote him a letter—'

'Wrote him a letter? How quaint. What's wrong with email?'

Again she refused to let Caitlin knock her off her stride. 'Well, I just thought it was a bit impersonal, particularly if he's been ill, or his wife's been ill.'

'Really? How do you know that?'

'Well, I don't actually. He just said club meetings had been cancelled due to "unforeseen circumstances".'

'Well, that could be anything, couldn't it? Maybe he just wants a break from you lot.'

'Right, well. Do you have his address or not?'

'His address? When did you ask me for his address?'

'Didn't I? Well I meant to. There. I've asked you now.'

'I've got it somewhere. It's on our Christmas card labels, I think. Why don't I email it to you? The fast and easy method of communication.'

'That would be lovely, darling, thank you.'

A couple of hours later she checked her emails and there it was: 20 Woodford Grove, Edinburgh. Not really her part of town but she knew it well enough. Solid stone villas made up so much of pre-war suburban Edinburgh. The little villages that respectfully encircled Edinburgh's historic and elegant centre might not have the grandeur of their lofty neighbours but then they were never intended to be in competition. Strangely enough it wasn't quite what she had in mind when she'd imagined the flamboyant Mr Stuart's choice of residence.

She wrote the name and address on the front of the envelope, picked her purse out her bag and removed the book of first-class stamps from the inside wallet. But then she stopped.

Why not take the letter round personally? Would that not be friendlier? Writing the letter had seemed more personal than the circulation email but actually putting a stamp on and sending the thing through the third-party officialdom of the Royal Mail felt really quite *im*personal.

Before she knew what she was doing, she had caught a bus across town and was wandering down the steep hill to Woodford Grove. She looked up at the first house she came to. Number Two. It looked very neat, very tidy, but it was the garden that drew her attention. Reminded her of Sandra and Brian's house. Inordinately green grass again. How did anyone grow that stuff? Where did it come from? The only thing that didn't quite rhyme with the picture of suburban uniformity was a brown jacket slung over the fence at the far side. An act of thoughtless abandon in a world of pristine order.

A low brick wall ran the length of the front of the property and just as she got to its end, an elderly gentleman popped up, trowel in hand. He was wearing a frayed yellowing shirt and brown trousers that obviously accompanied the suit jacket. Interesting. Gardening in a suit.

'Good afternoon,' he barked.

'Oh, good afternoon. Sorry, you gave me a fright there.'

'Ha, yes. I do that. When I'm down here. Wife tells me to emerge rather than shoot up like that. Always scaring the less robust neighbours, if you know what I mean. Not of course that I'm suggesting you're not robust.'

'No, it's fine, honestly. You didn't give me that much of a fright.'

'Can I help you with anything?'

'Just looking for number twenty.'

'Oh, that's down there on the left. Just keep going on this side.' He stopped smiling and his face contorted slightly. 'That'll be the Stuarts you're looking for then.'

'Yes, that's right. The Stuarts.'

He looked to be searching her for something. A justification or at least an explanation as to the purpose of her expedition.

She approached number twenty with a new sense of foreboding. *Wonder what sort of reaction I would have got if I'd said number eighteen*, she thought. Interestingly, number twenty was the one house that had bucked the orderly trend of uniformity in construct and style. There was an odd porch attached to its side. It looked as though it had been propped up against the outside wall – left there as a temporary feature. It was even painted differently to the rest of the house. A dull pink or mauve. And then the garden. It wasn't a complete mess, but it was less well kempt than its neighbours. The grass was too long; there were bare patches and a few scattered weeds. It was almost worse than if the thing had been left to grow wild. Wild gardens could be interesting. But this was someone who really couldn't be bothered. Someone who couldn't give a toss what his neighbours thought.

She took the envelope out of her bag. I could just pop this through the letterbox, she thought. But she didn't, of course she didn't. She rang the bell instead. After a while and just as she was on the verge of leaving, the door slowly opened. A small, thin woman emerged from the dimness of the hallway. Her cheeks appeared pulled in, like she was sucking at something unpleasant. She stared, unsmiling, at Sheila with large, watery dark eyes.

CHAPTER 17

Sheila fixed on the woman's eyes. She couldn't really do anything else. They felt like they were trying to draw something out.

'Oh hello, I'm sorry to bother you. I was just wondering if Harry was in. My name's Sheila, from his history club.' Best to identify herself upfront before the woman started to create wildly inaccurate scenarios in her head. The woman said nothing and continued to stare.

'It's just I've got something for Harry. A letter.' The silence continued. She suddenly felt unsure of herself. What was she really doing here? She broke away from the stare and looked down at the letter in her hands. 'It's nothing really. Just a note about a visit to Linlithgow Palace next week.' Her voice seemed to be fading away to nothing. 'Just a note. That's all.'

'Come in,' the woman replied and turned to walk back into the darkness.

She entered the dimly lit hallway. The wallpaper, an insipid beige by way of background, was covered with a repeating pattern of yellow swirls. She remembered similarly patterned duvet covers in the seventies. And there was that smell again. Slightly dank and musty. Just like Colin's lodge house. But she'd always attributed the smell of his house to the fact that it was centuries-old stone, covered in moss, sucking up the mud and drinking in the dampness spawned by the water running just yards from his front door. So why the similar odour? The reek of something.

'Come through to the back room. The front room is full of Harry's stuff. There's nowhere to sit down in there.'

Sheila followed as instructed and was suddenly hit by a much more acrid smell. The woman walked to the back of the dark room and pulled sharply at closed curtains. An onslaught of high-pitched chirping welcomed the new light.

'You can get a seat right there by the window.'

Sheila struggled to see the seat by the window, her vision obscured by small cages filled with indeterminate species of colourful birds. Exotic birds, shrilly tweeting, trapped within the confines of cages made to look like little houses. She tried desperately to ignore the smell of ammonia from the bird droppings covering the floors of these strange little dwellings, dotted around the makeshift aviary. Tiptoeing over piles of scrunched-up newspaper and bags of bird feed, she finally made it to the torn black leather couch pushed up under the windowsill. Half covered by a knitted multicoloured throw, the thing was filthy, but she had to sit down.

The woman stood watching her, framed by the doorway that led off to the kitchen. It was the first time Sheila had really had the opportunity to take in her overall appearance. The woman wore a pale pink dress.

She couldn't be sure, but it looked vaguely fashionable, although the original colour appeared to have been washed out over time. She wore no make-up and her hair was scraped back off her face, but her skin was flawless and her eyes were dark and piercing. Sheila could see a once-beautiful woman looking hesitant and unsure of herself. She tried not to move her head as her eyes dropped to the woman's padded slippers, each sporting a robin motif thrusting a bright red chest out to the world. Well, maybe just to the floor. Could this be Harry's wife?

'Tea, would you like tea?'

The thought almost made Sheila gag. 'No really. I was just passing and wanted to hand this in. But thank you.'

'I'm Harry's wife.' It was a statement of fact delivered without any sentiment.

'Oh right. I see. Well, it's lovely to meet you. He's not in then?' Well, that clarified things. She looked down at the letter, gripping its edges ever more tightly and then quickly handed it over.

'Thank you, I'll make sure he gets it. I don't know where he is. I don't know when he'll be back. Sure you wouldn't like a cup? I've just boiled the kettle.' Suddenly her face softened and she smiled. But it wasn't a particularly happy smile. It was more pleading than anything else.

'Okay then. Just a small one.'

Harry's wife turned into the kitchen. Sheila didn't want to go in. She didn't want to see what might be lurking; what other animal species might have made it their home.

'My name's Mary by the way.'

After a while Mary emerged from the kitchen and handed her a small cup of milky tea. At first glance all seemed perfectly well. No traces of grime or bird poo. Mary sat at the other end of the black couch. They were at the window but, still, it felt inordinately gloomy.

'So you go to Harry's club. Do you enjoy going there? Do you enjoy his lectures?'

Their clipped conversation was conducted against a backdrop of varying pitches of bird sound. Mary seemed inured to the noise, but it scratched at Sheila's brain.

'Yes. Yes, it's good fun. He's a good teacher.'

She felt nervous again as Mary stared at her, giving her the once-over. It wasn't subtle.

'Mind you, it's more of a discussion group than lectures. How was your holiday? Did you enjoy Pitlochry?' She was conscious of her voice going up in pitch.

'Pitlochry? What made you think we were going to Pitlochry?'

Damn Caitlin and her wild hypotheses. 'Oh, I don't know. I thought he'd said something about Pitlochry but maybe I'm mixing you up with some friends of ours. People that like to go to Pitlochry. John and I like to go to Pitlochry too – sometimes. John's my husband.'

'We didn't go anywhere. We just stayed at home. I'm not at my best at the moment and Harry didn't think it would be good if we went to a hotel. Funny you should say Pitlochry though. I've always liked going there.' Mary smiled briefly, clearly enjoying the memory of something until the sadness quickly returned. 'It's a bit quiet for Harry and he thinks it's full of old people. Old people just make you feel old, drag you down, Harry says. Anyway, we normally go to Fishers, when we do go, but then people get dressed up for dinner and well Harry just thought…'

Her voice trailed off. She looked very tired.

'Oh, I'm sorry if you've not been well.' Sheila put her cup down on the floor at the side of the sofa. 'I'll not put you to any more trouble.'

'No, it's nothing like that. I've not been ill. I just don't get out much now and so…' She stared down at the letter in her hands. 'It just wouldn't be right. Me going to a hotel, I mean. Not at the moment anyway. Not like this.'

Some people, maybe even Caitlin, would deduce that this was a woman who wasn't taking proper care of herself. But as Sheila listened, the words and the tone spoke of something more complex. She didn't understand what it was and she didn't understand why it should feel at all important to her. Harry's flamboyance, his flattery, seemed to suddenly all feel like a bit of a sham.

'Maybe you should come along to the club sometime. Or come on one of our outings. Come on the visit to Linlithgow Palace next week.'

Sheila could see immediately that the prospect of this form of sojourn into the world beyond these pitiful walls had been entirely the wrong way to go. Even as she'd finished speaking the words, she knew herself it was the last thing Mary Stuart needed. To be out with strangers and in the company of her husband.

Mary said nothing. Just stared. And so she decided it was time to go. What was she doing here anyway? This wasn't her problem. None of this was her problem.

As she stood up and plotted her path past the birds to the familiar, clean air of the outside world, she spotted a framed photo on the bureau in the far corner of the room. It had been masked slightly by an untidy display of small mirrors. But standing at this angle she could make out what was clearly a wedding photograph. The bride wore a pretty tea-length dress with an embroidered bodice and her new husband looked resplendent in a smart red kilt and black Argyle jacket. She was smiling, a carefree kind of smile. Something that suggested only good times ahead. He looked like the cat who'd got the cream.

'I know what you're thinking.' Mary looked up at her.

Sheila turned. 'What? Oh, yes what a lovely photo. Your wedding, I assume.'

'Yes. Can't believe it's the same woman, can you? Looking at me now, like this. You can't believe it.'

'No, not at all. That's not what I was thinking at all. I just wondered why you would hide it behind all these little mirrors.' She tried to relax into a quiet little laugh. 'That's quite a lot of mirrors.'

'Can't you see? They're for the birds. There's so much more for them to see if they look in the mirrors. Makes their world bigger.'

*

Sheila was beginning to wonder why she'd suggested this outing to Linlithgow Palace. The responses to her email were dispiriting to say the least.

'I hope we're not all taking cars. What a ridiculous blight on the environment that would be.' (Leonard.) 'But of course I don't drive anymore so somebody would need to give me a lift.'

'I'll get a bus. What bus goes there?' (Paddy.)

'Will there be a central pickup point or will the designated driver(s) trail round everyone's houses? (Sandra.)

'What about Harry? Has anyone told Harry? Should we be doing this without Harry? (Magda.)

The last point was particularly grating. There was no reason whatsoever why Harry Stuart needed to be there. He hadn't even had the courtesy to reply to her letter and, in any case, she couldn't imagine what he could possibly add to proceedings. This was a Mary Queen of Scots Society event for goodness' sake. No one could possibly know more about Mary and her birthplace than that lot.

She sat back from the computer and its depressing message trail. She wondered why Harry hadn't bothered to get in touch. He didn't have to use snail mail. He had her email and could easily have sent a message. Maybe Magda was right. Maybe they shouldn't be out doing things on their own. Maybe she'd get sent to the naughty step at the next club meeting. She smiled to herself. How ridiculous. Then the thought occurred that he might be more annoyed at her turning up at his door unannounced, than anything to do with the trip. Thinking about it, she probably wouldn't have gone if she'd known what she was walking into.

Bit too late to bother about that now. Sheila shut down her computer and shook the thought from her mind.

The day before the planned trip to the palace, she was in the home office putting together some information packs for her fellow history buffs. She'd downloaded some material from the internet and also copied extracts from the MQoS Journal on the society's fundraising efforts and commissioning of the statue. Everyone was to be given a little clear plastic wallet with a label denoting their name at the top right-hand corner. The traumas of transportation had been resolved and Sheila was going to pick everyone up in Charlotte Square at 10.30 prompt. Everyone except Paddy – he was resolutely sticking to his plan to take the bus.

The phone rang just as Sheila was about to begin stuffing the wallets. She left her papers and folders neatly arranged on the dining room table to answer the extension in the hall.

'Oh Mum, good, you're in.' There was an uncharacteristic weariness in Caitlin's voice.

'Yes, just sorting out some papers. Why? Are you coming round?'

'Oh no. I've felt dreadful all day. Don't know if it's the flu or a stomach bug. Something I've eaten maybe. Simon stayed at home, thank goodness. No way I could have looked after Milo. It's been both ends for most of the day.' The words, short and to the point, were delivered almost as if anything too superfluous or rambling might usher in another bout of sickness.

'Oh no, darling. How awful. How on earth did you get something like that?'

'I'm sure it's these bloody mother-and-toddler things. Honestly, Mum, they're absolute breeding grounds for all sorts of crap. You should have warned me.'

Sheila brushed past yet another example of her parenting negligence. 'Well hopefully it's just one of those twenty-four-hour things.'

'Thing is, Simon needs to go in tomorrow. Quarterly meeting with the partners from Head Office. I'm just so washed out. Don't know how I'm going to manage. Could you be a love and come round tomorrow? I just can't lift a finger. Maybe bring round some soup? Some of your broth? I might feel like that tomorrow.'

The stuttering voice suddenly stopped. She couldn't let her frustration, her disappointment, spill over into the conversation. If they'd been sitting right in front of each other, Caitlin might have seen it in her face, but she wasn't going to let her hear it in her voice. 'Of course, darling. Of course I'll come round.'

It was the right thing to do, of course it was, but she couldn't help feel disappointed. First thing she'd done off her own bat in a long time. Something she'd organised from scratch on her own and without anyone else standing over her, signing off their approval. It was small beer of course, but still… She tried to shrug it off, after all, that was life. You bend and yield. As a mother, a wife, a PA, you always bend and yield.

Then it hit her. A moment in time that she'd shut away but one that came back to slap her. Bending and yielding. Who was she kidding? Caitlin aged seven, wakening and coughing, her little chest straining. Sheila's mind full of sets of papers to copy, amendments to be tabled, trying to hurry her along. Get dressed, Caitlin. Eat something, Caitlin. Wrap up warm, Caitlin. Right – in the car and off to school, Caitlin.

Now are you sure you're okay? Sheila had looked at her in her rear-view mirror. The pale little girl with watering eyes nodded in the back of the car. Good. All fine in the back then. Quick drop off and then full Council meeting in the Chambers.

But of course she hadn't been okay. The school hadn't been able to contact Sheila and had called John's office instead. He'd picked his daughter up and taken her straight round to the doctor's. No appointment or anything. Sat in the waiting room for an hour until a locum could see her.

A bad chest infection. Antibiotics were prescribed.

'Couldn't you see she was ill?' He'd looked at her like she was a stranger.

'Well, of course not. She wasn't that bad this morning and I did ask her. I did ask you, Caitlin, didn't I?

Caitlin had nodded but never looked at her mother. But John had looked at her. Stared incredulously at her. She'd turned away from both of them and sobbed. Well, it was fine for him. He marched off to work every morning, immune to the storms of everyday life, and never looked behind him. And then, when she'd got it wrong, the one time she'd got it wrong and messed up her priorities, there he'd been to save the day. Heroic Daddy coming to the rescue. And now his look had turned to pity and he'd bent down to hold her.

She never did forget that look. Or the fact that nothing he said or did on that day made her feel any better about herself.

Over the years, that look occasionally resurfaced, even if the memory of that day had dimmed. All the while the relationship between her husband and daughter grew closer and Sheila felt more and more shut out. If she had been true to herself for a moment, she would have realised that was the time. The time when the family dynamic had formed and settled. Neither John nor Caitlin ever made reference again to what had happened, but they didn't need to. The evidence of their bond was enough to poke and prod at her. But children grow to adults, families change shape and here they were now – reconnecting and reforming as a family. Caitlin was ill and she was going to be there. She wanted to take care of her daughter, take care of Milo, even Simon.

It was just that she couldn't help but feel disappointed about the outing. Surely there was nothing wrong with that. Just as long as no one else knew.

She rang Sandra. 'Hi Sandra, it's me. Look Caitlin's not well and I'm going to have to go round there tomorrow. Sorry about that but I wondered if you would mind driving them out to Linlithgow. I'll pop round now with some information I've put together if that's okay. Just some stuff I thought folk might find useful.'

'Oh no, that's a shame. Why don't we just abort the whole operation? Make a trip when you and Harry are both back in circulation.'

'Oh no, no. I really think it would be wonderful for you to be at the unveiling. Such a special moment, I wouldn't want you to miss it. And I spoke to Leonard the other day. He's so looking forward to it. Hasn't been out much. Something about his son again. Didn't quite catch it but no, Sandra, if you don't mind, I think it would be great if you all went.' It had been fun organising the trip but now she wouldn't be able to see it through. She hated that. Not seeing things through. 'We can catch up in a day or two and you can tell me how it went.'

They said their goodbyes. Sheila sighed, picked up the neatly stacked clean plastic folders and the car keys from the hall table. How annoying. Annoying and *so* disappointing.

She made her way to Sandra's house and found her friend in a slightly anxious state. 'But who's going to lead the thing? I mean without Harry there and now you, what are we actually going to do?' Sandra was playing with the tassels of a multicoloured poncho that she'd bought at a craft fair the previous November. Authentic Mexican, she'd told Sheila and Agnes. How authentic Mexican had made its way to a muddy farm field just outside Edinburgh was anyone's guess.

'You don't have to do anything. I'll tell the branch chair that you're all going. Just that I won't be there, that's all.'

'Nobody has to speak or anything? And you're not asking me to take charge, are you?'

'No, no one has to take charge and nobody has to speak. Unless you want to of course. I mean maybe one of the others will want to say something. Talk to the people in the society.'

'Can't imagine anyone wanting to do that. Different if Harry was there.'

Sheila raised her eyebrows.

'Or you, of course.'

'Look Sandra, this is supposed to be fun. This whole history club thing is supposed to be fun. Just enjoy the day. Take a tour of the palace; go for lunch. For God's sake, just enjoy yourselves.'

CHAPTER 18

Sheila arrived at Caitlin and Simon's house just before eight. She rang the bell and then watched through the frosted glass in the door as a ghostly apparition made its way down the hall. The fuzzy form seemed to sway from side to side, as it got closer to the door. Then came the sound of the door unlocking and opening but barely enough for Sheila to see inside.

'Caitlin?'

'Yes, just come in. I can't stand the light. Oh, and don't touch anything just in case this thing's really contagious.'

Tricky, Sheila thought. How on earth was she going to see to Milo and her daughter if she couldn't touch anything? And then the overwhelming smell of bleach, so strong it was burning all the little hairs in her nostrils.

'You've not been cleaning, have you?'

'No. I told Simon just to do the bathroom and then clean down all the surfaces. Just trying to limit the spread.' Caitlin turned and walked slowly along the long hallway and into the lounge, barely lifting her feet as she went.

It occurred to her that this wasn't the sort of house you wanted to be ill in. All hard floors and cold colours. Her poor daughter seemed to be railing against the harshness in her large towelling robe, thick bed socks and sheepskin slippers.

Caitlin tightened the belt on the robe, lay down on the cream couch and covered herself in a cream check blanket. There was a white side table next to the couch with a mug, box of tissues and pile of magazines all within easy reach. She had set up camp.

Sheila quickly took off her coat and put down her bags. 'Right, where's Milo? Is he still asleep? I'll see to him and then come back and get you sorted, shall I? Or is there anything I can get for you now?'

Caitlin placed a flannel over her eyes. 'Oh, don't worry about Milo. Simon has dropped him off at Nana Reid's. They're quite excited to have him – Nana and Papa Reid. They think he's old enough to have his own toy trumpet. Did I tell you that? Well, I say toy, but I think it's actually a real trumpet just in miniature. They think he's ready.'

'He's only two for God's sake.' She hadn't meant to sound quite so sharp.

Caitlin was starting to sound a bit croaky. 'Oh, I know. But they're happy and Milo seems happy. As long as he gets to make noise in someone else's house. Actually, I was thinking that maybe they'll want to spend more time with him – now they've both retired that is.'

Rupert Reid had been French horn with the Scottish Chamber Orchestra and his wife Fenella had just retired as a piano tutor. John couldn't stand Simon's parents. They moved in the sort of Edinburgh cultural circles that he found completely nauseating. It was a different world, but she liked spending time in different worlds.

'But then again they've discovered cruising.' Caitlin attempted a laugh. 'Oh but of course you know, that's why they weren't at Simon's birthday and they're off again soon to the Caribbean.' Caitlin paused for thought. 'No, we're fine as we are with Milo, don't you think?'

'Yes, yes of course. Absolutely fine.' Sheila smiled.

'Just nice when they do decide to dock that we can park him with them for a while. And Simon thinks it would be nice if we can nurture any budding musical talent. *He* doesn't have any you see which has been such a disappointment to Rupert and Fenella.'

All this was relayed while Caitlin lay prostrate on the couch with half her face covered. Sheila thought fleetingly of her history chums, all piling into Sandra's car about now, hoping they were all looking forward to their day out. She sighed. Best get on and see to her daughter.

They spent the morning quietly until Caitlin emerged slowly from her dark pit of illness. 'I'm keeping things down now so some of your soup would be lovely.' The flannel was quickly removed from her eyes. 'It is your broth, isn't it?'

'Yes, dear, of course it is.' Sheila laid down her book and pulled herself up from the white leather recliner.

'What's that you're reading?'

'Oh, it's a book about tapestries. Mary Queen of Scots' tapestries.'

'Oh, gosh. Harry's history club. Forgot all about that.' Caitlin's devilish grin signalled a further spell of interrogation. 'You two certainly hit it off at Simon's party. You were quite the life and soul.'

'Oh, I wouldn't say that. We just get on quite well, that's all. Sometimes you just make a connection…' She brushed down imaginary hairs on her black trousers, all the while avoiding her daughter's gaze. 'Right, I'll go and get that soup heated up.'

Would these conflicted feelings ever leave her? Sheila stood over the pot on the German turbo-charged hob, slowly stirring her Scotch broth. Honestly, how was she meant to square it all off? She felt happy to be in somebody's company. Just to be in their company, mind you. Nothing else. And now she found herself feeling embarrassed, guilty, even questioning her own judgment. What had this opened up? Was it something that had always been there or was it something new? That sense of wanting to expand horizons; to be open to different thoughts and ideas.

Her absent-minded stirring was brought to a sudden halt when she realised that bits of barley were sticking to the bottom of the pan. She quickly turned off the jet-propelled stream of gas and went to cut some bread.

'This is lovely, Mum. Just what I needed.' Thankfully Caitlin had forgotten all about Harry.

She noticed some colour coming back into her daughter's cheeks as she greedily slurped down her soup. She'd turned a corner. That was what Scotch broth did for you. Helped you turn the corner.

In the afternoon, she busied herself with some housework although most of the cleaning was surplus to requirements after Simon's bleach onslaught. She took the vacuum upstairs and tidied away Milo's toys. Caitlin had emerged like a butterfly from its chrysalis after lunch and was now showering in the en suite. Showers were another sign that Sheila often thought marked the beginning of recovery from illness. The body yearned for hot soothing baths when exhaustedly fighting off germs but once rid, it demanded an invigorating cleanse to mark a return to normality.

Late in the afternoon Simon arrived home, having left work early to pick up Milo from his grandparents.

The little boy toddled hurriedly into the lounge, banged right up against Sheila's legs as she sat on the sofa beside Caitlin and promptly rested his head on her lap. She wasn't sure if he was delighted to see her or was just exhausted from playing the trumpet all day.

Simon made directly for his wife, planting a kiss on her forehead. 'You're looking better.'

Caitlin turned and smiled at her mother. 'Well, that's what Mum's broth does for you, darling. Definitely feeling much better. Think I've turned a corner.'

'And how are you, Sheila?'

'Fine, yes.' She'd picked her grandson up, sat him on her knee and buried her face in his soft silky hair.

'Harry was in today. Meeting one of the guys for lunch. Said he was sorry he'd missed you when you called round.'

Simon didn't look directly at her as he spoke. He was scanning the room for something in a kind of absent-minded way. But she could feel Caitlin's eyes on her. She could feel her chest starting to burn and the heat travelling up her throat to her face. She tore herself away from the warmth and the innocence of cuddles with Milo just in time to see Caitlin demanding an explanation from across the room. Even without uttering a word, her expression demanded it.

'Oh yes. I was just taking round a note about our trip to Linlithgow Palace. It's today actually so I'm not sure if he managed to go but I just wanted to make sure he knew about it.'

Caitlin looked quizzical.

'Anyway, it was something I'd arranged for the history club. They've got a lovely day for it, don't you think? Just sorry I couldn't go myself, but there you go. Family comes first, doesn't it? Family comes first because, well, that's what family is all about.'

'Yes, yes. Quite.' Simon was still scanning the room. Words didn't seem terribly important to him right now. 'Thanks though, Sheila. Thanks for coming round. Where's yesterday's *FT*? Anyone seen yesterday's *FT*?'

Caitlin smiled. It was a funny little smile and she wasn't quite sure what to make of it.

Simon left the lounge to continue his search and left a cavernous silence in his wake. She clung on to her grandson who was showing signs of restlessness. He began to squirm about in her ever-tighter embrace until she had no option but to let him slip to the floor and toddle over to his mother.

'Oh Milo, no. Mummy's still not very well.'

'He's fine, Mum. I'm fine. Sure, I'm not contagious now anyway.'

She smoothed out her barely crumpled trousers and, in the absence of knowing what to do next, smoothed them out again.

'Why did you go round to Harry's house? I thought you were just writing him a note?'

'I know, silly really. Don't know what came over me. Think I was curious. He's such an odd character. Maybe not so much odd, just different, and I think I was genuinely curious about where he lived. Just to place him really.'

Caitlin was staring at her, interested in what she was saying but without that judgmental look that had so often made an appearance during mother and daughter conversations. It gave her the courage to carry on and just tell it how it was.

'And I have to admit I was a bit curious about his wife. I mean I just think it's odd that he's never mentioned a wife. Even when we all get together for coffee or lunch after class, we share snippets from our home life. It just seems a natural thing to do and everyone does – even poor Leonard will say something about the wayward son. But Harry's never said a thing. And so when you talked about his wife and holidays to Pitlochry – well, I guess my nose just got the better of me.'

'And...?' Caitlin was now ignoring her son, pulling her dressing gown tighter round about her, and perching expectantly on the edge of the sofa.

'And what?'

'What did she look like?' All vestiges of a nerve-dulling virus had clearly left Caitlin's body.

'Not what I expected. Not what I expected at all.'

'Tall? Slim? Blonde? Dark? What?'

'No, it's not that. Not what she looked like. Just everything about her seemed damaged. I think she'd been ill, but it was more than that – like all of life, or all that can be interesting about life had gone – been taken from her somehow. Something or someone has taken anything meaningful, anything good away from that woman.' Sheila paused. 'Except for her birds. There were birds in cages all over the place.' She looked down at her feet. 'I felt sorry for her but then so uncomfortable too. I shouldn't have been there. I know I should never have gone. And now I feel like I've crossed a line. Gone somewhere I had no place going.' She was back in amongst the feathers, the smells and the sad eyes, wondering again what on earth she'd been doing there.

'Hey, Mum.' Caitlin got up and sat on the arm of Sheila's chair and placed an arm round her shoulder. 'I knew there was something a bit off about Harry Stuart. But look, you didn't do anything wrong. You just went round with a note. You went round with a note, that's *all* you did. It's not an outrageous thing to do.'

Sheila looked up at her daughter with a questioning look.

'Well, it might seem as though you were being a bit nosy, but that's all. Hardly the crime of the decade.'

*

It was Festival time in Edinburgh and like so many born-and-bred residents, Sheila and John found themselves skirting the centre of the city for its duration. Of course they would go to preplanned concerts, plays and book readings but these were carefully picked out as soon as the programmes were launched and involved only very brief incursions into the city centre with its unrelenting hordes of festival-goers.

This particular Saturday morning, they left the sanctuary of their home for an amble through the New Town. She looked at the green Virginia creeper sweeping down the side of their building as it burst through the black wrought-iron railings, crowning their boundary wall. When they returned from France, the leaves would be turning colour and a vivid red carpet would soon transform the cold grey stone. She smiled at the thought.

They made their way up the hill towards Abercromby Place, a curved street that sat just over the hill from its broader, busier and better-known neighbours. Queen Street, George Street and, of course, Princes Street kept the influx of tourists traversing speedily from one side of the city to the other. But over the hill, where no one could see them, was where New Town residents kept themselves to themselves as they travelled east to west and vice versa. The locked gardens on the other side of the street merely added to the illusion of a place set apart, shutting out the chaos just over the hill.

She held on to John's arm as they meandered along in the early morning sunshine. Until suddenly a young man, all blonde hair and wide toothy smile, bounded up to them from across the street and thrust a brightly coloured pamphlet into John's hand. 'Every evening at seven o'clock up at the Pleasance. An hour that will have you laughing till your cheeks hurt.'

John just looked at him blankly.

Undeterred, the boy cocked his head to one side and winked. 'Promise.'

'I don't think so, son.' John handed back the printed offering.

The boy stood for a moment looking perplexed, unsure where he'd gone wrong. Then the bounciness returned and he was off running up the street. 'That's an hour of happiness you've let slip through your fingers,' he called as he ran.

'We'll live,' John muttered under his breath.

'You could have just taken the thing. He's only trying to get people to come to his show. No harm in that,' Sheila remonstrated.

'Thought we were safe down here. Only needs to start with one. Harmless enough you might think and then before you know it they're swarming all over the place. Best not to give them any encouragement.'

She said nothing else on the subject. He was right of course. Best not to give some people any kind of encouragement.

She turned towards him, holding his arm that little bit tighter. 'We'll need to start thinking about Provence.' After the unwanted intrusion her mind was drifting to more peaceful surroundings. The uncommon warmth of the Edinburgh air also made her think of their summer home. A place where everything slowed, even her husband, for three weeks at the end of summer. It was a place where they both found the time to just enjoy each other. A place where he wasn't distracted and the only big decision of the day was chilled white or rosé.

John stopped, turned and placed his hand on top of hers. 'Yes, Provence.'

He sighed and as he did so Sheila could feel the light and warmth of their morning amble begin to fade.

'I should have mentioned this earlier but it's just I think we might have to postpone things for a few weeks.'

She looked at him but said nothing. She wasn't capable of hiding her disappointment and she knew he wouldn't have expected her to be anything other than disappointed.

'But we could head off towards the end of the month. Weather will still be good, maybe not quite so warm but that's no bad thing is it? And if we can't use it in September maybe the kids could?'

She couldn't even be bothered to ask why. It would be something to do with work – it always was – but the disappointment trumped everything. Explanations, justifications, everything.

They resumed walking and he carried on with his reasoning. 'It's just a critical time for the trams. The operational side, I mean. We've got the business model sorted now, I'm pretty sure of that, but everyone wants to know when the bloody things are going to start running and the next few weeks are going to be crucial. I have to make sure, doubly sure actually, that everything we say *now* to the government, to the media, to the public, is absolutely spot on. If we announce a commencement date, then there can be no going back on that. I can't have postponements or extensions. It just won't wash, not with everything that's gone on.'

No postponements for the First Minister, no postponements for the hacks who were ready to pounce on anything that might sully his reputation and no postponements for the masses who never wanted the bloody thing in the first place. Just a postponement of holiday time with his wife.

'You do understand, don't you, darling?' His eyes were pleading and she at least had her confirmation that this had not been something he relished telling her. He knew what it meant, what it meant for both of them, and it wasn't something he'd considered lightly. That at least made the whole thing vaguely bearable.

She looked into his eyes. 'Of course. End of September then. We're definitely going end of September.'

'Yes, definitely.'

When they arrived back at the house, Sheila took some time to check the pots under the window. They needed watering and when she glanced round the borders, she saw there was weeding to be done. She would need to think about rearranging their time in France, but a spot of therapeutic gardening might help get things into perspective. John had left the door open for her and she saw, as she entered the vestibule, that the postman had been. John stood with a white envelope in one hand and a small card in the other.

'Well, well. Colin Meikle is having a drinks party. What about that?' He turned to look at Sheila. 'That's not very Colin, is it? Never known him to throw a party of any kind, even when his wife was alive. Have you?'

A strange prickly feeling made her squirm slightly. 'It's an invitation, is it? To his house?'

'Yes. Week on Saturday. You okay with that?' There was that look of concern again.

'Yes, of course I'm okay with that.' Sheila smiled, fetched her gardening gloves, trowel and a small bin they kept under the coat rack for depositing wretched weeds.

CHAPTER 19

'Darling, it's for you. Sandra.' John stood at the door, phone in hand just as Sheila had torn out the last weed from the cracks between the old paving stones. As she took off her gardening gloves to take the phone from him, he kissed the top of her head.

Turned out Sandra had invited the history club round to her house for 'a bit of a social'. By all accounts they had had a lovely day at Linlithgow Palace and the bonds of friendship were strengthening.

'Yes, it was lovely. Place itself was a bit bleak but we had an interesting tour guide and your chums in the Mary Queen of Scots Society were great fun. And that's a big bloody statue that they unveiled. Anyway, we all trooped off to the local pub afterwards for some lunch and that really got everyone chatting – and not just about history, much to Ag's relief. Leonard was an absolute gem, I must say. He likes to share his knowledge in a very gentle way. And maybe because he is so gentle you just listen more. Take more in. Different from Harry – he likes to get a debate going of course, so forthright and sure of himself all the time.'

Interesting, she thought. *How relaxed and enjoyable the whole thing had been for them.*

After giving Sheila the low-down on Linlithgow, Sandra pressed the case for the Friday afternoon soiree. 'Other good thing is, Brian will be at a Roman history convention in Perth so we can whoop it up as much as we like.'

Poor Brian. If only he knew what wild things his wife got up to when he went off to Roman history conventions. 'Great. I'm looking forward to hearing all about it. And so what about Harry? Has anyone actually heard from him?'

'Not a peep. And to be honest, I think everyone was just so much more chilled on our day out. I know I was a bit anxious about going without him but old Leonard kind of took the lead. He has so much to offer, you know. Loads of interesting stories to tell and little insights. Just little snippets about Mary, about the Stuart line. Stuff that just added to the whole experience. And it's stuff that I'm not sure Harry would actually know or maybe just wouldn't think was all that important. And of course no barking questions all the time.'

Sheila thought about jumping to his defence again, but she stopped herself. What was it that she was defending?

'Agnes and I were just saying there's an awful lot of noise when Harry's around and that just makes us zone out a lot of the time. Well, that's what we were saying but then I don't think you *do* zone out, do you?'

'Maybe not, but I'm glad that others are finding their voice. Particularly Leonard. I think he does keep his counsel around Harry and I agree, I think he's got so much to offer.'

The conversation settled Sheila. With everything that had gone on, she'd felt things had just got a bit out of hand. Harry had moved from an attractive and stimulating personality to something that was beginning to feel too dominant in her life, her thoughts. She'd brought a lot of this on herself, she knew that. But it could only be a good thing if there was a bit of redress now. Time to listen to others – the quieter voices.

'So you'll be round for lunch? I do hope everyone can make it and for God's sake don't bring the car. We'll be having drinks.'

'Have you invited Harry?'

'No.' She could sense the tension in Sandra's voice. 'Not this time. I mean as you said he's been posted missing so let's just keep it between us. It'll be more fun.'

Friday afternoon arrived and Sheila did indeed walk to Sandra's house. She ambled along her neat little cobbled street to the widening thoroughfare that suddenly dropped into the hustle and bustle of Stockbridge – a busy little village in the heart of the city full of smart artisan shops regularly frequented by Edinburgh's New Towners. She picked up some goat's cheese, as requested by Sandra, and walked further along to the florists. She had already decided on a mix of bright summer blooms to match her mood. She always bought flowers to match her mood regardless, never really thinking of matching to the recipient's home colour schemes. Caitlin, on the other hand, would always go for pale neutrals in her choice of flowers. Whites, creams and pale yellows could pretty much stand up to anyone's choice of décor, she'd once told Sheila.

She had smiled to herself as she watched the florist tear a large section of brown paper in which to enclose the long thin stalks, leaving only the pretty heads exposed. Where had the preference for all things neutral come from? Like so much else about her daughter, she had struggled to understand the basis for another fixed idea. But now that she thought about it, maybe neutral wasn't such a bad option.

She strode out now, leaving village life behind her and entering the suburban road that eventually led to the Queensferry Road and the fast route out of the city, north to Fife or west to Glasgow. As she approached Sandra and Brian's bungalow, she saw Leonard coming from the opposite direction. He tipped his fedora hat and she smiled and waved in response.

He waited for her at the gate and when she caught up to him, he nodded slightly and offered an outstretched arm to guide her up the path. There was no affectation, no over-the-top gesture, nothing that suggested an ulterior motive. It just seemed to be something innate. Something that merely marked Leonard out as a gentleman.

'How are you, Leonard? Haven't seen you in a while.' Sheila let Leonard ring the bell, given her hands were full of flowers and cheese, and now they stood waiting for the hostess to open the front door.

'Very well actually, Sheila. Thank you for asking. I do feel that life might just be on the up.'

His turn of phrase made her smile. 'Well, you can't ask for more than that.'

'No, no you can't. Being on the up is a very good place to be, all things considered.'

Before she could enquire any further, the door swung open and there stood Sandra – a vision in canary yellow.

'Come in, come in.' Sandra turned and flounced off in the direction of the lounge. Her unbuttoned overshirt flapped about her thighs and her wide-legged trousers swept across the carpet. 'Everyone's here.'

Everyone said their hellos and she handed over her offerings. Leonard, in turn, presented Sandra with a small box of chocolates tied up with a neat pink ribbon. Sandra looked quite overwhelmed as she slapped her hand to her chest.

'Oh really, you shouldn't have. I told you just to bring yourselves.'

Not entirely true, thought Sheila, *but never mind*. The thwacking hand of gratitude was not for her benefit after all.

After a short while, Sheila noticed how relaxed everyone looked. Paddy and Magda were on the sofa chatting, smiling, easing into each other when they found something mutually amusing. Agnes was standing by the fireplace with Leonard, engaged in what appeared to be a quite serious discussion. But that too was interspersed with short bursts of laughter. And then Sandra, tight black top under all that canary yellow, was acting out the role of Queen Bee, summoning her guests to pour drinks and heap up side plates as she stood in the middle of the room surveying her domain.

'This is lovely, Sandra. What a spread. And I must say it's really nice to be back with our little group. Very nice indeed.'

'Yes, they're a good bunch. And you know, I'm not sure why, but since our little trip we've just all really bonded. Maybe it was the whole venturing out on our own thing. It felt like we'd branched out, broken free a bit and you know it was *so* lovely to be led by Leonard. The Mary Queen of Scots gang loved him too, but I thought – *No, hands off. He's ours!*'

She had wondered about telling Sandra and Agnes all about her visit to Harry's house, but this wasn't the right time. And the more she thought about it the more she knew they wouldn't understand. Might even start concocting their own outlandish theories. After all, she didn't understand it much herself, so best to just let things lie.

Agnes had peeled away from Leonard at the fireplace to help Sandra in the kitchen. Sheila took her opportunity and wandered across the room to pick up the conversation she and Leonard had left at the front door.

'So tell me why life is on the up? Always good to hear why people's lives are on the up.' She held up her glass as if to toast Leonard's good fortune whatever it might be.

'What about you, dear? Is your life not on the up?'

She wasn't prepared for the conversation to turn quite so quickly. 'Well, I suppose it might be. I don't really know – if it isn't on the up, it certainly isn't on the down.' She laughed.

'Well, from what I gather you have a very lovely life, Sheila. Beautiful home, successful marriage. A daughter, whom you are very close to, and an adorable grandson. And to top it all off, you've just retired. World's your oyster.'

The upward inflection in Leonard's last words made them sound more like a question rather than a statement of fact. Everyone else had been telling her the world was her oyster whether it was or not.

'Yes, I am very lucky. I know I am. Everyone tells me I am.'

Leonard smiled. 'The facts as presented don't always reveal the true story, though, do they, my dear? Everything I've just said, in and of itself, doesn't necessarily equate to life being on the up or even in a steady state, come to that. It'll only ever be on the up if you decide it is. Perhaps even make the changes required to make it so.' He took a sip from his wine glass, all the time looking at her.

'Well, it's not always about making things different for yourself, though, is it? There are others to consider. What's good for you isn't necessarily always good for anyone else.'

'True. But the decisions you make don't have to be selfish ones. If you make good choices, it might just be that life gets even better for those around you.' He played with a thin looping watch chain that trailed from the breast pocket of his waistcoat before suddenly pulling the ancient timepiece from its dark snug. 'I can't stay too long. Need to get back to my books.'

Sheila didn't want to think any more about choices, good or bad. She placed her glass on the mantelpiece and looked straight into his dark twinkling eyes. 'Okay, well back to you, Leonard. I don't want you rushing off until you tell me why things are suddenly on the up?'

'I went to see my son last week.' He stopped playing with his glass and put the watch back in its pocket.

Sheila remembered that he'd mentioned a son but that he never saw him, and Sandra, of course, had delighted in confirming the snippet of gossip. The information had been offered up at an early meeting of the club and so she hadn't pressed him any further. It hadn't really been of any importance to her at the time. And although the thought had quickly left her mind, it always popped back in when she saw Leonard, no matter how briefly. What could possibly have happened that led to such an estrangement? After all he seemed such a kind, thoughtful man. But then, as she was quickly discovering, we didn't ever really know what went on in other people's lives.

She didn't say anything but just waited. Time for Leonard to open up if he wanted to.

'My son was a brilliant mathematician. He read maths at Oxford and followed that up with a PHD in graph theory. I should have noticed in the last year of his time at Oxford. But I didn't. I didn't see the signs but then I didn't know what I was looking for.' He paused and looked down at the floor. 'Drugs. Cocaine then heroin.'

He almost spat out the words.

'I just don't know them. I've never been around them – their insidious grip on life. I just thought he was overworking. He was down, tired, but then he always put so much pressure on himself. And my wife had died some years back so there wasn't really anyone to share my concerns with.'

'All right, you two?' Sandra shouted from the entrance to the kitchen.

'Yes,' they exclaimed in unison perhaps a bit too forcefully. Sandra quickly turned and went back to her buffet.

'Do you understand, my dear? I'm not a stupid man but I watched my son descend into a hell that I just never knew existed. Well, I knew *of* it but not in my life, not in anyone I knew's life. He came home to live with me after the university had been in contact and we managed to get him into drug rehabilitation. Interesting word – rehabilitation. From the Latin – to make fit again. But was he fit in the first place? Was he damaged before he even left home? And if so how? Had we created in him, all the necessary ingredients to nurture addiction?'

'Oh, I don't think—'

'It's all right, my dear. I don't think these thoughts now. You see when he came out of "rehab" as they call it, he lived with me. That was when he robbed the local newsagent to get money for his habit. I discovered what he'd done, confronted him with the facts and, after a while, he turned himself into the police. Hardest thing I've ever had to watch. Well since then, he's been in prison and back into rehabilitation.'

'So that's why you never saw him?'

'That's right. He wanted nothing to do with me. I kept writing to him, but nothing came back. But the point is that I never gave up on him. I didn't feel any differently about the boy. Never have, never would. But I saw him last week after five years. He's living in something called supported accommodation.'

'What changed? Why did he want to see you now?'

'Maybe I just wore him down but to be honest I believe it's been down to the therapy he's been getting. I think he's had to look inwardly quite a bit, look at the choices he's made along the way. I've never really set any great store by the notion of introspection, but it certainly seems to have worked for him.' He fiddled with the watch chain again. 'He said he wanted to tell me that none of it had been my fault.'

'Well, that's good isn't it? At least you don't have to keep torturing yourself about that.'

'Oh no, my dear, that had stopped a long time ago. I couldn't keep thinking like that. *I* hadn't crossed the line. I hadn't robbed that poor man whom he'd managed to scare witless. That was all down to Jeff. His choices, his decisions. Sounds harsh perhaps, but I couldn't live my life believing somehow they were mine. That's the thing, Sheila. We're not responsible for other people's choices – the paths they alone decide to take. And so they should be the ones who have to live with the consequences.' Suddenly, his tone mellowed. 'Having said that, once all the dust has settled, and if you really care for someone, then you can start to think about moving forward. For everyone's sake.'

Sheila smiled at his sane, logical approach to a devastating episode in his life.

'Must have been hard when you thought you were somehow responsible, even if that clearly wasn't the case.' She looked down briefly. 'It's good that you've reconciled those thoughts. And, of course, managed to reconcile with your son.' She looked back up at Leonard. 'And so how was it? Meeting him again after all this time?'

'It was good. He seems to be getting his life back on track. And we talked, like we used to. Like father and son. About home, about politics, about holidays in Cornwall. Oh, and graph theory. We had a very good discussion about graph theory.'

CHAPTER 20

'So, who's going to this thing?' Sheila asked, laying out her outfit for the evening soirée at her former boss's house. Black trousers and a nice cream silk blouse, buttoned right up to the neck with a tight little bow.

'It's a strange one, I have to say.' John turned away from the mirror where he'd been doing up his Italian silk tie with an enthusiastic flourish. 'Looks like some of the Chamber of Commerce people are going along, but apart from that I don't really know. Didn't occur to me it would be a business thing. I'd thought it was more of a friends gathering. You know, get to meet the sort of people Colin Meikle likes to socialise with.' He raised an eyebrow and laughed.

'Well, we're not really his friends, John. We've only been along there a couple of times. No, I wouldn't call us friends. Had to be a business thing, that's the only explanation that makes any sense.'

'Oh, I don't know about that. You're his friend, darling. Well, you were until it all went a bit pear-shaped at that twinning event.'

He stopped and she saw the inner workings of his mind. Rolling back, rolling back until…

'We never really talked that through, did we?'

'Talk what through?' She walked over to the dressing table and focussed on picking out the earrings to match her outfit. Pearl studs. Pearl studs would do nicely.

'What happened. We didn't talk about what actually happened. I know you'd said he'd been a bit off, probably drinking too much. But was it something that we *should* have talked about? Properly, I mean.' He reached into the wardrobe for his jacket. 'Maybe we shouldn't go to this bloody thing, or maybe I need to have a word when we get there.' He laid his jacket down on the bed and joined her at the dresser. He started to empty his pockets of change, proceeding to stack the coins into orderly little piles. 'I mean, I'm not having you upset by him.'

'Oh John, no it was nothing. I told you we just didn't see eye to eye on how the whole thing was to be managed. And I think to be honest he was just a bit stressed out with it all. Things weren't going his way; councillors were getting on his back. Anyway, I was just happy to leave it all behind.' She turned, put her arms round his waist and head on his shoulder. 'It's fine. Look, it's a completely different context. I'm with you and it'll be good to catch up with some old faces from the Council. And actually, it was a bad way to leave things. I'm quite happy to be civil to the man as long as I don't have to work with him again.'

Half an hour later, they were ready to walk out the door.

John suddenly turned and held her hand. 'Your hair looks different.'

'I just had it done today. A few highlights to cover up the grey.' She grabbed her coat from the rack. The black Windsmoor.

'You're looking very businesslike. Lovely, but very businesslike. Not really in the party mood, are you?'

'Well, it's not like that, is it? You said yourself, a lot of businesspeople.'

John opened the door, ushering Sheila out. 'Yes, it's a strange one, that's for sure. He needs to be careful with this sort of thing, you know. If there's a developer there, maybe somebody tendering for contracts with the Council... it just takes one stupid remark, giving somebody the inside track, and he could land himself in bother.'

They decided to take the shortcut to Colin's house, round the corner to St Bernard's Bridge, down its sweeping Jacobean staircase and past the large stone well. There wasn't a pushchair to manoeuvre, so they could avoid the hustle and bustle of Stockbridge's main streets. Dusk was beginning to settle as they approached the top of the stone stairs. She clung on to John's arm and breathed in the familiar smell of well-worn tweed. It was dark, the street lighting here seemed dimmer and the ornate stone structures at this end of the Water of Leith were casting long shadows.

There was no one else around. Commuting cyclists and walkers had long since passed and late-night dog walkers had yet to appear. The only noise came from the chorus of small birds encouraging their friends and neighbours back to the roost. There was a sense of urgency to their calling and it increased in intensity as Sheila and John found the path at the foot of the steps.

'What a racket,' said John.

She concentrated on her footing and tried to ignore the shrill warnings.

'Hello, you two.'

She felt her head shake in fright as they both turned round quickly to see the tall figure of Jenny Blyth-Hume magically appear out of the gloom. It was her shockingly blonde hair that seemed to emerge first and then her gleaming white teeth. The nerves in Sheila's head stopped juddering.

'Hey, Jenny. Wasn't sure if you were coming to this thing.' John held out his hand to usher the shiny apparition towards Sheila. After kisses all round, the unlikely threesome started to make their way along the rough path to Colin's house. John strode out in the middle with the two women, one tall, one short, each taking an arm. She couldn't really make out the expression on his face, but she could sense a certain smugness.

'I've never been here before. If I'd known I might have had second thoughts about my footwear,' Jenny laughed, but Sheila could feel that her steps were tentative, unsure, struggling to keep up.

'Well, if you'd driven you could have parked up the top road. Would have been a quicker walk down but absolutely no lighting if you come that way. Think he'd get on to the Council about that.' John sniggered at his own joke.

'Driven? I don't think so. Drink will need to be taken tonight, just to get through it. Can't believe I accepted the invitation. He's just such a bore.'

Sheila wasn't sure if the ensuing pause meant Jenny, once again, remembered that she'd been Colin's PA for years, but the silence didn't last, regardless.

'Has he ever done this sort of thing before? Sheila, you know him well. Never seemed like a sort of party-throwing kind of chap to me but there we go. What do I know?'

'Well, I only really know him in a work context. We've hardly done any socialising with him, have we, John? He's had a couple of drinks things at home but just at Christmas for mulled wine. I don't really know what to expect tonight.'

'He's up to something. Not sure what.' John finished the conversation as they approached the dark outline of the lodge house. Gloomy in the daylight it looked positively forbidding in the falling dark of evening.

The front door had been left slightly ajar and the contrast as they entered Colin's mysterious world was stark. Bursts of laughter and something that sounded like Brazilian bossa nova drifted down the hallway. A little bit of Ipanema had found its way down the Water of Leith.

They took their coats off in the hall and hung them up. Normally small and oppressive, the narrow corridor seemed bigger and brighter. Then it came to her – he'd painted. That was what it was. Okay, it looked like a bog-standard version of pale magnolia, but what a difference. Really freshened the place up.

She stood with John at the edge of the lounge looking in. She didn't recognise anyone and couldn't see their host until John suddenly waved over everyone's heads. Colin came bounding towards them, looking slightly flushed.

She immediately recognised the signs. In Jenny's words, drink had been taken. In fact, whisky had been taken. She could smell it.

'John, great. So glad you could make it. You'll know quite a lot of these guys.' He turned to Sheila and Jenny just as John shifted his gaze to spot any recognisable faces in the crowd.

'Jenny, great. And Sheila, what a nice surprise. Good of you to come.' His expression gave nothing away. He just stared at her.

She suddenly felt as though she wasn't supposed to be there. That it had all been a terrible misunderstanding. The invitation had been for John alone, of course it had. Why hadn't she thought of that. John had just made an assumption. She moved to be closer to her husband, but Colin had already turned and grabbed him by the arm. She stood rooted to the spot as Colin ushered her husband away.

Whatever this evening was designed to achieve, she couldn't quite fathom yet. It was something about John, Colin and the new 'guys' and she was an unwelcome intrusion.

John suddenly stopped and turned. 'Darling?'

At the same time Jenny took her arm. 'Oh, come with me, Sheila. I've seen some folk I know head for the kitchen. Think you'll find them interesting. Get you away from the man of the moment.'

Sheila smiled at her husband and waved him on. He could handle Colin no problem. She followed Jenny and joined a small group of Chamber of Commerce people who'd taken up residence in the country-style kitchen where finger food and drinks were within easy reach.

'Why man of the moment?' Sheila asked, unsure if Jenny had been referring to John or Colin.

'What's with the Latin jazz theme?' Jenny appeared distracted. 'Does the man have gin? Really could do with a gin. Oh yes, sorry. He's telling everyone he's going to retire from the Council. Feels this is the right time for a move into the private sector. I mean seriously, Sheila; he's got to be kidding. He hasn't a cat in hell's chance. But he's trying to sell himself to some serious players out there.'

'Has anyone told him he hasn't a cat in hell's chance?'

'Hope that's what your hubby's doing right now.'

The chat in the kitchen was amiable enough. It was a younger crowd, clearly not overly impressed with the Brazilian rhythm section next door. They looked to be Jenny's age. Not that she had any idea how old Jenny Blyth-Hume was, she just seemed that bit younger. But then maybe it was all her dazzle that suggested youth, vitality.

'Been married a long time, Sheila?' Jenny was opening and closing kitchen cupboards until she finally found the elusive bottle of gin.

'Oh yes, over thirty years now. And you? Are you married?'

'Oh God, no. Couldn't stick with the same man for any length of time. Do my head in mostly. I just find that no matter how "modern" and "right on" they are with the equality stuff, the world still seems to revolve round them. When I've started to go down that road, I've just always seemed to find myself *seeing t*o a man. What does he want, what does he need? It's exhausting. You must find that with John?'

'Well, yes. I suppose. You get used to it.' She watched the young men gradually drift back into the lounge. 'I mean it's not all like that of course. You share things. Enjoy things together.'

'Glasses, Sheila, and grab the tonic. And what about Colin? You were quite the partnership, weren't you? Or so he was telling me.'

'Really? A partnership? That's how he described it?'

Someone Sheila recognised from one of the big banks briefly distracted Jenny on a quest for ice. Jenny chatted to him while he fought to prise cubes from a bendy plastic tray under the sink. As the water flowed and the cubes crashed, Sheila thought back to the word. Yes, they'd made a good team but partnership felt like a step up. That wasn't the relationship. That wasn't it at all.

Eventually the banker, who had managed to fill his glass of malt with what appeared to be a small ice floe, smiled and returned to the lounge. Sacrilege to John, drowning perfectly good malt like that.

'When did he say that? About a partnership I mean.' Gin, tonic and ice but no lemon. Not even a sliver this time.

Jenny drew her fingers through her hair, but the blonde crown barely shifted.

'Oh, he's always going on about you, Sheila. He comes along to all the Chamber of Commerce dos and I get bored listening to how much a good PA is worth her weight in gold and how you'd made a really strong partnership.' She leant in towards Sheila. 'Oh, and by the way it's all John's fault that you were forced to dissolve said partnership.' Jenny slugged back her gin.

That word had been said too many times now and was swirling round her head, clashing with the reality of their encounter at the end of the twinning event. If 'partnership' had ever been a remotely accurate description surely his words, his actions on that night had completely destroyed the notion. The damage was irreparable – he must see that. The only reason she was here tonight was to show that his behaviour couldn't possibly intimidate her. She could be perfectly civil to him because he meant absolutely nothing *to* her.

She and Jenny stayed in the kitchen talking mainly about favourite restaurants, theatre productions and books. It surprised her that they seemed to share similar interests and tastes. In fact, she found herself really enjoying Jenny's company until, one by one, everyone drifted back to the lounge or hallway. Both women enjoyed the peace and quiet for a while until deciding it was best to be moderately sociable. As they walked into the lounge, Sheila was surprised to discover that all of the other guests had sloped off. Better things to do on a Saturday night. Colin, however, was still bouncing about the room – switching CDs and snapping his fingers in time with the rhythm. Suddenly he stopped.

'Getting a bit chilly, don't you think? I'll get this fire going.' He took a bit of time to get down onto his knees and then started to pull bits of newspaper and firelighters from a brass box at the side of the hearth. 'Just like José Feliciano. Come on baby, light my fire.'

'Right, that's me. I've shown face, think I'll make my escape,' Jenny whispered in Sheila's ear.

'Emphasis on the second beat, John. Get that?' Fire lighting over, Colin stood up and closed his eyes, swaying to the sound of Feliciano's guitar.

She didn't know where to look and she could see that John was clearly struggling not to laugh. Jenny stood transfixed in the corner of the room until she turned to eye up a watercolour of St Bernard's Well. Sheila found it best in situations like these to transport herself clean away from the sounds and images crashing wildly in front of her. Her mind took her off to France. To their small house with its brightly painted windows, sunflowers aplenty and the gentle wafting in of heady lavender scent from the adjacent fields.

Eventually Colin stopped and walked somewhat unsteadily over to the other side of the room to kill the South American musical tutorial. Jenny turned away from her feigned interest in local art and they all stood, uncomfortably in the silence, looking at each other.

'Well Colin…' John, thank heavens, moved to shake Colin's hand. Sheila dropped her shoulders, put her glass down, knowing that this was the hoped-for signal to leave. Jenny looked at her knowingly, perhaps even gratefully.

'Yes, yes of course. Just wanted to show you one thing before you go, though John. Ladies, care to join us?'

She didn't say anything. What was there to say? Best to ignore the feeling of nausea and get on with it. Sooner they saw whatever it was, sooner they got out of there. She could see Jenny's eyes burning with anger, but Sheila took her arm firmly as they walked a little behind the two men.

'Patronising bastard,' Jenny muttered.

They headed for a door at the back of the kitchen. She had noticed it earlier and had assumed it led to an old-fashioned pantry or modern utility room. Colin opened the door slowly and turned on a shadeless light.

'Careful now,' Colin called as he descended a set of wooden stairs, positioned in the centre of the small space.

She noticed that dank, musty smell again, sucking all the clean air away. What on earth could they possibly be going to see? She went slowly down after John, hoping to God that Jenny's high heels would negotiate their way without incident or they might all take a tumble. She imagined the four of them, lying crumpled at the foot of the stairs. No one would know they were there.

When they reached the bottom, Colin flicked another switch to reveal a cavernous room. There were old desks and bureaus wedged up against the cold stone walls and a series of wooden racks. Wine racks.

'What do you think of this then, John? I've put a lot of this stuff down for my retirement. Bit of an investment in the future.'

It was cold down there and any uplifting effects from the alcohol served upstairs were quickly dissipating. She watched John inspect the bottles, occasionally turning one to look at the label.

'What's the temperature down here, Colin? Humidity levels?' John asked firmly, directly.

Colin looked confused. 'Oh, I don't know. There's always been a cellar down here though so must be okay.'

The men walked further down past the rows of bottles. She turned to see Jenny standing in front of one of the old bureaus. She was lifting up the roll-top and pulling out some of the drawers. She was either inordinately bored or too drunk to worry about the host's reaction to her prying behaviour.

John shook his head. 'Can't ever fall below twenty-five degrees Fahrenheit, Colin. Too warm is just as much of a disaster. If the temperature fluctuates too dramatically then the wine can expand and contract quickly – then you've got the danger of letting air in.' He put his hand on Colin's shoulder. 'Bought myself one of these artificial cellars last year. Best investment I ever made. Everything under control then, you see. Nothing left to chance.'

'Sheila, look, come over here and see this,' Jenny was whispering loudly. It was on the cusp of turning into a screech.

John wasn't for stopping. 'It's like a large fridge but keeps reds and whites at preordained temperatures. Best way to do it. Then you know you're not wasting money. You've got some good stuff down here, but it could all end up being ruined if you don't know how to keep it properly.'

She couldn't quite make out Colin's face, but she could sense his simmering resentment. It was John at his best or his worst, however you wanted to see it.

'Sheila.'

'Coming. What?' She turned away from the scene of Colin's latest humiliation to find Jenny laying out a number of folders across the desktop of the bureau.

'Look. I saw the edge of a photograph sticking out the side here and thought I'd take a closer look. I thought it was you.'

Sheila recognised folders from various civic events that she had helped organise over the years and had labelled accordingly. She didn't want to touch anything. None of it belonged to her anymore. None of it had any place in her world.

Then she noticed. Two folders with her name written on them in large black capitals. Jenny had emptied the contents and was now starting to spread everything out, displaying the material in front of her. Photographs she didn't recognise, had no recollection of ever having been taken, stretching back ten years at least. Nothing but photographs. No embossed invites, guest lists, printed running orders. None of the detritus that normally accompanied the administration of civic events.

Only images of a smart-brained, sharp-suited PA, collected and saved as if in homage. A weird, perverted homage.

*

There were different poses; colours; outfits. There was laughter; solemnity; eagerness; diffidence. Close-ups; distance shots; front angles; side angles and back shots. Photos taken from the back at the photocopier, from the side at the water cooler and from a distance just sitting at her desk. She sensed a pain in her stomach now. Nausea, sickness. No, *this* was a sickness. In front of her here – some kind of weird, obsessional sickness.

'What the...' Jenny was scanning the images, her eyes darting from side to side.

Sheila could hear the men's voices as they walked further down the cavernous, dank, musty hole of a cellar. Her mind clicked over. Scrambled thoughts became ever more coherent.

'Put everything back in the folders.'

'What? You can't just leave this without asking for an explanation.'

She turned to look straight at Jenny. 'Just do it.' Afterwards she would think back to how she had barked orders at the Chief Executive of a luxury knitwear business and had watched her obey with the minimum of fuss.

'Okay. Got everything?'

Jenny nodded.

'Right, upstairs quickly.'

The two women hurried towards the foot of the stairs and without a word climbed quietly to the top.

Back in the kitchen, Sheila turned to look up at her accomplice. The colour had drained from Jenny's face and she stood, shoulders slightly hunched, against the kitchen cabinets. 'What now?'

'I don't know, I just need to get rid of these.' Then she remembered the fire in the lounge. 'Come with me, and bring the folders.'

As they walked through, Sheila began to shiver. It felt as though South American beaches had been all but eroded by a dark bilge lapping at the foundations of the house.

'Give them here.' She took out the photos and flung them one by one on to the blazing fire. She watched the flames devour each image until she couldn't bear to look any more. It was easier now just to grab at the photos and throw a handful in at a time. The flames crackled and spat at her melting face and body and the room began to fill with an acrid, choking smell. She threw the empty folders to the floor and turned to find Jenny. Poor Jenny, she looked pained.

'Right, out here. Come on,' Sheila urged. The women grabbed their coats, left the house and stood for a few moments under the protection of the stone vestibule. It took a little while for her eyes to adjust to the darkness but then, just as the gnarled trees and bushes began to take shape, they started to walk gingerly down the path. The only sound was the water below them, across the other side of the walkway, rushing and tumbling against the rocks.

'What about John?' Jenny cried.

'We'll wait for him here. I can't bear to be in that house one second more.'

They walked closer towards the walkway, closer to home.

Just then, John and Colin appeared at the porch and her husband rushed down the path and grabbed her by the arm. 'What's going on? What the hell is all that stuff burning in the fire? I thought it looked like – well, some of it looked like you.'

'That old creep had folders filled with photographs of your wife down in that disgusting cellar.' Jenny had stretched back to full height now.

'Photographs? What do you mean photographs? Sheila, what does she mean – photographs?'

Sheila stood, watching the outline of the man she had once so admired, stand at the entrance to his home. He might just be able to see her through the gloom, but he would never see the contempt, feel the disdain, or sense the pity.

'Oh John, nothing like that, nothing sordid.' Jenny explained. 'Just photos of your wife at work, at receptions, dinners. But so obviously taken without her knowing. Loads of them from all sorts of angles. And then kept by him. Down there. Actually, it *is* pretty sordid when you come to think of it.'

'Sheila, speak to me.'

He was close to her now, his arm round her shoulder. 'What the hell is he playing at? What the fuck is wrong with the man?'

She stood, quaking with anger.

'God, you're freezing. Come on, put your coat on.' She let John place the black Windsmoor over her shoulders but still she didn't move. She watched, staring into the blackness until the shady form turned, walked back into the house and quietly shut the door.

'I'm going to have it out with that creep. What the hell does he think he's doing? Wait for me here.' He shouted his words and started to move away. Sheila blinked hard. The heat from the fire and the smoke were still stinging her eyes and scratching at the back of her throat.

She pulled her husband back. 'No need, John. It's done. There's nothing left here.' She slipped her hand into his. 'Come on, let's go home. I just want to go home.'

CHAPTER 21

'I've been thinking. We should call the police.' John had returned from the local bakery with a bag of morning rolls. His eyes were heavy, his voice hoarse after a night of fitful sleep.

'The police?' Sheila turned away from the plates, the mugs, the cafetière. Everything that suggested a domestic norm. She was back in the cellar. Back in his cold, dank lair.

'Yes. That's bloody pervy behaviour, Sheila. And God knows he might have a history of this sort of thing. Could have done it to other women or might even be thinking about doing it to someone else.'

'Yes, but he hasn't actually *done* anything. It's creepy, it makes my skin crawl, of course it does, but they're just photos. Photos taken at work. *He's* more likely to call the police to report an act of criminal damage.' She opened the fridge and pulled out the canister of Peruvian coffee. She twisted the lid and released the deeply satisfying aromas of chocolate and dark maple syrup. It was the coffee they always drank and its smell cocooned her. 'I mean it's not like he set up cameras in the toilets or snapped me taking my clothes off. They mean nothing, these photos. The police would just laugh at us.'

John threw the rolls down on the worktop. 'It's not bloody right. It's not normal. And you never noticed him. With a camera, I mean? Or coming on to you? I mean, did he actually come on to you – ever?'

She walked up and put her arms round his waist. 'No, I never noticed him and no he never came on to me. It's not right and it's not normal but I don't want to think about it anymore. Look, that's him, his issues. I just want to leave it all there. Please. Let's just have breakfast.' She kissed his cheek and returned to her coffee-making. 'Eggs? Bacon?'

He stood now with his hands in his pockets, looking down at the floor. 'No, thank you. Just the coffee and the rolls. I got the floured ones. Thought it best to leave the well-fired ones alone today.'

They smiled and laughed. Forced laughter but it sounded good to Sheila. Good to drown out last night's smells, last night's images.

They talked more during that breakfast than they had for a long time. It felt like the more mundane the conversation, the better. Topics that would normally have prompted John to hide behind his newspaper, or drift off back to his own world of transport management, were enthusiastically pounced upon. Breakfast suddenly became a flurry of anecdotes, of quick-fire banter. Oh, and the garden. Yes, the garden. There was so much to do that they would need to get really stuck in before the end of September. So much to do, that it all needed to be discussed and decided upon, right there and then.

After they'd talked, eaten and drunk endless cups of coffee, the breakfast discourse had to come to its end. John got up, walked round the table, and kissed his wife on the top of her head. 'I'm just going to clean the golf clubs. Just gave them a quick wipe down the other day but they're filthy really. The dirt gets engrained, you see. Right into the grooves.' He was speaking about golf clubs, but his eyes spoke of something else. Something else entirely.

She looked up at him and tried a reassuring smile. He seemed to understand, squeezed her shoulder and went out to the garage.

Sheila got up, carried plates and cups through to the kitchen and began to stack the dishwasher. Back to the normal now, back to the everyday. If you say you don't want to think about something, then that should be that. Except that it wasn't. She couldn't stop thinking about it. She didn't really know what any of it meant, all these images, but they wouldn't stop swirling about inside her head. Again, she tried to think, think back over the years. Had there been a trigger? Had she done something to set off this warped behaviour? Was it the way she looked? The way she spoke?

She went back through to the dining room to wash down the table. Trying to think back to times and events, some of which had taken place years ago, started to make her head hurt. She was pressing her memory, forcing it to reveal truths, obvious truths that she just hadn't seen. My God, when you thought about how some women behaved. All that flirting. Jenny Blyth-Hume was a flirt but no one seemed to mind that. And then the Christmas parties in the Chambers. People got off with each other all the time. Locked offices, locked stationery cupboards. Furtive looks, secret signals.

Where were the placemats? What had she done with the placemats? Then she remembered she'd taken them through to the kitchen. But they needed to go in the sideboard, in the drawer in the sideboard.

She stopped what she was doing and forgot about placemats for a moment. Of course she'd never consciously flirted. Definitely not consciously. With Colin Meikle? No one had ever flirted with Colin Meikle. But then there was all that stuff with Harry. She hadn't meant to flirt with him, but everyone seemed to suggest she had.

She walked through to the kitchen and turned her attention back to the placemats, vigorously wiping them down. Was this some mid-life crisis? Had she forgotten how to behave normally and was now giving off some strange hormonal aura. How was she to know? How did anyone ever know these things?

Over the next few days she tortured herself with hugely unproductive bouts of introspection. John, meanwhile, wandered about the house like a wounded lion. Slightly weakened by the whole affair, he looked ready to lash out at the slightest provocation.

'Jenny rang me,' he announced when he'd got in from work, a few days later.

'You never said.' Sheila steadied herself against the worktop. Gin and tonics would need to wait. 'What did she want?'

'She didn't want anything. She was just asking how you were. How both of us were.' He looked straight at her. 'And she was wondering what we were going to do about it.'

'Look, we're not doing anything. Nothing. I've told you, there's nothing more to be done.' She whacked the bright yellow lemon down by the side of the sink and made for the sanctuary of the bedroom.

It was impossible. Impossible to keep going down this track that led absolutely nowhere. Still fully clothed, she got in under the duvet and lifted it up and over her head. She felt like a child again, waiting for her father to come up and tell her to stop wallowing, get out of bed, wash her face and talk to him like an adult. But she didn't want to be an adult. She hadn't then and she didn't now. Not right now. How, at the age of sixty, could it all have got so ridiculously complicated?

After some minutes, she heard the bedroom door slowly open. 'Don't you want to come down? We could go for a walk. It's still light enough. I won't talk about it anymore. Promise.' She was so tired of the whole thing she could barely move and there were no words that she could think of to say. Absolutely none.

'Okay, well, I'll just be downstairs. Downstairs. If you need me.' The door slowly shut again and she returned to her silent cave filled with downy feathers.

It was dark when she woke. Really dark. She normally stirred at first light or first birdsong, but this was the darkest, quietest time of the night and her sleep had been truly deep and dreamless. Her mouth was dry, so dry that there was barely enough moisture to soften her lips. They broke apart eventually and she took a long deep breath. She was sure she could still taste the smoke, the char, drying out and cracking her lips. The bottom half of her body felt warm, too warm, but then it occurred to her that she still had her trousers on. It was her shoulders that were cold. She couldn't remember taking her top off, but she must have. Or John perhaps? Surely she'd have woken when he did that – touched her, come near her. Surely she'd have noticed that, noticed him. After all, he knew she liked to sleep with her shoulders covered.

He was there, of course, next to her but she didn't want to wake him. On his side, his sleeping side, but she couldn't even remember him getting into bed. Had he spoken to her, had he held her?

She peered at the red glimmer from her digital alarm and saw that it was barely three in the morning. She got out of bed, walked silently into the en suite, washed her face and brushed her teeth. When she returned, she picked up her discarded blouse, hung it neatly over the back of the bedroom chair and slipped quietly back into bed.

After he'd got up, her body seemed to relax. She heard the shower, the powerful jets disrupted as he started to wash his hair and then, quite quickly, a blanket of tiredness came over her. The whirring stopped.

Sheila didn't know how long she'd been sleeping but she was woken abruptly.

'It's that Leonard chap. From your history club. On the phone.' John was standing over her, phone in hand and whispering loudly.

She felt groggy, almost hung-over. That horrible, early morning sleep that neither soothed nor revived.

John put his hand over the mouthpiece. 'Will I tell him to call back?'

'I'll call him. Shortly. When I'm up, washed. Don't tell him I'm still in bed for God's sake.'

John walked off, talking down the phone to the one man she actually did feel like having a conversation with.

'Hi Leonard. Sorry I couldn't take your call. How are you?' After a quick shower, she felt something approaching normal.

'I'm fine, my dear. Absolutely fine. Very much enjoyed our little chat at Sandra's the other week.'

'Oh, me too. Very much.' She relaxed back into the chair at the corner of the French windows, looking out into the garden. John was pacing, inspecting his herbaceous borders.

'Anyway, my dear, I won't keep you but it's just to let you know that Harry's been on the phone.'

'Oh really?' So, he's been on the phone to Leonard. Couldn't bring himself to pick up the phone and get in touch with her, but never mind.

'Yes. He was so sorry that he missed our little trip to Linlithgow Palace and was wondering if there might be a reprise. To be honest I'm not sure if any of our group would want to go again. There's not an awful lot to see and once you've been there, I don't really know why you'd necessarily want to go back. However, as you missed the trip, my dear, I would be more than happy to come along. We could have a nice lunch afterwards.' He paused momentarily. 'Might be quite interesting to hear what Harry has to say about the place.'

She'd put the whole Palace trip to the back of her mind after everything that had happened. And now that she was *having* to think about it, she struggled to ignore Harry's ignorant behaviour when thinking about the history club's successful outing. And then, of course, there'd been the stupid decision to go round to Harry's house. A decision she regretted but one that she could do absolutely nothing about now. None of it made a trip to Linlithgow Palace with Harry Stuart sound terribly appealing.

'I don't know, Leonard. There's so much up in the air just now, I'm not even sure about continuing with the club. We'll be off to France in a few weeks as well…' She tailed off.

'Ah well. Never mind. Just thought it would be something you might enjoy. Particularly given your enthusiasm for our initial trip. You'd put so much into its organisation I just didn't want you to miss out. But I understand if the timing isn't right.'

She didn't say anything. Maybe he could sense her world-weariness. It wasn't the trip, it wasn't the Palace, even being around Harry wasn't that much of an obstacle. Like it or not, Colin Meikle seemed to have tainted everything around her and she was struggling to see the joy in anything.

'Look, let me think about it and I'll come back to you. Later today or tomorrow, is that okay?'

They said their goodbyes and Sheila sat back in the chair watching her husband. Tears filled her eyes. Nothing terrible had happened, not really, but she wasn't sure she could convince John of that. She would get over this, they both would and then life would go on as normal. Maybe she would just trim back on her own ventures a bit. There would be no working at the Council – that had been decided already – so that was okay. No Chamber of Commerce events – she couldn't bear the thought of bumping into Colin although John would make sure he was never invited to anything else again. And the history club, with or without Harry. She did enjoy it most of the time and she was so fond of Leonard but her overwhelming desire at that moment was to rein everything in. Just be with her family, the people she trusted and loved most in the world.

She got up and flung the French windows open. The warm air and scents of summer flowers hit her as soon as she stepped out onto the small patio. She walked up to John, put her arms round his waist and rested her head on his back. She wanted to drink in his smell, everything about him, everything she loved.

'Hey there. What's this all about?' He turned round and held at her arm's length.

She couldn't speak. She didn't really know what was wrong with her.

'I've told you, just say the words and I'll go round there.'

'No, no, it's not just Colin. I don't know what it is, John. It's given me a bit of a knock and things just feel very muddled. Things I was sure of, I just don't know anymore.'

He held her closer. 'Look, you can't start doubting yourself because of his weird behaviour. You're a good judge of character. Married me, didn't you?' He laughed, but none of it was funny. 'Look, I'm not the best at saying what I mean. I know I'm not, but I've always tried to be – oh, I don't know.

Consistent. What I feel I mean. You say you can't be sure about anything, but you can be damn well sure about that.'

She smiled at him. It was a funny thing to say and it was the right thing to say.

Later that evening after dinner they sat quietly in the lounge. John had the usual pile of papers in front of him, but she could tell he wasn't really concentrating.

'So what did Leonard want?' He took his reading glasses off and looked straight across at her.

'He's going to arrange another trip to Linlithgow Palace with Harry Stuart. Thought I might like to go along, given I'd missed out last time.' She put down her magazine. 'I don't know though. Don't know if I feel up to it.'

'Well, I think you should. Be nice to have something positive to focus on. You enjoy their company, it's stuff you're interested in and then after that you'll have France to look forward to.'

'Yes, France.'

'Oh, I meant to ask. Are the kids not going to bother taking the place for a couple of weeks?'

'No. Simon can't get away and they'd already planned to go to Tuscany with the Reids in any case. Same time we're away I think.'

'Christ. Wonder if our wee lad will have to take his trumpet to Italy. He'll be playing Puccini before we know it, poor wee sod.'

She laughed at the image he'd conjured up and John responded with a rather self-satisfied smile. Reassured as to her state of mind, he put his glasses back on and returned to all things transport.

'John?'

'Yes.' He took his glasses off and looked across at her.

'I was worried, you know. Work schedules and then my retiring and you just ploughing on.' It felt odd, talking like this, but he'd opened a door earlier and she wasn't going to shut it now. 'Felt we were drifting a bit.'

'Really? That's a strange thing to think. I mean it never crossed my mind.' He got up and walked past her chair to switch on the standard lamp in the corner of the room. As he passed, he brushed the top of her head with his lips. 'No, we'll never drift, darling. I mean, tell me if you think we are and I'll do something about it. But no, we'll never drift.'

She smiled as he puzzled over the concept.

*

She rang Leonard the very next morning. 'Yes Leonard, that would be lovely. I think I'd really enjoy it actually. I'll get some of my reading material back out again.'

'Oh, that's such good news, my dear.' He sounded genuinely pleased.

'So maybe if you could get possible dates from Harry, we could tie things up over the next week or so?'

'Yes, of course that's absolutely no problem at all. I'll not bother the others. It'll just be the three of us. Wonderful, I'm really looking forward to seeing you again, my dear.'

'Me too, Leonard. Really looking forward to it. Oh, and Leonard, does Harry know I might be coming too?'

'Oh yes. When I mentioned that you'd missed the original trip, he thought it would be a grand idea for you to join us.'

'Oh, that's good. I am pleased.'

A grand idea. Well that's all fine then, she thought to herself.

*

'Do you think that's wise?' Caitlin was munching at a Danish pastry and the yellow custard was oozing out of the sides and on to her fingers. She lapped it up, left hand fingers first, then right hand.

Sheila sat opposite wondering if any of the gooey substance was going to make it onto John's armchair. She had opted for the smaller and altogether easier to eat Chelsea bun from the home bakery and little Milo was on the floor happily sticking his tongue into the centre of a jammy dodger.

'What do you mean?'

'Well, after going round to his house and everything. I mean you haven't spoken since then, have you?'

'No, but then you were the one who told me I'd done nothing wrong by going round.'

'Well, no, of course you didn't. I mean I don't think you did anything wrong but, you know, others might.' Caitlin shifted her gaze down to her sticky fingers.

'What others?' She hadn't shared the news of this little adventure with John and she'd expressly asked Caitlin not to bother her father with any of it.

'Well, Simon thought it was a bit odd, that's all.'

'Simon. You told Simon.'

Caitlin suddenly looked all wide-eyed and innocent. 'Gosh, Mummy. It was just everyday conversation. Nothing to look quite so shocked about.'

She wanted to get up and leave her daughter and grandson to their messy eating. Get up and go somewhere, anywhere.

'Look, he's just a bit of an oddball, that's all. But don't listen to me. If he hasn't said anything to you then he's probably just forgotten all about it. Actually, come to think of it, it's probably a good idea that you're on this little trip together and you can put all that behind you. New chapter. New chapter in your quest for historical truths.' Caitlin smiled. She looked quite pleased with her quirky little turn of phrase. 'And of course Leonard will be with you and he seems to be a good sort so I'm sure everything will be fine.'

CHAPTER 22

Sheila had made up a couple of extra information packs for the original trip to Linlithgow and now pulled them out of their filing place in the home office. She had a whole section in there now. Well, two shelves anyway. She'd carefully moved some of John's older files and placed them in plastic boxes under the stairs. She'd mentioned her intention to create space, but he'd barely acknowledged the fact, so she stuck labels at the front of the shelves 'Ad hoc speeches are now under the stairs'.

She looked at the neat A4 folders in front of her and considered the pros and cons of taking her little pile of fun-filled facts along to the trip with Leonard and Harry but began to worry that they might think she was being a bit – what though? Presumptuous because she assumed they didn't know as much as she did, or pretentious because she looked like she was trying to impress them? It was the sort of thing she would have done as a matter of course in her working life. You always had to be prepared at Council meetings or on field trips with councillors. Somebody always forgot his or her papers. It was her job to cover every eventuality and plug any potential information gaps. But then maybe that was what people found so annoying about her. Never ruffled, always on top of her game. For God's sake, it wasn't a crime to be organised.

She looked at the front index inside the wallet folder and her list of subject headings. (1) Phases of construction; (2) Birthplace of Mary Queen of Scots; (3) Statue of Mary; (4) Rooms of special interest; (5) Life at Court. Probably pretty superfluous stuff as far as Leonard and Harry were concerned. On reflection, it would probably be best just to take one along for her own interest. That's what she would do. She would organise and inform herself. No one could possibly have any objection to that.

'How are you getting there, my dear?' Leonard had called to make arrangements for their trip the following day. It must have been perfectly obvious to him that she would be driving.

'Well, I'm taking the car if you'd like a lift.'

'Ah, wonderful yes. That would be very kind, my dear. Very kind.'

'What about Harry? What's he doing?'

'I did ask but he's going to make his own way there. Think he's going on somewhere else straight after.'

Convenient, she thought, perhaps uncharitably. He wouldn't have to come across town to pick anyone else up.

'Will I pick you up? You're not too far way, are you?'

'Oh no, my dear, I wouldn't want to put you to any trouble. I'll get a bus down to you. Shall we say 10.30?'

'Yes. 10.30 would be just fine.'

*

It was a dull morning. The kind of morning that felt more like autumn than late summer. She opened her front door and walked down the path just to gauge the level of chill in the air. It was a necessary precursor to going out for the day, given Edinburgh weather wasn't always as it seemed. Looking out to a cloudless sky gave no hint of the cold air that often accompanied bursting sunlight. Likewise a dull, overcast sky might have held the freezing haar at bay. Always best to test the conditions. She strolled down to the gate and looked across at the smart terrace opposite where lights were still turned on in drawing rooms and hallways.

No goosebumps and no shivers. Dull but reasonably warm was the verdict, which meant light layers and a raincoat and umbrella – just in case. John had left about two hours earlier with a quick squeeze of her shoulder, kiss on the forehead and a very clear instruction to enjoy herself and forget all about 'that bastard Colin Meikle'. If only life were that simple. But then it needed to be for John and so she nodded, kissed him back and assured him it was her every intention to have a lovely day out.

Leonard arrived dead on time, wearing an old-fashioned gabardine raincoat over his tweed suit and carrying a small umbrella. She smiled. Another proper assessment of weather conditions had been undertaken.

After a quick cup of tea, they headed out in her Volkswagen Golf, travelling inland of the Firth of Forth toward their destination. The sky seemed to have got progressively darker as they headed west.

'Looks like rain,' Leonard remarked, as they sped along the motorway.

After about forty-five minutes, they arrived into Linlithgow and began to drive along the High Street. It seemed to Sheila that the stone buildings in the ancient town had a dark, morose air about them. She had been to Linlithgow before, many years ago, but it hadn't felt like this. But then the sun would probably have been shining and she would have been preoccupied with Caitlin and the need to find ice cream or chips. Anything to stop the moaning about the Sunday car trip. Caitlin had always hated Sundays out with her parents. She always wanted to be left on her own to play or to go with Daddy to the driving range. She never seemed to enjoy the three of them being all together. Images of her daughter's contorted face flashed before her until Sheila quickly remembered to turn into the municipal car park around the corner from the Palace.

'Where are we meeting Harry?' Sheila was keen to see him to get any potential awkwardness out the way as soon as possible. She'd already rehearsed a little quick-fire monologue about her visit to Woodford Grove. How she'd really wanted to make sure he didn't miss out on the trip; how she'd hoped to catch him in; and how lovely it had been to meet his wife. Short and to the point. She'd supposed that there would be nothing further to say on the matter and they would be able to proceed with their tour, unburdened by worry and suspicion.

She checked herself in the mirror on the car's sun visor.

'You look very nice my dear.'

'Oh no. I wasn't looking at myself really. Just checking hair, lipstick.'

Leonard just smiled.

The sky had turned steel grey and looked much less forbidding. Maybe it wouldn't rain after all.

'He said he'd see us at the gift shop.' They walked up the cobbled street and through the archway of the outer gate, passed St Michael's Church and then through the main entrance to the Palace. The gift shop was on the left – a small space crammed with all things Mary. Placemats, key rings, mugs. Standard Historic Scotland fare.

A small dark-haired lady came out from behind her counter. 'Can I help you with anything? Have you been here before? Where have you come from?' Her hands were clasped tightly in front of her as she waited for a response.

'Oh, we've just come from Edinburgh. But it's such a long time since I've been here. I was probably at school I think.'

'Ah, yes. People from Edinburgh don't tend to travel outside the city very much.' A smile cracked but brought little warmth to her expression. 'Certainly, that's what we find out here and we're only half an hour away.'

Sheila just smiled. Of course they leave the city – maybe not so much to Linlithgow Palace. As she looked round, there wasn't really a lot to tempt Edinburghers out to these bleak surroundings. And there certainly wasn't any point in setting out all the problems associated with traversing the city that would have knocked her half-hour travel time into a cocked hat.

The little woman retreated back into the shadows behind her counter in the corner of the shop.

'He's late.' Leonard stood tapping his watch.

'Only ten minutes. He's probably stuck in traffic.' Sheila raised her voice slightly and spoke in the direction of the woman in the shadows, but she didn't speak, didn't move.

'Hello you two.' Suddenly he was there filling the entrance to the shop. The sun had forced its way through the metal skies right at that moment and Harry was silhouetted in the doorway. His outline made him almost look like a Highland chieftain. The red hair, beard and some kind of long tartan coat. As he moved towards them, she could see that the garment in question was a frock coat. Stuart tartan, obviously, with matching Stuart tartan trews. God, he'd gone full pelt with the Darnley connection, that was for sure.

'Harry, my lad. You look resplendent I must say.' Leonard shook his hand vigorously.

'Well, I like to look the part. Try to match the sartorial elegance of my much-maligned ancestor.' He winked.

Sartorial elegance of a debauched, drunken, pox-ridden rogue more like – but she didn't say anything, just smiled. 'Lovely to see you, Harry, it's been ages. Hope everything's well.'

He nodded but said nothing. Looking at him again, he seemed quite different to her now. The anticipation of the next provocative remark, the lure of the challenging debate had all fallen away. The bold tartan suddenly looked a bit threadbare in places. The once bright smiling eyes appeared dimmed now and the sharpness of his brogue just sounded harsh and caustic.

'Shall we go?' Leonard took the lead much to Sheila's relief.

'Tickets. You haven't bought any tickets.' The woman barked from behind the counter.

'Ah yes. We're all members of Historic Scotland. Everyone got their cards to show...' Leonard peered at the woman's chest, '...June? Yes, can we show our cards to June?'

June looked slightly taken aback that these ignoramuses from the big city were actually members, but she smiled, recorded the card numbers and handed out three adult tickets.

Sheila walked alongside the two men into the central courtyard, dominated by an ornate fountain and with square towers situated in each corner of the vast open space. She shifted her gaze upwards. The Palace was roofless with black gaping holes for windows. It was indeed bleak, soulless even.

As a wild wind swirled around them, Sheila struggled hard to envisage a once magnificent palace, but Leonard appeared to have no such problem. He seemed to recreate every facet of the place in his mind and described the rooms, imagined the feasts, the sweeping procession of successive Stuart kings. All the while Harry walked around, staring at the walls, hands in pockets and saying nothing.

They made their way into the Great Hall and Leonard's voice again filled the room with magnificent items of furniture and intricate tapestries. The food, the festivities were all being brought to life right in front of her and finally her mind began to travel back.

The wind stopped, the cold shifted. This was why she loved history. She could see the raging fire in the massive fireplace, the heavy dress fabrics and ornate cloaks sweeping past, the silver trays laden with food and fruit. The smoked and chargrilled taste of assorted animals and birds killed and cooked for the delectation of the royal household. It all filled her senses until she could no longer see the dark moss on the walls or taste the dry stone dust filling the air.

Leonard stood, looking up, hands clasped over his chest. He was there too. Then after a few moments of silence he announced 'Birthplace of Mary Queen of Scots, whose line of succession can be traced right up to our present Queen. Now isn't that something?' The bold statement seemed to bring him right back into the present day and Sheila followed reluctantly. 'So, my dear. Are you all for a little bit more exploring?'

Harry turned round quickly and stared down Leonard but the old man remained unmoved.

'Yes, of course. Harry?' As she turned towards him, the chill wind returned and so she turned the collar of her coat up and sank her chin down into her scarf.

Suddenly Harry's mood seemed to pick up as though casting off its ancestral shadow. 'Yes, why not. Why don't we climb up one of the towers? Great views across the loch from up there.'

'Oh, not for me, I'm afraid. I'll stick to the ground-floor rooms. Old knees won't take it, I'm afraid.' Leonard's voice seemed to falter slightly, losing some of its authority.

She felt Harry might be smirking at the old man's admission of weakness but didn't want to look to find out. Instead, she turned to Leonard. 'But I'm so enjoying your descriptions. You make everything come alive.'

Harry said nothing. She turned to see him brushing down the front of his frock coat and looking down at his feet.

'I'll go into the kitchens I think, the storerooms. Like to try and work out how everything connects, how they made it all work.' Leonard took her arm. 'When you come back down, we'll go out and have a look at the Queen's statue. When we were here last time at the unveiling, a pigeon flew across and emptied itself all over her head.' He let out a little laugh. 'I do hope they've cleaned it off.'

Suddenly he was gone, disappeared through another gaping hole in the wall. Sheila and Harry walked towards the corner of the Palace to the bottom of one of the corner towers and then in through the entrance to the turnpike stairs.

'Are you okay going up here?' His voice sounded unusually gentle.

'Yes, of course.' Her mouth felt suddenly very dry as she started to climb round the tight spiral. She wished she'd brought water. Had there been any? In the shop? Probably not. Round each corner she climbed and the end never came. She was convinced the stone steps were getting shallower and the walls on either side narrower. Every breath became more constricted, not because she was particularly pushing herself, but because she felt like she was running out of air, running out of time. It didn't really take that long to get to the top, till she could breathe fresh air again. But when she finally could see the vivid green of the grass and the trees in the distance, it all just made her want to curl up and sit down on the cold stone ledge.

Why come up here really? What was the point? Phobias attacked her from all sides trying to topple her from the great roof. Stand there, don't stand there. Go back inside, don't go back inside. Sit down, stand up. Agoraphobia and claustrophobia joining forces to wreak havoc with any kind of rational thought. She reached back and caught his arm. 'Sorry, Harry, no. I can't do this. I need to get down. I need to get down, now.'

'Okay, okay, don't panic. We'll go back down. I'll go first – don't worry. Just hang on to me if you like.' She stepped down gingerly behind him, grabbing onto his coat and trying not to think about the walls. He moved at just the right pace, in time with her steps until they were back into the courtyard.

'Thank you – I'm sorry. I'm usually okay with heights. I don't know what came over me.' She swept the hair back off her face and with it, the residual dust from the stone.

'It's fine. Nothing to worry about. Why don't we go in there?' He pointed to yet another slightly larger black hole. 'The old man might be wandering about in there. Think it's the wine cellar. Might be safer territory.' He smiled.

They walked into a long room with a high domed roof. The stone felt even colder here and the moss clinging to the walls seemed to have turned into a dark green slime. At the far end was a narrow slit of a window – the only source of brightness in the place. There was no Leonard, there was no one.

Harry walked toward the bright light and sat down on a small rectangular ledge under the window. He pointed to a mirror image of the small seat opposite. 'I don't understand why these windows are so narrow.' He sat peering out at what little there was to see and she began to wish she'd stuck with Leonard. Any enthusiasm for the place was beginning to wane but she did as instructed and sat down opposite Harry. It suddenly struck her that with a bit of face paint and some ridiculously oversized shoes, he would make the perfect clown.

The moment she sat down was the moment she realised everything had changed. The charismatic imagery had faded away completely now. It reminded her of the time she had watched a towering performance of King Lear only to find, minutes after the crushing finale, the fine Shakespearean lead actor smoking a fag and drinking from a can of lager by the stage door. The power of his performance, the impact of his words and movement just gone.

And now she couldn't see anything. Just the stone, the moss and this oddball of a man. A man who really wasn't anything to her any more.

'You enjoying yourself?' He kept looking out the window.

'Yes, it's been interesting. But it's awfully cold and damp in here.' She put her hands in her pocket and tugged her coat round her thighs. 'Let's go and look for Leonard.'

He turned to look at her. 'No, I mean are *you* enjoying yourself. Not this place, not this.'

'Sorry. What do you mean?'

'Did you think it was clever going round to my house?' He stood up to face the window, blocking out the sliver of light.

She couldn't speak because she couldn't see his face. Couldn't see the expression that would tell her what his words meant.

'Did you want a good look at the competition? Not much to write home about. Is that what you were thinking?'

Oh God. She felt faint.

'Looking down your nose at her, were you?'

'No, No. I just went round with a note for you. That's all I did. And then we had a cup of tea. That was all. We just had a cup of tea.' She wanted to stand up but her legs wouldn't move. 'She seemed very nice. Mary seemed very nice.'

Now he turned to look at her. 'So who are you trying to convince with that little story? Me or you?'

Suddenly worry turned to upset and she stood up. Her legs felt weak, but she had to stand. 'Look here, Harry. I just went round to your house with a note and had a cup of tea with your wife. And if you really want to know I felt a bit sorry for her. I don't know what's going on, it's absolutely none of my business but she did seem a bit down, a bit worn out. And we did discuss holidays – and then maybe I suggested something about going on one of our trips. But then it sounded like she didn't go out too much. She said you don't really think she's up to staying in a hotel.' She'd said too much, she knew she had. Why hadn't she just walked away? Why didn't she just walk away now? There was nothing to stop her.

Too late. He was standing right in front of her now and she could smell something woody. Strong and earthy. Like an old-fashioned cologne or aftershave. The smell coupled with the brutishness forced her to sit back down. And now he was on the same seat as her. The same narrow little stone ledge, thigh wedged up against hers. But this time there was no dubiety, no scope for misinterpretation.

'No, you're right. It's none of your business.' He suddenly slipped his hand inside her coat and pressed it against her stomach. She felt like she couldn't breathe.

'Do you think for one moment I buy any of that nonsense? I've seen the way you look at me.'

She couldn't move. She felt hemmed in from every angle.

'That's fine, Sheila, but it's the games I can't be bothered with. Flirting is just pathetic. All that coy behaviour gets on my wick. If you want it you can have it but there are rules. No coming round to the house and no imagined happy ever after. We're adults so start behaving like one.' He took his hand out and away and suddenly she could take in gulps of the damp, oppressive air. He swept his hair back from his face. A face filled with anger or desire; she couldn't tell which. And then he grabbed her thigh. 'So make up your mind, Sheila. If this is all some game because you're bored with your life, just want some imaginary romance to fill the empty hours, then quite honestly you can stop wasting my time.' His hand moved up and he slowly caressed her cheek. The gesture made her feel physically sick. 'But if you're serious then treat me like a grown-up.'

He got up and turned to head towards the exit back into the courtyard. 'I mean it, Sheila. Don't mess around with me. I like women who know what they want, know what they're doing.' He grabbed her by the arm and pulled her up from the cold stone. 'Right, come on, let's find that old bugger.'

She walked slowly out behind him feeling as though her legs might give way at any point. She tried to replay every word that had come out of his disgusting mouth. Like he'd been given a script and was reading his lines, but they weren't real. Not real words, not real sentences. All made up for effect just like a bad Fringe play. And then suddenly she saw Leonard.

'Are we doing lunch?' The old man's eyes twinkled in the gloom.

'Actually, if you don't mind, I think I would like to just go home. Think I might be coming down with something.'

'Suits me,' Harry said, face expressionless.

Leonard was about to say something when Harry turned and walked away leaving all his words behind. Words and actions designed to hurt and humiliate. Mission accomplished.

CHAPTER 23

When she got home, she went straight up to the bathroom and stared at her reflection in the vanity mirror above the sink. She moved in closer to see the hints of grey in the dyed auburn hair, the lines round the eyes, the wrinkled neck. She tried to see the woman Harry could see. Everything she thought she was, every aspect of her character was confused, fading before her eyes.

She stepped back quickly. It wasn't just his coarse language, or the physical assault that had really upset her. Was it an assault? What constituted an assault? There was no physical pain, no bruises. Nothing for the world to see.

No, it wasn't any of that. She just didn't know who she was looking at anymore.

She needed to get out, go somewhere normal, speak to someone normal. She splashed her face with cold water, walked through to the bedroom and picked up the phone.

Later that afternoon, she found herself sitting in a local cafe, staring down at a milky foam heart, slowly dissolving on top of her cappuccino. A young waitress smiled at her as she cleared a neighbouring table. She smiled back, momentarily enjoying a little piece of polite social discourse.

'Ah, here you are, sitting through the back.' She looked up to see Agnes take off her coat and hang it carefully over the back of a small wooden chair. 'I was looking for you out the front. All these little dogs out there. Quite funny. It's a new trend I think – small dogs in cafes.'

She listened to Agnes talk of the ordinary, the mundane. Little dogs in cafes. If only they could just sit and laugh and gossip about little dogs in cafes. She looked up at Agnes's kindly face and the tears suddenly spilt over. An elderly couple, with a toy poodle seated between them, glanced over but quickly returned to feeding their canine friend small pieces of toasted teacake. It would not do to watch over a poor stranger's meltdown.

'Oh, Sheila. What's going on? What's happened?'

She composed herself, pulled her chair closer into the table and proceeded to tell Agnes about Colin, about Harry, about everything.

'It's not that I haven't had to deal with difficult men in the past. Of course I have. But somehow at work I felt more in control. Well, at least more than I am now. And of course, I wasn't alone at work. These men were the usual suspects and we all just swotted away their unwanted attentions. And then came the rules, the policies and procedures and I think we all felt a little bit more protected after that. Maybe it was all just less overt. There were norms, expectations, and not so much bad behaviour on display. And now I'm just finding it difficult to work out exactly what's happened and what part I've played in all this mess. What's happened to me, Agnes?'

'Oh my goodness, Sheila. You're the same person you've always been.' Agnes leant over and took her hand. 'This isn't about you, about who you are. You've had the misfortune to bump up against two men who, for whatever reason, seem incapable of behaving normally around women. I don't know why, you don't know why. And you shouldn't have to. Nothing they've done can be excused.' She leaned in across the table. 'That kind of behaviour is desperate and sad and downright intolerable. You shouldn't have to put up with that sort of nonsense.' She suddenly sat back. 'Have you thought about the police? '

'Oh no, not the police.' Sheila's body stiffened.

'Okay, okay. Don't panic. You deal with it however you think best but they can't change how you see yourself, or the life you have. They're not worth getting upset about.' Agnes paused for a minute. 'Have you spoken to John?'

'Some. Not about all of it. I mean we've talked about Colin, obviously. I just don't want this to mess up my life – our lives. Not now. Not when I feel we're starting to look forward.' She smiled at her friend and felt the heaviness begin to shift. 'I'll think about it though. What to say to him, I mean.' She sipped at her lukewarm coffee. 'Funny, isn't it, that I've been so focussed on studying the lives of strong women and here I am crumbling in the face of a dose of toxic masculinity.'

'Toxic masculinity. Where did that come from?'

'Oh, I read about it in a magazine. Anyway, I wonder what Elsie Inglis or Mary Queen of Scots would do?'

'Well, I think Elsie would navigate a way round all the nonsense but I'm afraid poor Mary's decision-making wasn't the best. She'd probably marry one of them and have the other killed.'

She laughed, Agnes laughed with her and the small poodle looked up and barked.

In the hours that followed she thought about how to start such a conversation with John, but she couldn't decide what she wanted to tell him. If she combined the visit to Harry's house with his cruel behaviour at the Palace, then would John wonder what she'd done? Had she led Harry on, encouraged him? Would he think she'd overstepped the mark? But then, if she told him how disgusted, how frightened she'd been, did she risk more upset, worry and anger? And all on top of the Colin Meikle episode. Everything might start to move beyond her control.

It was exhausting. Nothing she did seemed to stop the images circulating and thoughts tumbling. Every time she moved to speak to her husband, Harry Stuart's red face and burning eyes would appear and she would stop herself from saying a word.

In bed that night, she felt her heart beat at an alarming rate. She turned to look at John but only saw the space between them and the space panicked her. He didn't like to have his sleep disturbed but the caustic voices and the pressing hands were all beginning to crowd in around her. She rolled over on to her side and lay against his back. She pressed her face into the warmth of his neck and slid her arm around his waist. Just as she began to feel him stir, he covered her hand with his.

*

Three days after the disastrous expedition, she spent the morning with Caitlin and Milo, baking and talking mothers and toddlers, chickenpox outbreaks and Milo's instinctive problem-solving skills. It was all reassuringly safe and mundane. The phone rang just as she was waving them off down the path. Sheila closed the door, caught a glimpse of her reflection in the hall mirror, pulled her hair back from her face and picked up the phone. It was Leonard.

'Just wanted to make sure you were quite all right, my dear. You didn't seem quite yourself the other day. Some kind of virus, do you think?'

'Yes, probably. Just came on all of a sudden.'

'They quite often do. I'm sure you'll shake it off with a bit of rest. And then I'd like to talk to you about something. When you're feeling better, when it's all out of your system. This sort of thing's quite short lived I think you'll find.'

'I'm sure you're right. I'll speak to you soon.'

She was just about to say her goodbyes when she suddenly became aware of a momentary pause at the other end of the line. Just as she was about to speak, Leonard resumed. 'Remember, there are always choices, Sheila. Different paths to take. The important thing is that you are in control. You must decide the right path for you. The path that feels right, both for you and those closest to you.'

She wasn't quite herself, but the old man's words coupled with Agnes's little pep talk gave her a degree of comfort and a measure of resolve, right at the moment she needed them most. Had Leonard known? How could he? But he'd guessed something was wrong and she was thankful for that.

The following day she decided to visit her father. She'd missed her visit the previous week, which was a rare occurrence and one she felt badly about. But more than that – she'd missed *him*. She chose not to tell John or Caitlin in the unlikely event that they would choose to accompany her. At that particular moment she just wanted to be alone with him.

It was a dull, overcast afternoon as she drove up to the entrance of the care home. She'd deliberately decided not to bring the photo album this time. It wasn't the past that she wanted to rediscover with him – it was the here and now. Whatever world he inhabited, whatever state he was in, he was still her father and it was her father that she needed. It was unrealistic, of course, and she knew it.

She got out of the car and began the solemn walk up the driveway. Suddenly there was singing. At first she couldn't work out where it was coming from. She looked around at the elegant villas either side of the home until she realised the beautiful sound of young voices was drifting out through the open windows of her father's comfortable prison. The music was instantly recognisable although she couldn't put a name to it. Soulful, haunting, it made her want to cry – cry about everything and nothing. But she didn't. She steadied herself and just as she was about to ring the bell, Carole opened the door.

'Saw you coming up the path. Aren't they wonderful? Youngsters from the music school are popping round all the care homes during the Festival.' Carole took Sheila by the arm like she was a long-lost friend and walked her along the corridor, footsteps echoing the length of their walk, until they arrived at the entrance to the communal lounge. 'Let's just stand here and listen a while.'

They stood in silence, listening to the voices undulate, reaching crescendos and then gently falling back. Young girl sopranos holding interminably long notes till a wave of boys gently and seamlessly followed in behind. 'Barber's Adagio – the choral arrangement. It has a name, but I can't remember what it's called now.' Carole looked puzzled. Her mind for a few moments was escaping the complexities of feeding and medication regimes.

Carole had spoken quietly but Sheila didn't want to hear anything other than the melodious tones coming from the far end of the room. Something magical might break, might be lost forever if harsh words interrupted the flow. She broke away from Carole and looked round the room. The normally twisted, contorted faces were for the most part enraptured. Even her father, whose gaze remained resolutely fixed, as it always did, out towards the gardens, seemed at peace with his surroundings. He might not know what he was looking at or what he was even hearing but it looked as though every beautiful note was flowing over and through him like a stream of crystal-clear water, unencumbered by rocks, stones or other obstacles to its gentle meanderings.

Suddenly the angelic voices stopped and there was a moment of silence. A moment when the young people, perhaps used to some form of acclaim that would have come almost immediately the performance ended, began to look around at their surroundings and then, slightly uncomfortably, at each other. A burst of short, sharp claps broke their discomfort. A small bird-like lady sitting right up front was eagerly showing her appreciation. Like a small child she bounced up and down on her seat and squealed in delight. The young men and women of the Royal Edinburgh Musical Academy smiled at her and nodded.

And then a man at the back of the room, near to Sheila's father, let out an excruciatingly painful wail. A horrible sound that brought Sheila, and everyone else for that matter, right back into the here and now. Carole took that as her cue to bring a close to the magical interlude and marched up to the choir, shaking hands and thanking each of them enthusiastically. They looked relieved that it was over, that they could soon escape back into their own reality.

Sheila turned to move towards her father. He had been completely undisturbed by the wailing episode, but his expression was no longer peaceful. He looked frightened again, sitting bolt upright in his high-backed chair.

She sat beside him and gently covered his withered hand with hers. Head bent down, she stared at the dark blue veins covering his skin like a map of endless tributaries. She began to cry. The tears fell toward her mouth till she could taste their saltiness. A few dripped onto her hand. She couldn't look up, couldn't look at anything, but just closed her eyes in a hopeless bid to stop the flow.

And then she felt it. Felt the warmth and comfort. The absolute surety that she was loved and cared for. By her family, by her friends. No matter what happened, she always would be. The tears stopped as her father laid his hand gently on top of hers.

*

She had told John something of the trip to Linlithgow Palace. Not everything; she hadn't wanted him to know about the unwanted physical contact. That might have provoked something she couldn't control but she did tell him about the twisting of words and conjuring up scenarios that didn't exist – which never could exist. Not for her. She'd told him that Leonard could see it, that something was wrong and that they'd decided to move on without Harry. There would be no more history club with Harry Stuart.

Maybe it was how she'd told it, maybe she'd been just a bit flippant, but his response had surprised her slightly. He'd laughed off Harry as some ridiculous buffoon who could never be taken seriously. But then he had seemed to reset and looked at her a little panic-stricken as though studying her face for something. She couldn't say anything more and he'd seemed to understand. Everything that had happened with Colin and Harry needed to be let go now.

She was in the dining room, which she'd now turned into a makeshift office. She'd kept the table but got John to store the chairs in the garage until they could work out a more permanent solution. He had half-heartedly offered up his study but she couldn't bear the thought of being surrounded by planning consents, financial projections and emissions targets. 'What about one of the small bedrooms upstairs?' he'd suggested. Perhaps in time. Not right now. She had plans.

She needed a space that would allow her mind to travel back in time, to conjure up images from the past and at the same time let her organisational skills flourish. Historical texts properly categorised and displayed. She could wheel about in her swivel chair and pick out the right reference book at a moment's notice. Ornaments and decanters replaced by Lady Antonia Fraser.

And of course she had the French windows. Peaceful contemplation while looking out onto her display of purple asters and sweet bergamot. It was perfect, her own little historical dominion.

She had been sitting back in her brand-new, Swedish-designed, automatically reclining ergonomic chair when John came in from golf one day. '*How much?*' he had screeched. She'd smiled at him. Her money, her chair.

On that particularly sunny day she was unwrapping a newly purchased laminator. She liked laminating things. 'A clean protective barrier against unwanted stains,' the box screamed when suddenly the phone rang in the hall.

'Hello, my dear. Just wondered if you'd got the email.' It was Leonard.

'Ah, the email. Yes, fascinating, isn't it? Not so much as a peep and now Harry wants to start up his pet project again.'

'Do you want to reply to him or would you like me to?'

She thought for a moment. 'It's fine, Leonard. I'll get something out to him this afternoon. Will you tell the others what's happening? I mean they might want to join up with him again, but I can't really see it.'

'No, I don't think so, Sheila, not after the group's last discussion.'

'Do you want me to run a draft past you?'

'No, no. I think you know exactly what needs to be said.'

She walked through to the kitchen, made a small cafetière of coffee and returned to her domain. She took a sip, opened up her laptop and began.

> *Thank you for the email, Harry. I do hope you and Mary have been enjoying the lovely weather and have managed to get away for a while.*
>
> *With regard to the history club well I have to tell you that things have moved on apace while you've been away and in fact we've decided to form our own society. It's going to be on a bit of a firmer footing than history club and we might also look at charitable status but that's probably some way off. According to Leonard there are pros and cons. Anyway the critical distinction for us is really to expand our reach and to invite in a variety of speakers and also, when we decide to focus on any one period of history, to ensure that we invite a variety of opinions and standpoints. In addition, we feel that it is important for members to take the lead in areas they find to be of specific interest. I'm sure you will agree that the dominance of any one view in an interest group like this can only stifle growth and learning.*
>
> *I have to say that I was both surprised and honoured to be elected the chair of the society at our*

inaugural meeting and with Leonard as secretary and Agnes as treasurer I'm sure we will flourish.

I'm sorry that your little project seemed to founder but then sometimes these things happen when we lose our way a bit and other unhelpful pressures and distractions take over our lives. The sooner things can be turned around the better, I think. Making good choices is a new little mantra I'm certainly now committed to following.

Anyway, I must dash, we have an impressive programme planned for the rest of the year, which won't just happen on its own. I do hope you have some success with whatever your next venture might be, Harry.

With all good wishes
Sheila.

CHAPTER 24

Sheila and Caitlin were lying back in matching white towelling robes with thin pads covering their eyes. There was something very cooling being administered through these slivers of cotton, but she didn't know what. After the heady and slightly nauseating onslaught of aromatherapy oils swirling around the massage room, the cold, odourless application was a welcome relief.

She had tried to relax throughout the treatment sessions. Body massage, head massage, facial, pedicure but all the while she couldn't help feeling that it was all a bit of an ordeal. Get through this treatment and then we'll move on to the next onslaught of prodding hands and detoxification. Caitlin by contrast had succumbed to the whole process as soon as they'd walked through the doors. Sheila could see her daughter's limbs suddenly loosen the minute the heavy robe was donned. She smiled and watched her happily pick at tiny pieces of cut-up melon and sip from a glass of lime-infused water, brought by a cheery young therapist before the sessions began. And then they had been marched off to separate chambers. Anything might happen. Mind-cleansing might get rid of all the unhappy memories from the last few weeks.

And now they had entered the end stage of Mind and Body Cleanse – a gift from John. Mother-and-daughter time at the local spa. The spa outing demonstrated John's need to fix things. He didn't quite know what was to be fixed but he had to do something. She had loved the gesture even if spas had never really been her thing and had hugged him in gratitude and told him it was perfect.

The two women lay side by side on their wooden recliners until Sheila could hear her daughter's gentle snoring. She didn't think anyone else was in the relaxation suite but then she heard the door slowly open and the sound of whispering voices. It was time to wake Caitlin up. She leant across and gently squeezed her arm. The action induced a low groan followed by a short expletive. Enough to prompt Sheila to whip the cotton pads off her eyes.

'Oh God, I was really away there.' Caitlin was sitting upright and rubbing her face vigorously.

'Yes, you were.'

Three women in the towelling uniform of the spa worshipper took up their positions in recliners at the opposite end of the room.

'So nice of Daddy to do this for us. Don't you think?'

'Yes. It was very thoughtful.'

'I was going to ask you about this new project you've got going before I dozed off. This historical thing. What is it, again?'

She could make out Caitlin's screwed-up face in the dim light. All the benefits of exfoliating and toning gone in a flash.

'It's a historical society. Proper society with a constitution and everything and I've been made chair.' She hoped she didn't sound too boastful. Proud, but not boastful.

'And what about old Harry? Is he not running the show then?'

She winced slightly at the sound of his name. 'No. This has nothing to do with Harry. I really don't know what he's doing with himself.'

Caitlin swung her legs round, sat on the edge of the recliner and leant over towards Sheila. 'I tell you something he's *not* doing and that's going home to his wife. She's up and left him. Gone to live with her sister in the Borders. According to Simon it's given him a real knock. He didn't see it coming at all, apparently.'

'Yes, well, some men don't.' She didn't meet Caitlin's intense gaze. She just stared at the blank wall in front of her. Of course, none of that was anything to do with her, nothing to do with her life, but still she felt an immeasurable amount of pleasure on hearing the news. It was like finishing off the stitching in her own small tapestry. The conversation with Mary Stuart was the one thing that had felt unresolved but now there was a complete picture in front of her and everything was in its rightful place.

An hour or so later Sheila had dropped Caitlin back at her house.

'Coming in for a cup of tea?'

'No, thank you, darling. I think I'll just head. It was lovely though. Really lovely.'

Caitlin peered back into the car and smiled. 'Yes, it was. *Really* lovely.'

Sheila turned the car round and drove off. She wanted to get home and see John.

As she drove through Stockbridge, she noticed the boards outside the newsagent's proclaiming the arrival of the trams in two weeks' time. Her husband's ambition and reputation on show for the entire city to see. She felt the muscles in her stomach tighten.

She turned into their cobbled street and parked. As she got out of the car, something caught her eye. Did neighbours' curtains move? Then the creaking sound of a wheelie bin being dragged down a path. Far too early for bins to go out, surely. Were the conservation overlords secretly furious that someone in their midst now bore the responsibility for the trams fiasco or were they just hacked off by all the media hype? The sheer crassness of heralding the arrival of something they found to be an obscene waste of money and completely surplus to *their* requirements. The things people got in a lather about. She hurried up the path, away from prying eyes and into the house she shared with the trams supremo.

*

'Sheila?'

She jumped. She hadn't heard him come in and the short, sharp call of her name took her aback. She was upstairs looking at summer clothes. France clothes. 'Coming.' She shut the wardrobe and made her way back down to the kitchen.

John was in the fridge pulling out ham, cheese, and tomatoes. 'Just going to make a quick sandwich and then

I'm going back in I'm afraid, darling. It's all hands on deck now. Going to be like this for the next two weeks I'm afraid.' He turned and gave her one of his sore kisses right on her cheekbone. 'I'll have a quick shower and change. God knows when I'll be home. Might end up sleeping in the bloody office.'

Why did she ever worry about him? This was John in his element. Pressure was piling on and he couldn't get enough of it. It was like a small boy going on an adventure holiday. He couldn't be absolutely sure about how the thing was going to pan out but the anticipation of setting up camp, dealing with the unexpected and challenging himself was more excitement than he could ever have hoped for.

And that was the moment she decided. She'd been mulling it over in her mind, of course. Weighing up pros and cons as she did with most things, but it was time to make the good choice.

'I'm going to head to France. In the next couple of days. I'm going to go. By myself.'

'But I thought we were going at the end of the month. The two of us.' The packet of ham was swiftly discarded.

'Well, yes, but you're so caught up with the trams and everything.' She clasped her hands tightly. 'I just want to go.'

'But how? How will you get there?'

'How we always get there. I'll fly to Marseille and then hire a car.'

'But you've never driven on your own in France.' John leant back against the worktop as though the incredulity of it all might just send him falling to the ground.

'I always drive in France.'

'Yes, but *I* always navigate. You won't know how to *actually* get there.'

'I'll use sat nav.'

'We never use sat nav in France.' Now he was gripping hard on to the edge of the worktop.

She smiled. 'Well, there's a first time for everything.'

She had booked flights, arranged the hire car and was now packing a case. They kept a certain amount of clothes in their little stone villa, but she always topped up with extras. As she carefully folded and laid tops over trousers she thought of the blue-tipped lavender gently swaying in the wind, pink and white roses scenting the air and scarlet- and salmon-coloured geraniums in their window boxes. Most would have died back now, she thought, but other scents and sights would fill her senses.

Suddenly he was in the doorway, leaning against the frame with arms folded.

'I didn't think you were coming home till late.'

'I'm going back in. I just wanted to make sure you had everything.' He stood upright and put his hands in his pockets. 'Wondered if you might have any questions. You know, about the water heater or whatever.'

She smothered a laugh. 'No. No questions.' She shut the case closed.

He walked up to her and put his arms round her waist. 'Do you remember our first flat?'

'Of course. I loved that flat. Always did. In fact, I never wanted to move if you remember.' She lifted a strand of hair away from his eyes.

'It was the top floor.' He was looking straight into her eyes. She couldn't move. She didn't want to move. Not now, not when he was taking her back to that precious time when it was just the two of them. Everything new, everything exciting. The first pot of soup she ever made, the first time curling up on their brand-new sofa, arms and legs entwined. Who knew where one body began and the other ended?

'Yes.' She remembered it well. 'Just as well we moved before Caitlin was born. Would have been impossible carting everything up to the top floor.'

'People do. People manage.'

'Yes, well, mostly women. Mostly women manage.'

He smiled and nodded. 'I'm going to miss you, you know.'

What a strange thing love was. Most of the time it was just there and you didn't really notice it but then there were moments when it filled you up like an extravagant gourmet meal. There just seemed to be so much of everything, and all of it, everything that was right in front of you, looked delicious and tasted wonderful.

'Well, it's only two weeks and then you'll be with me. We'll be together again.'

He moved away from her and then stopped. 'The flat.'

'Yes?'

'The stairs. All the stairs.'

'Oh yes, the stairs. When we first moved in you used to take an age. I'd lift the bell pull and wonder if you'd changed your mind halfway up.' The memory made her laugh, but he didn't laugh.

'No, it wasn't that. I took so long because I was savouring what was ahead of me.' He turned and left the bedroom. 'I'll try not to wake you,' he shouted back at her as he ran down the stairs.

*

There had been talk of air traffic control strikes but nothing materialised and Sheila's flight was smooth and uninterrupted save for the crackled recording of a bugle blast announcing their arrival at Marseille. She filed through passport control, waited at baggage reclaim with her fellow travellers and then walked straight through to the car hire reception. She watched other people spinning round looking for the right counter. Peering at names, pointing in different directions. People who thought they knew where they were going.

The car was the exact same make and model that they always used. John had been quite insistent on that point and she had nodded in agreement. She was always going to hire the same make of car. Did he think she would suddenly want to plump for a top-of-the-range sporty number? It was baking hot when she stepped into her black Renault Mégane, set up the sat nav and set off on the thirty-minute drive to the villa. Instead of John barking instructions and then quickly changing his mind, she had the monotone voice of Ursula guiding her calmly and sedately right up the rough bouldered drive to the front door.

She opened all the shutters wide on arrival. The stone kept the house cool inside, but it felt musty, unlived in.

She desperately wanted to fill the place with freshly cut flowers, but everything was beginning to die back. She'd have to wait till morning to get to the market.

In the days that followed, Sheila stripped everything back. She decluttered rooms, aired crisp white sheets by hanging them in the garden and letting them billow in the warm breeze. She decided she would eat mostly from the market and make the short trip to the supermarket just for milk and yoghurt. She ate small meals of rotisserie chicken, ham and salad and filled her fruit bowls with green and scarlet apples, pears and melon.

She found herself drawn to the small writing desk that looked out on to the terraced garden. Creative endeavours weren't part of the plan but then there wasn't, for the first time in her life, any kind of real plan. No structured outline, no keyboard, no electronic whirring in the background – just a pile of notebooks and pens and imaginings. She wondered what John would think. After all, the beautifully crafted desk, fashioned out of walnut, had been purchased for purely decorative purposes. Now she looked down at the small tight knots that swirled across the surface, beckoning her to follow their flow. She sat down, clicked the end of her pen and began to write. She couldn't stop. Her mind was filled with possibilities, endless roads to travel.

Some time into her second week, Sheila broke away from her new world and took a cup of coffee outside. The lavender blooms had gone but their aroma still seemed to fill the air. Remnants of harvesting, perhaps. She smiled, lifted her face up to the cooling breeze and drew her fingers through her hair. Leonard would love this. He would love what she was doing but also this place. The way time suddenly became your own here, no one else's. Maybe they could invite him out for a few days. Maybe next summer.

Two days before John was due to arrive Sheila forced herself to drive to the supermarket. She needed gin. Gin was not something she ever enjoyed drinking on her own. She didn't know why. Wine, yes. Gin, no. And then processed cheese and marmalade. She didn't know anyone, other than her husband, who ate Bavarian smoked cheese. It was the round hard stuff she bought back home and it always surprised her to see it abroad. It got stuck in your teeth and had all the texture of chewy plastic, but John loved it. Earlier that day at the market she'd spotted red mullet at the fish stall, scales glistening in the sun as it rested serenely on a bed of melting ice. That would be supper on Saturday, she'd decided. Fresh fish, grilled on the barbecue, and salad. And as much Bavarian smoked cheese as he could stomach.

Back home, she put the shopping away and decided to take her notebooks out into the sun and think a little about story, plot, characters.

She looked up from her writing and watched a couple of cyclists meandering along the bottom road towards the village. God, it was a hot day for cycling. Humid as well as hot. They trundled along, heavy panniers slowing their progress. And then she saw a poor man, slightly hunched, dragging a weight behind him. Something to sell at the market perhaps. Whatever it was seemed to be sending a huge plume of dust up behind him. *Poor soul*, she thought. He didn't have far to travel, mind you, but still pretty miserable in this weather. She half thought of going down the drive and offering him a lift but decided against, preferring to watch his slow but steady march. It might not be one of her better choices but at this point in her life it felt like a necessary one. Suddenly the man started to turn up the drive to her house. She sat bolt upright, quickly locating her mobile phone in her mind until the image grew less hazy and she could finally see him. Properly see him.

'Bloody car broke down about a mile away,' he shouted up the drive. 'Phone out of battery. Bloody car hire firm. Not using them again.' The sweat-inducing heat would not allow whole sentences or flowing phrases. He looked shattered.

She jumped out of her seat and rushed to him. 'What on earth are you doing here? You're not due until Saturday. I was going to pick you up.' She flung her arms round him and started to kiss away the salty sweat from his face. She blinked as her tears mixed with his.

He dropped his wheelie case and held her in close, his wet shirt sticking to her. 'It was supposed to be a surprise.'

'But what about the trams? Is everything okay? Did it all happen?'

'Yes, yes all good. Lord Provost cut the tape yesterday morning at five o'clock and now we're fully operational.' He stepped back and held her hands. 'That was it, you see. When the tape was cut. That was it. I decided. So I met the Chairman of the Board yesterday lunchtime and told him

I'm going. I'll give them six months but then that's it.'

It was everything she'd hoped for. Of course it was. But still…

'Don't worry, darling. I know. It'll be fine. Time to take stock, I think. I've got lots of ideas swirling around in my head. Things I'd like to have a go at.' He smiled. 'I know you have too.'

'Well, actually, I've been doing some writing.'

'Writing? Come on then. Tell me.' He put his arm around her shoulder and she clung on to his waist as they walked back up the drive. Suddenly he stopped and looked out at the terraces in front of the house. 'We could also do with getting this place into better shape. It's been left to its own devices for far too long.'

'Yes, yes. I was just thinking that. Look at that wall over there. Must have been like that for years but I hadn't really noticed before.' In the corner of their French country garden stood an ancient gnarled olive tree, impervious to the passage of time and to the lives of those who had chosen to make this place their home. Behind the tree, the wall had collapsed. 'Do you think we should get someone from the village to fix it?'

John bent down to conduct a more forensic inspection. 'Oh, it's only a small breach. Might have been a dislodged stone and then one of the farm animals has toppled the rest over.'

She smiled. 'So, nothing serious then. Nothing we can't fix ourselves.'

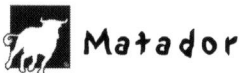

For exclusive discounts on Matador titles,
sign up to our occasional newsletter at
troubador.co.uk/bookshop